ST. MARTIN'S

MINOTAUR

MYSTERIES

W9-CFC-682

GET A CLUE!

Be the first to hear the latest mystery book news...

With the St. Martin's Minotaur monthly newsletter, you'll learn about the hottest new Minotaur books, receive advance excerpts from newly published works, read exclusive original material from featured mystery writers, and be able to enter to win free books!

Sign up on the Minotaur Web site at:
www.minotaurbooks.com

Praise for DONNA ANDREWS
and her Meg Langslow Mysteries

No Nest for the Wicket

"Andrews strikes just the right balance between comedy and suspense to keep the reader laughing and on the edge of one's seat. . . . Fans of this series will no doubt enjoy this installment, while new readers . . . will be headed to the bookstore for the earlier books."
—Romantic Times BOOKreviews (4 stars)

"Any day when I start reading about Meg is cause for delight. Ending the book makes me yearn for more than one per year. Hint."
—Deadly Pleasures

"As usual, Andrews is a reliable source for those who like their murder with plenty of mayhem."
—Kirkus Reviews

Owls Well That Ends Well

"A loony, utterly delightful affair."
—Booklist

"It's a hoot . . . a supporting cast of endearingly eccentric characters, perfectly pitched dialogue and a fine sense of humor make this a treat."
—Publishers Weekly

"Death by yard sale epitomizes the 'everyday people' humor that Andrews does so well . . . for readers who prefer their mysteries light . . . Andrews may be the next best thing to Janet Evanovich."
—Rocky Mountain News

"Andrews delivers another wonderfully comic story. . . . This is a fun read, as are all the books in the series. Andrews playfully creates laughable, wacky scenes that are the backdrop for her criminally devious plot. Settle back, dear reader, and enjoy another visit to Meg's anything-but-ordinary world."
—Romantic Times (starred review)

More . . .

We'll Always Have Parrots

"Laughter, more laughter, we need laughter, so Donna Andrews is giving us *We'll Always Have Parrots* . . . to help us survive February."
—*Washington Times*

"Perfectly showcases Donna Andrews' gift for deadpan comedy."
—*Denver Post*

"Always heavy on the humor, Andrews' most recent Meg Langslow outing is her most over-the-top adventure to date."
—*Booklist*

"I can't say enough good things about this series, and this entry in it."
—*Deadly Pleasures*

"Hilarious . . . another winner . . . keeps you turning pages."
—*Mystery Lovers News*

Crouching Buzzard, Leaping Loon

"There's a smile on every page and at least one chuckle per chapter."
—*Publishers Weekly*

"This may be the funniest installment of Andrews' wonderfully wacky series yet. It takes a deft hand to make slapstick or physical comedy appealing, yet Andrews masterfully manages it (the climax will have you in stitches.)"
—*Romantic Times*

Revenge of the Wrought-Iron Flamingos

"At the top of the list . . . a fearless protagonist, remarkable supporting characters, lively action, and a keen wit."
—*Library Journal*

"What a lighthearted gem of a juggling act . . . with her trademark witty dialogue and fine sense of the ridiculous, Andrews keeps all her balls in the air with skill and verve."
—*Publishers Weekly*

"Genuinely fascinating. A better-than-average entry in a consistently entertaining . . . series."
—*Booklist*

Murder with Puffins

"Muddy trails, old secrets, and plenty of homespun humor."
—*St. Petersburg Times*

"The well-realized island atmosphere, the puffin lore, and the ubiquitous birders only add to the fun."
—*Denver Post*

"Another hit for Andrews . . . entertaining and filled with fun characters."
—*Daily Press*

"Andrews's tale of two puffins has much to recommend it, and will leave readers cawing for another adventure featuring the appealing Meg and Michael."
—*Publishers Weekly*

"The puffin angle proves very amusing . . . an enjoyable flight of fancy."
—*Booklist*

Murder with Peacocks

"The first novel is so clever, funny, and original that lots of wannabe authors will throw up their hands in envy and get jobs in a coffee shop."
—*Contra Costa Times*

"Loquacious dialogue, persistent humor . . . a fun, breezy read."
—*Library Journal*

"Half Jane Austen, half battery acid . . . will leave you helpless with heartless laughter . . . Andrews combines murder and madcap hilarity with a cast of eccentric oddballs in a small Southern town."
—*Kirkus Reviews*

"Andrews's debut provides plenty of laughs for readers who like their mysteries on the cozy side."
—*Publishers Weekly*

Other Meg Langslow Mysteries By
Donna Andrews

No Nest
for the Wicket

Donna Andrews

St. Martin's Paperbacks

This is a work of fiction. All of the characters, organizations and events portrayed in this novel are either products of the author's imagination or are used fictitiously.

NO NEST FOR THE WICKET

Copyright © 2006 by Donna Andrews.
Excerpt from *The Penguin Who Knew Too Much* copyright © 2007 by Donna Andrews.

Library of Congress Catalog Card Number: 2006040420

ISBN: 0-312-99791-4
EAN: 9780312-99791-5

Printed in the United States of America

St. Martin's Press hardcover edition / August 2006
St. Martin's Paperbacks edition / July 2007

St. Martin's Paperbacks are published by St. Martin's Press, 175 Fifth Avenue, New York, NY 10010.

10 9 8 7 6 5 4 3 2

Acknowledgments

Thank you!

To everyone at St. Martin's Press, especially Toni Plummer for her efficiency, and (as always) Ruth Cavin for pushing me to make it the book it can be.

To Ellen Geiger at Frances Goldin Literary Agency and Anna Abreu at Curtis Brown for taking such good care of the practical stuff.

To the Connecticut eXtreme Croquet Society for introducing me to the sport and allowing me to play with it in the book.

To the friends who help me brainstorm about plot and then read the results: Dana Cameron (who helped with the history but is blameless for any misuse I made of it), Carla Coupe, Ellen Crosby, Kathy Deligianis, Suzanne Frisbee, Maria Lima, Dave Niemi, and the Rector Lane Irregulars.

To Dad for helping inspire Meg's father, and Mom for being nothing at all like Meg's mother.

And to all the readers who enjoy Meg's adventures.

No Nest

for the Wicket

Chapter One

"Move," I said. "You're blocking my shot."

The cow chewed her cud and gazed at me with placid bovine calm.

"Go away!" I ran toward her, waving my arms wildly, only to pull up short before I ran into her. She was bigger than I was. Half a ton at least. Maybe three-quarters.

I turned my croquet mallet around and prodded her black-and-white flank with the handle. Not hard—I didn't want to hurt her; I just wanted her to move.

She turned her head slightly to see what I was doing.

I prodded harder. She watched with mild interest.

"Hamburger!" I shouted. "Flank steak! Filet mignon!"

She ignored me.

Of course, those words held no menace for her. Mr. Shiffley, her owner, was a dairy farmer.

I walked a few yards away, feet squelching in the mud. I could see why the cow insisted on lounging where she was. The evergreen tree overhead protected her from the March drizzle, and she'd claimed the only high ground in sight.

I glanced down. My croquet ball was sinking into the mud. Did the rules of eXtreme croquet allow me to pull it out? Probably not.

The little two-way radio in my pocket crackled.

"Meg—turn!" my brother, Rob, said.

"Roger," I said. The cow still lay in front of—or possibly on—the wicket, but I had to move before the mud ate my ball. Didn't mud that ate things count as quicksand? I set down the radio and whacked my ball. It bounced off the cow's flank. She didn't seem to mind. She had closed her eyes and was chewing more slowly, with an expression of vacuous ecstasy.

"Done," I said, grabbing the radio before it sank. "I need a cow removal here at wicket nine."

"Which one is that?" Rob asked.

"The one by the bog."

"Which bog?"

"The one just beside the brier patch. Near the steep hill with the icy stream at the bottom."

"Oh, that bog," Rob said. "Be right over."

I pocketed the radio and smiled menacingly at the cow.

"Be afraid," I said. "Be very afraid."

She ignored me.

I leaned against a tree and waited. The radio crackled occasionally as Rob notified the scattered players of their turns and they reported when they'd finished.

In the distance, I heard a high-pitched cackle of

laughter, which meant my team captain, Mrs. Fenniman, had made a difficult shot. Or, more likely, had just roqueted some unlucky opponent, which she told me was the technical term for whacking someone's ball into the next county. Annoying in any croquet game, but downright maddening in eXtreme croquet, where the whole point was to make the playing field as rugged as possible. On this field, being roqueted could mean half an hour's detour through even boggier portions of the cow pasture.

I pulled the cell phone out of my other pocket. Time to see what was happening back at the house—the construction site that would eventually be a house again, if all went well. Today we'd begun demolition of the unrepairable parts, and it was driving me crazy, not being there. I'd left detailed instructions with the workmen, but I didn't have much confidence that they'd follow them. They were all Shiffleys, nephews of Mr. Shiffley the dairy farmer. Everyone in Caerphilly knew that if you wanted some manual labor done, you hired a Shiffley or two—or a dozen, if you liked; there was never a shortage. They were cheerful, honest, hardworking, and reliable, as long as you didn't need anything done during hunting season.

Everyone in Caerphilly also knew that when you had Shiffleys on the job, you needed someone else in charge. Not that they were stupid—some were and some weren't, same as any other family—but they were stubborn and opinionated, every one of them, and you needed someone equally stubborn and opinionated telling them what to do. Me, for instance. Not only was I stubborn enough but, thanks to my work as a blacksmith, they halfway respected my opinions about related crafts like carpentry and plumbing. Michael, my fiancé, would do in a pinch, as long as he remembered to suppress his innate niceness. Unfortunately, Michael was in town, attending the dreaded all-day Caerphilly College faculty meeting. We had Dad in charge. I was worried.

"Come on, Dad, pick up," I muttered as his phone rang on unanswered. I heard rustling in the shrubbery—either another competitor approaching or Rob arriving for cow removal. Either would cut short my time for talking.

"Meg!" Dad exclaimed when he finally answered. "How's the game?"

"I'm stuck in a bog with a cow sitting on my wicket," I said. "How's the demolition going?"

"Fine the last time I looked."

"The last time you—Dad, aren't you at the house?"

"I'm up at the duck pond."

I closed my eyes and sighed. Two weeks ago, when I'd left Dad in charge of another crew of Shiffleys to install the new septic field, he'd talked them into excavating a duck pond. Apparently, Duck, my nephew's pet duck, needed a place to paddle while visiting us. Or perhaps Dad thought Michael and I would soon acquire ducks of our own. Anyway, he'd sited the pond uphill from the septic field, but in a spot with exceptionally good drainage—so good that the pond didn't hold water. Which hadn't stopped Dad from trying to keep it full.

"Let's talk about the pond later," I said. "I need

you to keep an eye on the demolition crew. See that they don't get carried away with the sledgehammers."

"Roger," he said. "I'll run right down. Oh, about those boxes in the front hall—the Shiffleys can work around them today, but next week—"

"The boxes will be long gone by next week," I said. "The professor from UVa should come by before five to haul them off; keep an eye out for her, will you?"

"Roger. By the way, speaking of the duck pond—"

"Gotta go," I said. "Rob's here for the cow."

I had spotted Rob peering through some shrubbery.

"Man, I thought last month's course was tough," Rob said. "Who set this one up?"

"Mrs. Fenniman," I said. "Possibly with diabolical assistance. Did you bring Spike?"

"Right here," Rob said. He pushed through the thicket and set down a plastic dog carrier. He'd gouged a small notch in its door opening so he could put Spike inside without detaching the leash. Smart.

I peered in through the mesh.

"Cow, Spike," I said. He growled in anticipation. I could see he'd already done cow duty elsewhere— his fluffy white coat had disappeared under a thick layer of mud.

"Here we go," Rob said, grabbing the leash. "Go get her, Spike!"

A small brown blur shot toward the cow, barking and snarling. The cow must have met Spike before. She lurched to her feet with surprising agility and trotted off.

Annoying that an eight-and-a-half-pound fur ball

could strike fear in the heart of a cow when I couldn't even keep her awake.

"I'll just move her a little farther while we're at it," Rob said. He grabbed the dog carrier and ambled off.

"Not too far," I said. "And remember, you're supposed to get the milk out of the cow before churning it."

"Don't worry," Rob called over his shoulder.

I hadn't been worrying, only hoping Spike wouldn't chase the cow quite so far off. Cows were welcome as long as they refrained from lying on the stakes and wickets—the rules of eXtreme croquet defined any livestock on the course as walking wickets. Hitting the ball between the legs of a standing cow would give me a much-needed extra shot. I didn't want Spike chasing her toward a rival player.

Yes, the cow had been lying on the wicket. I bent the battered wire into an approximation of its original shape, pounded it into the ground, and leaned against a tree to await my turn.

But before it came, another player arrived. Henrietta Pruitt. I smiled and hoped it looked sincere. Mrs. Pruitt was captain of the Dames of Caerphilly, a team whose members were all big wheels in local society. I had no idea why they were here. When the *Caerphilly Clarion* ran the article announcing that Mrs. Fenniman had planned an eXtreme croquet tournament, I thought the townspeople would either laugh themselves silly or ignore the whole thing. Instead, we'd had to make room for two local teams.

Either they were too embarrassed to withdraw

when they learned this wasn't a normal croquet tournament or they really wanted to play eXtreme croquet. All day, they'd slogged through the mud as if born to it. Maybe I'd misjudged them.

"Well, fancy meeting you here," Mrs. Pruitt said. "After you passed me a few wickets ago, I thought you'd be at the finishing stake by now."

Damn. Apparently, I'd had the lead for several wickets and never noticed. Of course, someone else could have passed both of us while we were stuck in various bogs.

"This wicket's tough," I said.

Not for her. Her ball sailed through on the first try, avoided the roots, and rolled down to tap my ball with a firm but gentle click.

"Good shot," I said. "All that golf and tennis pays off."

Maybe if I flattered her, she wouldn't roquet me.

"Yes," she said. She looked left, down the hill toward the icy stream, then right, toward the brier patch. "It's important to keep in shape, isn't it?"

She raised her mallet. I closed my eyes and tried not to wince at the sharp crack that sent my ball flying.

I plunged into the thornbushes to find it while Mrs. Pruitt played on. I dodged poison ivy, cow pies, protruding roots, and the bleached and scattered bones of a sheep.

Suddenly, I found myself perched on the edge of a steep bank, looking down at a gulley filled with more thornbushes and, by way of a change, lots of sharp, pointy rocks.

"I think I'll take a detour," I muttered. But before I

could retreat, the bank crumbled, and I found myself sliding down toward the thorns and pointy rocks.

My mallet hit me in the stomach when I landed. For long seconds, I lay with my eyes closed, fighting to breathe.

"Meg! Turn!" my radio said.

I opened my eyes to answer and found myself staring into a pair of blue eyes. Strands of long blond hair fell around them, partly obscuring the woman's face but not the eyes, which stared at me with unnerving intensity.

"Are you all right?" I wheezed, shoving myself upright.

No, she wasn't.

Someone had bashed in the back of her head.

Chapter Two

I jumped when the radio crackled again.

"Meg? Your turn," Rob said.

"Not now," I muttered, although not into the radio.

I squirmed farther from the corpse while fumbling in my pocket for the cell phone, and whacked myself in the stomach again with my own mallet.

My mallet. I glanced at it, and then at the dead woman's head. Maybe I was jumping to conclusions. Maybe she'd just fallen, as I had, and been less lucky. Hit her head on one of the rocks.

I inched over so I could see her head wound. Then I held my own croquet mallet as close to it as I could.

Looked like a match to me.

For a horrible moment I wondered if I'd done this accidentally when I fell. No, my mallet showed traces of mud and leaves—more than traces—but no blood. I took a deep breath and checked the woman's wrist. No pulse, and while she was still warm, she definitely wasn't body temperature. She'd been dead before I fell.

But not long before. Which meant the killer might still be nearby. I dropped her wrist, scooted away until I had my back against the bank of the gulley, and flipped open the cell phone to call the police.

Debbie Anne, the dispatcher, shrieked and dropped the phone when I told her why I was calling. In a few seconds, Chief Burke was on the line.

"You're reporting what?"

"A murder," I said. "Female, blond hair, blue eyes, late thirties. Tall, I think, though that's hard to tell—she's lying down. Not someone I know."

"You're sure she's dead?"

I glanced up and met the blank blue eyes.

"Yeah, someone bashed her head in," I said. "But send an ambulance if you don't believe me."

"And you have no idea who she is?"

"I don't know her, and I haven't searched her for an ID."

"Keep it that way," he said. I nodded. Though now my curiosity was aroused—most women carried a purse, but when I stood up and scanned the area, I didn't see one.

"The ambulance is on the way," the chief said. "And I'm sending a couple of deputies to secure the scene—just where is the scene, anyway?"

"Somewhere in Mr. Shiffley's cow pasture," I said. "The boggy part, near the stream. Have the deputies stop at the house and someone can probably lead them up here. Dad, or maybe one of the other players."

"Other players?" the chief asked. "Good Lord,

please tell me you're not out there playing paintball again."

"Not paintball," I said. "Croquet."

"In Fred Shiffley's pasture? What's wrong with your backyard?"

"Too tame," I said. "This isn't normal croquet. It's eXtreme croquet. You have to play it in extreme conditions. Mr. Shiffley's pasture's perfect—plenty of hills, trees, rocks, quicksand, thornbushes, poison ivy—"

"Something your family invented?" the chief growled.

"Actually, something Mrs. Fenniman read about in *Smithsonian* magazine," I said. "Extreme sports are very big these days, you know."

"Sounds damned strange to me," he muttered.

I agreed, but family loyalty kept me from saying so.

"Fred Shiffley know you're doing this?" he asked.

"We have his permission," I said. "In writing."

Which was true. Dad got along beautifully with the neighboring farmers. I wasn't sure whether his endless curiosity about every detail of farm life had won them over or his free medical advice, but he'd charmed them into letting us play—not just Mr. Shiffley but also Mr. Early, who owned the nearby sheep pasture, where another croquet game was currently going on.

Unless the other game had ended earlier than ours. What if it had, and the other players wandered over to watch our game? I needed to call Dad and—

"Minerva's here," the chief said, interrupting my worrying. "We'll be out as soon as we can."

Minerva? Much as I liked Mrs. Burke, I wondered why he'd bring her to a crime scene. Not my business to pry.

"Fine," I said aloud. "What do you want me to do until the officers arrive?" I was hoping he'd order me to go back to the house. Away from the body.

"How much of a crowd do you have gawking at the body?"

"No crowd at all," I said. "This isn't exactly a spectator sport."

"The other players aren't standing around gawking?"

"The field's at least two acres," I said. "I can't even see the other players at the moment."

A short silence.

"I'm sure it will all make sense when I see it," he said finally. "Don't touch anything till I get there."

With that, he hung up.

"Meg!" my radio squawked. "Your turn."

I realized Rob had probably been calling me all during my conversation with Chief Burke. I grabbed the radio.

"I'm still looking for my ball," I said.

I heard tittering. Probably from Mrs. Pruitt and the other Dames.

"Try closing your eyes and letting the ball call to you," said another voice. My cousin Rose Noire—Rosemary Keenan to the IRS and our mothers. "Imagine the ball emitting a guiding beacon of white light."

"Can we get on with it?" Mrs. Pruitt snapped.

"Not until I find my ball," I said. "And no sneaking extra shots while I'm looking. Everyone stays right where they are—understood?"

"Roger. Everyone, report your whereabouts!" Mrs. Fenniman said in her best field marshal's voice. "Claire and I will stay here by the turning post."

Claire, presumably, was the woman I still couldn't bring myself to call anything but Mrs. Wentworth—wife of the history department chairman.

"We'll concentrate on beaming positive energy for your search," Rose Noire said. "Won't we?"

"Or if you want some real help, give us a call," Mrs. Pruitt said. I heard her in the background, rather than directly, so evidently she was with Rose Noire.

"Could someone please come and chase this cow away?" Lacie Butler whined. "I think it's planning to attack me."

"Good grief; it'll be killer rabbits next," I muttered, though not into the radio. I'd never met anyone as timid and anxious as Lacie. I hadn't quite decided whether I felt sorry for her or just found her terminally annoying. Maybe if I ever ran into her when she wasn't gophering for Mrs. Pruitt and Mrs. Wentworth, I'd find out.

"I'll bring Spike," Rob said.

"Oh, would you?" Lacie asked. Lucky for us, Lacie was a good fifteen years older than Rob, and married to boot. That breathless damsel in distress routine was exactly what my overly susceptible brother fell for—if the damsel was beautiful and on the fair side of thirty.

"I'll be right over as soon as I chase Duck away from wicket three," Rob said.

"Oh, did she lay another egg?" Rose Noire asked.

"Just sitting on some smooth rocks," Rob said. "But we don't want her getting used to nesting on the field."

No, especially now that the field had become a crime scene. I put the radio down and tuned out the continuing chitchat from the other players. I opened my cell phone again and called Dad.

"I'm up at the house," he said before I could speak. "I'm keeping a close eye on them—you don't have to worry about a thing."

Except perhaps Dad looking too closely over someone's shoulder and getting accidentally whacked by a sledgehammer. Or the very real possibility that the Shiffleys would mutiny against their unwanted overseer and go home to sulk. That was the downside of working with the Shiffleys—they were quite clannish. Offend one and you offended them all, and fat chance of getting anyone to do your carpentry, plumbing, wiring, tree cutting. . . .

"That's nice," I said. "We have another problem."

"What?"

I took a deep breath. Dad, an avid mystery buff, wouldn't see a problem, but a golden opportunity to kibbitz on Chief Burke's investigation.

"We have a suspicious death," I said. "Chief Burke is on the way, and he needs our help."

"He needs me to examine the body," Dad said, jumping to a predictable conclusion. "My medical bag's in the car."

"Examining the body comes later," I said. "First

we secure the crime scene and prevent suspects from leaving."

"Okay," he said. "What suspects?"

"The croquet players in the other field, for starters," I said. "And anyone else who looks suspicious."

I remembered the half dozen Shiffleys swarming over the house, each armed with a sledgehammer that looked remarkably like a croquet mallet.

"Including the Shiffleys," I said with a sigh. "And anyone else who's been hanging around today."

"Will do," Dad said. "Cousin Horace just drove up. I'll get him to help me."

"Good idea," I said. Cousin Horace was a crime-scene technician with the sheriff's department in my hometown of Yorktown. Like many of my relatives, he'd been spending more and more time here in Caerphilly lately—though in Horace's case, I suspect the attraction wasn't me but Rose Noire, the distant cousin with whom he was smitten.

"If you get a chance, could you call the teams that are supposed to show up tonight and head them off?" I added. "Odds are, we won't be playing tomorrow, with one field being a crime scene and all. But don't tell them why we're rescheduling. In fact, don't tell anyone."

"Of course not," Dad said. "So where is the body?"

"On the croquet field," I said, which was sufficiently vague to keep him from trotting up here to inspect it. "Oops! Gotta go; talk to you later."

As soon as I hung up, I wished I hadn't. What an hour ago I would have called peace and quiet settled over the gulley, only now it felt like oppressive silence.

I glanced over at the dead woman and realized that I resented her for getting murdered practically in my backyard. Illogical, and I didn't like myself for feeling that way. After all, she hadn't asked to be murdered here. Mrs. Fenniman was a much more logical target for resentment, wasn't she? It was her fault I was out here playing eXtreme croquet instead of back at the house minding my own business. She'd organized the tournament and then browbeaten me into playing hostess.

Of course, I hadn't had to go along with her plans. I'd gotten better at saying no to my relatives' crazier projects, but I still wasn't very good at continuing to say no until they heard it.

How long did it take to get here from town, anyway? And was it early enough to head off the other teams, or were they already en route—perhaps already here to complicate things even more? I glanced at my watch. Almost three o'clock.

"We keeping you from something?"

Chapter Three

I started, and suppressed an undignified shriek. Chief Burke stood at the top of the bank, almost directly over my head, staring down with an expression of mournful disapproval on his round brown face. Sammy, one of his young deputies, stood beside him.

"Is there an easier way down?" the chief asked, peering over the edge of the bank. "I'm not as agile as usual, thanks to this fool thing."

He indicated his right arm, which was encased in a cast and a neat black sling.

"Depends on your definition of easy," I said. "You could follow my example—just stand there till the bank caves in under you. Not fun, but it's pretty quick."

"I'd prefer something longer and less abrupt," he said, backing away slightly.

"Can't help you there," I said. "I surfed down. If I were you, I'd stay up there. In fact, if you're going to interrogate me now, can I come up?"

"Interview, not interrogate," he said. "If you're squeamish, come on up. And you a doctor's daughter."

"Dad's patients tend to be alive, as a general rule," I said as I stood and grabbed my knapsack. "They may not be healthy, but most of them are breathing."

I found a less crumbly part of the bank and Sammy gave me a hand up before scrambling down to take my place. He bent over the dead woman and frowned.

"I don't know her, Chief," he said, sounding surprised. "She must not be from around here."

The chief nodded.

"Soon as the rest of the officers get here, we'll do a preliminary search," he said.

The bank crumbled a little more, raining clods of dirt into the gully. The chief and I stepped farther back.

"Could be how it happened," the chief said, craning his neck. "She fell, hit her head on a rock."

"I doubt it," I said. "The wound's not that ragged, and besides, I don't see any bloody rocks, do you?"

"Oh, you've already done a preliminary medical examination and searched the area, have you?" he said, taking out his notebook.

"I nearly fell over her, and I'm not blind," I said. "Looks as if she was hit with a croquet mallet."

"Do tell," the chief said, frowning at the croquet mallet in my hand.

"Not my mallet, of course," I said. "But we've got five other people running around nearby with mallets, and another six up in Farmer Early's sheep pasture—there's another game up there. Plus the Shiffleys."

"They've taken up croquet, the Shiffleys?" the chief said, sounding dubious.

"No, sledgehammers," I said. "We've got them doing demolition up at the house. Sledgehammers look remarkably like croquet mallets, you know. Not that I know why they'd want to kill the poor woman, whoever she is."

"When we find out who she is, no doubt we'll find out why someone killed her," he said. "Contrary to what your father thinks, most murders aren't very mysterious."

Just then my radio came to life again.

"Meg?" Rob said. "Haven't you found your ball yet? 'Cause we're really getting behind on the game schedule."

"Do those fool people really think I'll let them keep playing croquet at a crime scene?" the chief said, incredulous.

"They don't know it's a crime scene," I said. "I just told them I was still looking for my ball. If I'd told them what really happened, they'd have all come over to mess up any evidence I haven't already messed up. I didn't think you wanted that."

"Of course not," the chief said.

"For heaven's sakes, just take the damned penalty and let's get on with it!" Mrs. Pruitt snapped over the radio.

"Who's that?" the chief growled.

"Mrs. Pruitt," I said. "Henrietta Pruitt," I added, forestalling his question. Pruitts were almost as common around Caerphilly as Shiffleys, though I suspected either family would react with profound indignation at being lumped with the other. "You know, the one who runs the Caerphilly Historical Society."

"I see," the chief said. He didn't sound thrilled. He had opened his notebook and was scribbling in it.

Just then, Horace and two uniformed officers showed up. The chief sent the officers out to round up the other players and Horace scrambled down to the body, taking large chunks of the bank with him. The chief and I backed farther away. After a few moments, we heard Horace's voice.

"We'll need the medical examiner for an exact time of death," he said. "But I doubt if she's been dead more than an hour or two. If that. Meg's probably right about the murder weapon. A croquet mallet would work fine."

I held my mallet out to the chief.

"No use handing it to me when I obviously don't have an evidence bag to put it in," he said. "Just hang on to it till we get back to your house. Come on."

He set off through the underbrush, muttering "Damn!" and "Blast!" at intervals—presumably when he hit a particularly thorny shrub. I followed a few feet behind, letting him break trail until we escaped the brier patch.

"So who else is out here playing full-contact croquet?" he asked, pausing to let me catch up.

"It's eXtreme croquet," I said, correcting him. "And don't you mean who are your other suspects?"

He looked over his glasses at me.

"All right," he said. "Who are my other suspects?"

"Here in the cow pasture, Henrietta Pruitt, Claire Wentworth, and Lacie Butler on one side," I said. "The Dames of Caerphilly, they call themselves. Mrs. Fenniman, my cousin Rose Noire, and me on the other, with my brother, Rob, as referee."

"I see," he said with a slight wince. At the prospect of interviewing more of my relatives, or the pain of dealing with Mrs. Pruitt and her socially prominent cronies? Possibly both. He'd slowed down and was scribbling in his notebook. "And at the other field?"

"Mrs. Briggs," I said. "I don't know her first name. Wife of the man who wants to build that outlet mall."

"I know him," the chief said. From the sound of it, he didn't like Mr. Briggs very much.

"She has those two Realtors on her team," I said. "The two Suzies. I don't remember their last names."

"The clones," the chief said, nodding. I was relieved I wasn't the only one who called the two Realtors that. They weren't clones, of course, but in addition to both being named Suzie, they were both petite, blond, and perky. I not only couldn't remember their last names; I couldn't reliably tell them apart.

"The other team in the sheep pasture I don't know at all," I said. "Three students from some college."

"You don't know which one?"

"We had teams sign up from five different colleges," I said. "I forget which one this is, but you can ask them."

"So this eXtreme croquet isn't just a bunch of lu-
natics fooling around?" he said, sounding baffled.
"It's an organized sport?"

"Not well organized," I said. "Some guys in Connecticut invented it—or at least popularized it. But
the tournament was Mrs. Fenniman's idea. She
couldn't even get many of the family to play with
her, so she announced a tournament, and suddenly
we had seven other teams."

We fell silent as we climbed the steep slope that
marked the approximate boundary between the
three acres Michael and I owned and Mr. Shiffley's
pasture, which surrounded us on three sides. Now
that we'd stopped talking, I heard fiddle music coming from our backyard.

"Not the best time for a party," the chief said,
puffing slightly.

"They don't know about the murder yet," I said.
Just then, we heard a cheer from the lawn above.

"Hmph," the chief snorted, as if to say that he'd
change that pretty darn soon.

The last few feet of the path were so steep that the
previous owners had put in a set of rustic stone
steps, though they were in such disrepair that they
weren't much of an improvement over the muddy
path. The chief sped up slightly; many people did, in
fact, to get the last stage of the hill over as quickly
as possible and reach the level ground of our backyard. As he put his foot on the bottom step, a figure
leaped into our view at the top of the hill.

"Yee-haw!" the figure shouted, springing into the
air and waving a cudgel.

Chapter Four

Chief Burke's hand darted inside his jacket, a reflex left over from his days as an urban police officer. Fortunately for the man at the top of the stairs, the chief no longer carried a gun. Not that he'd have had much luck drawing it with the cast on his arm.

"It's okay," I said. "I know him." Which probably didn't reassure Chief Burke that much. Fortunately, something must have convinced the chief that the figure was harmless, because he relaxed slightly. Perhaps, like me, he recognized the cudgel as a croquet mallet, though considering the crime scene we'd just left, it might have been shortsighted to consider a croquet mallet reassuring. There was nothing reassuring about his unearthly cry, a cross between a rebel yell and a yodel, that stopped us in our tracks with our mouths open, but following up this bloodcurdling sound with a smirk and a guffaw definitely reduced its effectiveness. Most likely, the chief figured a truly dangerous madman would charge down the steps instead of leaping up into the air and clicking his heels together to make all the bells strapped to his shins ring as loudly as possible. Then, as soon as his feet hit the ground, he bounded off like a kangaroo on fast forward.

"What the dickens is going on up there?" the chief asked as he raced up the steps.

"It's a player from the students' croquet team," I said, following him.

"Craziest damn fool kind of croquet I've ever seen," the chief said. He had paused at the top of the steps and was frowning down at our lawn.

"It's not croquet," I said. "It's Morris dancing."

"Morris dancing," the chief repeated.

"It's a form of English folk dancing," I said. "They put on traditional costumes, including about a million bells on their shins."

"I know what Morris dancing is," the chief said. "Not that I'd call that much of an example. Why are they doing it here, practically in the middle of my crime scene?"

He wasn't hurrying to stop the spectacle, though, and I had to admit that I felt a certain morbid fascination with the Mountain Morris Mallet Men's performance.

I'd already seen the costumes—white shirts, black knee breeches, and brightly colored X-shaped suspenders decorated with ribbons and rosettes—since they'd insisted on wearing them to play croquet in. Along with their bells—dozens of brass bells sewn in rows to pads that looked like truncated hockey shin guards.

All three students were prancing in a circle, lifting their knees as high as possible, then bringing their feet down sharply to get the maximum amount of noise out of the bells. They started out holding their croquet mallets in both hands, but as they worked up speed, they began waving the mallets overhead and whacking them together in time with the music.

"Now there's a concussion waiting to happen," the chief said, shaking his head.

"True," I said. "But your victim wasn't Morris dancing when she met her end. I'd have noticed the bells."

It was the bells that got to you. I'd thought the weeks of construction had made me immune to noise pollution, but I'd been ready to strangle all three students long before we hit the croquet field. I'd have tried to persuade them to doff their bells if not for Mrs. Pruitt.

"You simply cannot permit them to wear those ghastly bells," she had informed me halfway through this morning's prematch breakfast.

"There's nothing in the rules to prevent them," I said. I knew because Mrs. Fenniman and I had spent an hour studying her dog-eared copy of the rules, looking for a precedent to ban the bells. "You could refuse to take the field until they remove them."

Mrs. Pruitt smiled and inclined her head toward me in gracious thanks for my support.

"Although that would count as a forfeit," I added.

Her usual glare returned.

"Do you have any idea how annoying those bells are?" she snapped.

"Yes," I said. "They're sleeping in our barn, you

know; which wouldn't be as bad if Michael and I weren't camping out there ourselves during the construction."

"Do they sleep in the bells?"

"I have no idea," I said. "As far as I can tell, they don't actually sleep. They're college students, remember?"

"Do you mean you can't do anything about the bells?"

"They're only doing it to annoy us. If we ignore it, we'll annoy them back. Throw them off their game."

"Hmph," Mrs. Pruitt said, and strode off. I noticed afterward that she was being unusually gracious to the students. The students, for their part, took pains to shuffle their legs and tap their feet as much as possible in her presence. As soon as breakfast ended, I had sent them all down to the cow pasture to annoy one another while my team played a relatively straightforward match against Mrs. Briggs and the clones up in the sheep pasture.

In a just world, the Mountain Morris Mallet Men would have gone home after the Caerphilly Dames defeated them in the morning game, but the rules Mrs. Fenniman had devised for this tournament called for a complex multiple-elimination system. At least by beating the clones, my team got to play the Dames in the second match, which meant that I hadn't heard the bells all afternoon.

Although come to think of it, if we'd lost the morning game, I'd have been up in the sheep pasture, and someone else could have found the murdered woman.

I also realized that Mrs. Pruitt and her team had had two chances to learn their way around the playing field that contained the crime scene. My team and the Morris men had had only one—an interrupted game in our case—and Mrs. Briggs and the clones hadn't been there at all. Not that I knew of anyway. Should I mention this to the chief?

Maybe later. He was frowning at the Morris men.

"You didn't hear any bells while you were playing?" he asked.

"No," I said. "But they're not permanently attached. If one sneaked down to our field to murder someone, he'd have taken off his bells."

The chief nodded.

"Of course, that would imply premeditation," I said.

He ignored me. Or maybe he was fascinated by the Morris dancing. All the other males in the backyard were. My nephew Eric was already imitating the dancers, fortunately with a plastic toy baseball bat rather than a croquet mallet. Dad was observing them with the rapt attention our family found alarming, because it usually signaled that he'd found a new hobby. Joan of Arc and Napoléon were slackers compared to Dad in pursuit of a new hobby.

The Shiffleys were variously leaning against the side of the barn or squatting on their ankles, elbows on their knees, a position they seemed to find comfortable and could hold indefinitely, probably due to long years of practice. I wasn't quite sure why they liked to do this—perhaps to make people like me feel like city slickers.

They were tapping their feet and nodding their heads to the music. It was a lively tune played on a fiddle and an accordion—one of those songs that had migrated over to the Shenandoah Valley with early English and Irish settlers and taken root so thoroughly, you were surprised to find it had been born on the other side of the Atlantic.

"Co-ol," my brother, Rob, said behind me. "It's like a mating dance for Santa's reindeer!"

I glanced back and saw the rest of the croquet players straggling up the hill, escorted by two of the chief's deputies and Cousin Horace.

"Sammy," the chief said, gesturing toward the lawn. "Get the rest of these people into the house so we can question them."

Sammy scurried off. Horace, who was plumper than Sammy, arrived at the top of the hill slightly winded.

"You've got the photographs of Jane?" the chief asked.

Horace nodded.

"Oh, splendid!" I said. "You've identified her!"

"Jane as in Doe," the chief said.

"Oh," I said. "Sorry."

"How soon can you get copies printed out?" the chief asked Horace. "I want to show them to the witnesses and see if any of them know her. The sooner we get her identified, the better, but I don't want to drag every single person out here past the body."

"I could run down to your station and make some copies there," Horace said, sounding slightly breathless and not at all enthusiastic about the prospect of running anywhere. "But that would take a good forty-five minutes."

The chief growled again.

"If Meg has a color printer—" Horace added.

"It's in the barn," I said. "I'll show you."

"Just herd everybody into the living room and have them keep their mouths shut," I heard the chief say to one of his deputies as I accompanied Horace to the barn. "Don't want them contaminating one another's stories any more than they already have."

Fortunately, the barn's roof had been in decent shape when we bought the property, needing only new shingles. We'd waited until the worst of the winter cold had passed before starting major work on the house, since we planned to camp in the barn till the house was habitable again. We'd put a futon in a large stall to serve as a bedroom and turned the former tack room into an office, since we could pad-lock the door and keep the computers safe.

"Nice setup," Horace commented. "You should just make this your office permanently."

"Yes, apart from the lack of heat or air condition-ing, it's perfect," I said.

I hovered while Horace loaded the pictures into my computer and printed them. I offered to do the printing, but he refused, so I suspected the chief had told him not to let any of the photos out of his hands. A precaution probably aimed more at the press than at me, but I found myself wanting to circumvent it anyway. I found my chance when the toner ran out midway through printing.

"New cartridges in here," I said, opening the supply cabinet's door. "Which one's out, color or— yow! Damn it!"

Chapter Five

Horace leaped to my rescue, which wasn't neces-
sary. I wasn't in danger, just slightly hurt and seri-
ously annoyed. Duck, Eric's imaginatively named
pet duck, was sitting in the box that held the toner
cartridges, and when I'd reached in, she'd bitten me.
Luckily, since ducks have no teeth, she hadn't
drawn blood, but her beak was hard and her bite remarkably forceful. I'd have a bruise.

"Stupid duck!" I exclaimed, shaking my hand.
"Can you help me get her outside?"

Most of my family knew how to carry Duck
safely, though not all of them had the nerve to do it.
Luckily, Horace was a veteran duck wrangler and
had no difficulty seizing her with one hand while
holding her bill with the other. While he carried her
out of the barn, I tossed her egg out the window, so
she'd have no reason to linger if she did sneak back
into our temporary office.

Then I hid one of the completed printouts of Jane
Doe underneath the desk mat. Not that I had any-

thing in particular I wanted to do with it, but you never knew.

Horace deleted the files from my hard drive after he'd printed his copies and shredded the several washed-out copies that had printed while the toner was running low.

"Okay," he said, when he'd emptied the computer's recycle folder. "Let's take these to the chief."

Back at the house, the deputies had herded the croquet players, the Shiffleys, and assorted members of my family into the living room. A few of them sat on folding lawn chairs dragged in from the yard, but most were milling about under the watchful eyes of the deputies, sipping cups of tea and coffee. Apparently Mother, as usual, was determined to turn the occasion into a social gathering.

Periodically, Sammy escorted someone into the living room, consulted a piece of paper, and led someone else out—to be interviewed by the chief, I deduced. Short interviews—apparently most of them knew nothing of interest to the chief.

The third time Sammy reappeared, he spotted Horace and his face lighted up. He abandoned his list and headed our way.

"Chief's been asking every five minutes where you were with the photos," he said, motioning to the archway.

Horace nodded and scurried out. I went over to the card table that held the teapot and the coffee urn, where Mother stood, frowning with disapproval. I assumed she was upset by the decor—not just the lawn chairs and the card table but also the industrial-weight extension cords snaking through the room to power a few battered floor lamps. No doubt she'd rather have had the chief conduct his investigation by candlelight.

"I do hope Mrs. Pruitt and Mrs. Wentworth aren't too put out," she said as I poured myself some coffee. "And that other nice lady from the country club—what was her name? Lucy?"

"Lacie," I said. "Put out by what?"

"At being treated like common suspects," Mother said.

"You hope they're not too upset?" I said. "What about me and Rob? And Rose Noire and Mrs. Fenniman—your own family? We're suspects, too, you know."

"Well, anyone in the family understands that these little things sometimes happen," she said, waving dismissively. Yes, especially in our family. "But shouldn't we be doing something to keep Mrs. Pruitt and her teammates from being badgered and interrogated?"

"Not if they're guilty," I said. "If they're guilty, I want them badgered and interrogated until they confess. If you ask me, they're at least as likely to be guilty as anyone else here. Especially Mrs. Pruitt."

"You're not upset about that?"

"We're not close," I said. "I hope she's not the killer, but if it turns out she is, I think I can cope."

"What about the country club?"

"I'm sure everyone there would cope, too. They'd have a harder time winning golf and tennis tournaments, though."

"Yes, I'm sure," Mother said, sounding testy. "I meant, won't all this make it harder for you and Michael to join the country club?"

"Mother, we don't want to join the country club," I said. "It's expensive and boring. Only the older, stodgier faculty belong. We don't want to offend them by turning down an invitation—not while Michael's still working on tenure—so we're trying not to get invited."

"Trying *not* to get invited?" Mother repeated.

"I know it sounds crazy—"

"If Mrs. Pruitt is typical of the membership, it sounds remarkably sensible to me," she said. "Joining the country club won't help Michael's career?"

I shook my head.

"I wish you'd told me that earlier," she said with a sigh. "The time I wasted being nice to that woman."

"You can relax," I said. "You don't have to be nice to her at all on our account."

"That doesn't mean we should be gratuitously rude to her," Mother said.

"No, but isn't it a relief to know we don't have to be gratuitously chummy with her?"

"Dreadful woman," Mother murmured, and I suddenly felt more cheerful. Mother knew more ways to cause someone trouble without actually being rude than anyone I'd ever met. Mrs. Pruitt didn't stand a chance.

"I hope Burke knows what he's doing," Dad said, shaking his head as he helped himself to the tea. "He hasn't told us anything."

"Is that a hint?" I said. Dad's face brightened,

and after Mother left to cajole someone into brewing more coffee, I cheered Dad up by telling him what I knew.

Dad approved of everything I'd done—especially the things I'd glossed over when I told my story to the chief, like scanning the gully for Jane Doe's purse and matching the croquet mallet to the wound. But I should have known he'd find something I should have done differently. Dad read mysteries by the hundred and fancied himself quite an expert on detection.

"You got some good photos of the body?" he asked.

"Photos? I didn't have a camera."

"You had your cell phone," Dad said. "Doesn't it take photos?

"I have no idea," I said.

"You have the same model Rob has," he said. "His can take pictures."

"Does Rob actually take pictures with it?" I asked. I was genuinely curious. Only a week before, Rob had sought my help fixing his phone, and it turned out that he'd activated the keyguard during a game of Tetris and couldn't make calls for three days. Not that I'd tell Dad—Rob still owed me a large, as-yet-unspecified favor in return for not telling anyone else in the family.

"I don't expect *him* to," Dad said. "But I thought *you'd* have figured it out."

"Don't worry," I said. "Horace took photos. And they may need help identifying the victim, so I'm sure you'll get to look at them eventually."

I could tell this wasn't a satisfactory answer. He

wanted photos he could pore over, looking for clues. Not just a full-face photo but detailed close-ups of the wound, as well. He wandered off after giving me a reproachful look most parents wouldn't inflict on their kids unless they'd done something illegal or immoral.

Mother and Minerva Burke returned bearing plates of cookies, and we all stood back as the crowd descended on them like a flock of ravenous seagulls.

"What were you planning to do about dinner?" Mother asked, in a stage whisper.

"Nothing special," I said. "Michael will be tired from the faculty meeting, so I thought we'd stay in."

"I meant for your guests," Mother said.

"You mean the croquet players and the construction workers?" I said. "Send the locals home to find their own dinners, and give the students directions to Luigi's."

Mother shook her head. She should have realized by now that as a hostess, I'd never live up to her expectations. I usually exceeded her worst fears.

"Some of your guests aren't getting along," she murmured. I glanced up hastily. The last time she'd said that, I'd had to break up a fistfight between two cousins. This time, to my relief, no actual combat had begun. Mrs. Pruitt and the other Dames had gathered at one end of the room, pointedly not looking at Mrs. Briggs and the clones, who had clustered at the other end, ostentatiously ignoring Mrs. Pruitt and the Dames.

"Perhaps if you introduced them?" Mother suggested. "Drew them into conversation together?"

"Mother, it's a police investigation, not a party," I said. "If anyone's the host, it's Chief Burke."

"And he knows better than to expect those two lots to get along," Minerva Burke added. "You're lucky—they're behaving better than usual."

"It's a long-standing thing, then?" I asked. "I just assumed they were carrying the croquet rivalry too far."

"Where have you been, girl?" Minerva said. "Obviously not clawing your way up in Caerphilly society."

"Trying to avoid it," I said. "Why don't they like each other?"

"Mrs. Pruitt and her crowd make a big fuss about being descendants of the founding families of Caerphilly."

"And Mrs. Briggs and the clones aren't from around here," I said, nodding.

"Worse—they make money bringing in more people who aren't from around here," Mrs. Burke said. "May Briggs's husband built that development of town houses Mrs. Pruitt and her gang tried so hard to block. And Lady Pruitt still hasn't forgiven the clones for selling a house in Westlake to that professional basketball player. They did manage to stay civil to one another in public until the whole outlet-mall thing broke."

"Outlet mall?" Mother asked, her keen shopper's instincts coming to full alert.

"There's a rumor that Evan Briggs wants to build a big outlet mall in town," I said.

"More than a rumor," Mrs. Burke said. "He and

the clones have put together a formal proposal. Three million square feet—larger than Potomac Mills, which might make it the largest in the country. Henrietta Pruitt's leading the battle against it—the only useful thing I've seen her do in the four years we've been in town."

"Ah," I said. "So that's why they've all been so surly. Maybe I accidentally did something right, keeping them on different croquet fields all day. Probably prevented—well, who knows what."

I started to say bloodshed, then remembered Jane Doe.

"So what if the murdered woman is allied to one side or the other in the battle over the outlet mall?" I said aloud. "That might make anyone on the other side a logical suspect. We just have to look for the connection."

"If you find one, I'm sure Henry would be much obliged for the information," Mrs. Burke said, her tone sharper than usual.

"Naturally."

"How nice," Mother said. No doubt she'd heard Mrs. Burke's tone and thought another social rift needed mending. "I know Meg always enjoys assisting the police in their investigations—isn't that what they call it?"

"Usually, when the police say that, it means they're about to arrest the person, Mother," I said. "I'll just try not to get in the chief's way."

"I'm surprised you two aren't involved in the mall issue," Mrs. Burke said, dragging the conversation back to safe ground. "Considering how it affects you."

"Affects us?" I echoed. "What do you mean?" Though I had a sinking feeling I already knew.

"Well, they haven't named the location," Mrs. Burke said. "But if you look at the documents and know which local farmers haven't signed the protest petition—"

"Don't tell me," I said. "Mr. Shiffley's selling them his farm."

Chapter Six

I glared over at Mrs. Briggs and the clones. Then, for good measure, at the nearest Shiffleys. They were a close-knit clan; they had to know what their uncle was up to. Yet here they were, helping us beggar ourselves to fix up a house that might soon have the world's largest outlet mall in its backyard.

I figured I should volunteer to join Mrs. Pruitt's battle against the mall, even if it meant seeing more of her. If she was so gung ho on fighting the mall, why hadn't she enlisted Michael and me?

And in case Mrs. Pruitt and company lost the battle, shouldn't we halt all this expensive construction until we knew if we'd want to keep living here?

I looked up, to see Mrs. Burke studying me.

"Sorry," I said. "That's a lot to digest."

"Astonishing that no one told you anything about it before," Mrs. Burke said.

Which meant that if Jane Doe's murder proved related to the outlet-mall project, nobody in town would believe that Michael and I knew nothing about it. Or her.

The sooner they identified Jane, the better.

As if on cue, Chief Burke strode in. He paused dramatically in the doorway, expecting his arrival to quell the commotion, but conversation continued until Mother began tapping a spoon on her teacup. I quickly followed suit and we achieved a gratifyingly expectant hush.

"Thank you good people for coming here," the chief began. "We appreciate your cooperation."

"You're already gathering the suspects to tell us who done it?" Dad asked. "That was quick."

He sounded disappointed.

"No, of course not," the chief said, frowning and looking slightly flustered.

"How could he figure out who done it already?" I said. "We don't even know yet who's been done."

"You mean you don't even know her identity?" Dad asked, his good humor restored. "Amazing."

The chief had to rap sharply on the table to regain control of his meeting.

"That's what I'm hoping one of you can help me with," he said. "Do any of you know this woman?"

He held up a photo of Jane Doe.

He probably hoped someone would gasp out a name, or faint, or jump up to confess. But no one did. Seconds passed, then more seconds. People shifted from foot to foot.

"No one knows her?" the chief asked.

Mrs. Pruitt stared at the photo a few more seconds and shook her head. I could imagine her blackballing country club applicants just as coolly.

Mrs. Briggs's lips pursed disapprovingly and her

shrug suggested that she hadn't known the deceased and wouldn't have wanted to. Her husband gave the photo a cursory glance, shook his head, and put his hand on his wife's shoulder.

Both Suzies looked at the photo briefly and averted their eyes as if a streaker had crossed the room. Nice people didn't get murdered. Brought down property values.

Mrs. Wentworth gawked with obvious relish. She probably slowed to a crawl when passing traffic accidents.

Lacie Butler put both hands over her mouth and turned her face away slightly, while still peeking out of the corner of her eye. A silly reaction, though I'd seen plenty of women at scary movies doing much the same thing. At least Mrs. Wentworth was honest about her rubbernecking.

The six Shiffleys exchanged glances and, when they had settled the matter among themselves, crossed their arms or stuck their hands in their belt loops, shook their heads, and looked back at the chief in mute collective denial.

Dad stared as avidly as Mrs. Wentworth, though he had the excuse of wanting to draw medical conclusions.

Mrs. Fenniman was probably memorizing every detail, the better to gossip with later.

Rose Noire shook her head sadly and closed her eyes. I wasn't sure if she couldn't bear the violence implied by the photo or if she was performing some divination. Assessing the photo's aura perhaps. Doubtless we'd hear about it later.

The students shook their heads and their faces had a curiously familiar expression—one I'd seen often enough on Rob. The look of the habitual offender who didn't do it but expects to be blamed anyway. They shifted uneasily from foot to foot, and the muted jingling of their shin bells contrasted oddly with the somber mood of the room.

Rob showed more genuine emotion than anyone.

"Wow," he said, breaking the silence. "She was gorgeous. Wish I'd known her."

"I assume that means you didn't," the chief said. He sounded vexed. Not fair, taking out his disappointment on Rob that way, but Rob should learn to keep his mouth shut.

"Never even saw her," Rob said.

"None of you know her?" the chief asked, turning the frown on the rest of the company.

Much head shaking and a few murmurs.

"Someone must know her," the chief said, frowning.

"There're always the fingerprints, Chief," Sammy said.

The chief growled softly. Obviously he didn't think the fingerprints would help. I could understand his point. Having seen Jane Doe, I had a hard time imagining her getting fingerprinted. Manicured, yes, but fingerprinted?

The big meeting fizzled after that. The chief stomped out, obviously irritated. Sammy tried to make us all look at the photos again, but everybody ignored him. Instead, they all snuffled around the refreshment table, eating the last of the cookies and wearing the vexed expression of dinner guests left too long to forage on the appetizers.

Except for the college students. I wasn't sure whether to be annoyed or find their directness refreshing.

"So, what's for dinner?" one of them asked—the redhead who'd been flirting with me, and who seemed not to notice when I pointedly referred to the tall, dark, and handsome Michael as my fiancé.

"We thought people could fend for themselves," I said. "It's a college town—plenty of affordable places."

"Maybe you could recommend one?"

"Luigi's," I said. "Great pizza. Awesome selection of beers, or so I'm told; I'm not a big beer drinker."

"We'll have wine, then," he said. "My treat."

"Sorry," I said. "My fiancé and I have other plans."

"Ah, well," he said, shrugging. "Another time."

I gave him directions, ignoring the fact that he was giving me what my college roommate and I used to call "puppy dog eyes." I hadn't liked the whole mournful hangdog act then, and I didn't like it now. He snapped out of it fast enough when he rejoined his teammates and they all hurried out to their car.

Was I imagining things, or was their departure not just hasty but downright furtive?

What if I had misinterpreted their behavior when Chief Burke showed us Jane Doe's photo? I'd assumed it was the knee-jerk reaction of young men who expect to be blamed for anything that goes wrong when they're around. What if I'd seen real guilt? After all, none of the deputies knew her, which made it more plausible that none of the locals did, either. But someone knew her well enough to kill her. And the students, like Jane Doe, were strangers. What if—

"Meg?" asked Rob, standing at my elbow. "You okay? You have a funny look on your face."

"I'm fine," I said. Fine, except that I was starting to think like Dad, who saw everything as a potential clue in a real-life version of his beloved mysteries. The students probably just wanted to flee the company of so many old fogies. Evan Briggs, the developer, had spent the first half of our lunch break haranguing them for their feckless failure to major in business administration, and Mrs. Pruitt used the rest to interrogate them about their family histories and genealogies. Probably wise to vanish—Dad had recently developed a renewed interest in healthy eating, and had already remarked that he didn't think the students ate enough fiber.

For another thing, if I had to suspect someone of deception, why not Evan Briggs, who wanted to erect the world's largest outlet mall in our backyard? Who, after driving his wife to the game, couldn't possibly have spent every minute of the day watching the players and chatting with Dad. I glanced around to see what the developer was up to.

Talking with Rose Noire. And not enjoying it, from his expression. Rose Noire's intense interest in New Age subjects daunted most people. Her sweeping arm gestures suggested that she was telling him about the conversations she'd had this afternoon with the larger oak and poplar trees in Mr. Shiffley's woods. She'd developed a passionate interest in trees lately. I wondered how she'd react when she found out that Evan Briggs was planning to cut down hundreds of her beloved trees.

"What's up?" Dad said, appearing at my elbow. "Any good clues?"

Chapter Seven

"No clues," I said. "A few good motives." I brought him up to speed on Mr. Briggs's plans.

"Shocking," Dad said. "That would be an environmental catastrophe. You're right; he must be the killer."

"Not necessarily," I said. "Though he might be a suspect if we find out the dead woman's connected with Mrs. Pruitt's campaign against the mall. On the other hand, what if she's one of his employees and was killed by someone violently opposed to the mall?"

"Do you really think someone enlightened enough to oppose the mall would resort to violence?"

"Absolutely," I said. Dad looked startled—he hadn't spent as much time as I had with Mrs. Pruitt and the Dames. "You're right, though; Briggs seems more suspicious."

One of Mother's innumerable cousins dabbled in real estate development, though on a much smaller scale than Mr. Briggs. I knew from Cousin Ralph's misadventures that by the time developers presented a project to the county board, they'd have already spent a lot of money. Ralph barely escaped bankruptcy two or three times when community opposition shot down one of his projects. And worse, from Ralph's point of view, than community opposition—

"What if she's an environmentalist?" Dad said. "From the Sierra Club or the Fish and Wildlife Service?"

Cousin Ralph also had an uncanny gift for picking development sites already occupied by one or more endangered species. At parties, after a few too many glasses of punch, he sometimes become morose and said uncharitable things about the Virginia sneezeweed, the southern bog turtle, the Shenandoah salamander, the pink mucket, and the duskytail darter. Mother had forbidden everyone, on pain of banishment from all future family gatherings, to mention Ralph's particular bete noire, the Virginia fringed mountain snail, which he held personally responsible for his one actual bankruptcy.

Of course, Ralph was a mild-mannered soul who wouldn't have harmed the smallest fringe on the most hapless of mountain snails if his life as well as his solvency depended on it. But Briggs . . .

I savored the vision of Briggs being led off in handcuffs, his plans for the outlet mall crashing about his ears. Yes, I could live with Briggs as the killer. And much as I disliked her, if Mrs. Pruitt was leading the antimall forces, I hoped she hadn't done anything as stupid as killing one of the opposition. Surely if she had, we could argue it was the action of one unbalanced mind, and not—

I was thinking way too much like Dad. We had no idea who Jane Doe was, much less whether she'd had anything to do with the mall project. I decided I should leave detecting to Chief Burke and concentrate on getting through the weekend.

"Go talk to Mrs. Pruitt," I told Dad.

"You suspect her?"

"I suspect everyone. Engage her in conversation. But be subtle. Don't bring up the mall unless she does."

"Right," Dad said, hurrying off.

Not that I expected him to learn anything critical, but as long as he was talking to her, I didn't have to.

"We're taking off now," someone behind me said.

One of the Suzie clones. Both of whom were also involved in the outlet-mall project. They seemed less suspicious than Evan Briggs, but that was probably my innate prejudice. Why should a heavyset fiftyish killer in a two-button suit be easier to visualize than a perky thirty-something killer in expensive upscale leisure wear?

"We're so sorry," the other clone said. "Please let us know if there's anything we can do."

"We'll manage," I said. Which sounded a bit abrupt, but I couldn't say much more without giggling. Apparently, they'd decided to treat the murder like any other death in the household. One patted my hand solicitously.

"We'll be here with the food at ten-thirty tomorrow," the first clone said, as if reading my mind.

"Food?" I repeated. Did they plan to drop by with casseroles, as if we'd had a loss in the family?

"The picnic lunch for the players," she said. "You haven't forgotten that our team's doing lunch tomorrow?"

Actually, I had forgotten. Perhaps deliberately. When Mrs. Pruitt had suggested that the three local teams take turns organizing potluck meals for all the players, I'd tried to veto it, but Mother and Mrs. Fenniman overruled me. They were probably still chafing that I'd insisted on limiting the potluck meals to a Saturday lunch by the Realtors and a Sunday brunch by the Dames, with my team providing supplies for people to fix their own breakfasts. I didn't feel guilty—any sane person knows that a potluck meal always makes three times as much work for the person hosting it as for any of the cooks.

"Right," I said. "Though I doubt we'll play tomorrow."

"You'll still need to feed everyone," the clone said. "Chief Burke didn't want anyone leaving town."

"That's true," I said. "Won't be as large as planned, though—the other four teams won't be coming."

"Then the rest of us will just have to eat twice as much, won't we?" she said. "Can't waste all that potato salad!"

Her clone nodded and they tripped down the steps to their car. The Briggses followed. Mrs. Briggs gave me a characteristically wan, self-effacing smile. Mr. Briggs nodded curtly, as if anticipating what I'd say to him when I knew the outlet mall wasn't just a nasty rumor.

Which gave me an idea. I headed for the barn and

grabbed my cell phone to call my nephew Kevin, the family cyber whiz.

"Another problem with your computer?" he asked.

"Whatever happened to 'Hello, Aunt Meg, how are you, and is my little brother enjoying his visit?'"

"If you wanted to be sociable, you'd e-mail or call after dinner," he said. "It's okay, Mom; it's just Aunt Meg with another computer problem."

"Not a computer problem, a murder problem," I said. "Don't upset your mother; Eric's fine and he didn't see anything that would upset him."

"She says Eric's fine," he repeated. "I need to get on my computer to help her. Save me a piece of pie."

"I didn't mean to interrupt your dinner," I said.

"I was mostly finished anyway. So what's with your . . . problem?"

I filled Kevin in on the murder, deliberately leaving out any gory details, in the interest of maintaining my reputation as a responsible and trustworthy aunt. He pried them out of me anyway, but luckily the details weren't all that gory—not for a kid who'd grown up around Dad.

"So what do you want me to do?" he asked.

"See what you can find on this outlet-mall project."

"You think it's connected to the murder?"

"It might be," I said. "It's sure as heck connected to our property."

"Would it be so bad having a mall nearby?"

"It's not just a mall; it's a contender for the largest mall in the universe."

"Even cooler."

"Did I mention that they'd be building it where you and your friends played paintball last summer?"

"Gotcha," he said. "Definitely a threat to civilization as we know it. I'll let you know what I find."

"Thanks. About the murder—don't scare your mother."

"Right," he said, and hung up.

I felt better. If cyberspace contained any information about the outlet-mall project, Kevin would find it. I'd also accidentally given myself an out if Pam chastised me for not telling her about the murder. I'd said, "Don't scare your mother"—not "Don't tell her." If Kevin chose to interpret that as an order not to tell . . .

Yes, I definitely felt better. Then I glanced at my watch and realized Michael would be home soon. I felt a surge of relief so intense, it was almost physical. His return wouldn't solve anything, and I didn't plan to dump my troubles on him or let anyone else dump theirs. But having him around made me feel less stressed, more grounded. We'd get through this.

I reached under the desk mat and pulled out the photo of Jane Doe, mainly to make sure Horace hadn't seen through my act and confiscated it. Rob was right: she'd been beautiful. About my age, but she'd been one of those tall, slender blondes who made me feel so insecure about my brunette hair and more normal shape. Although her clothes were disheveled, she'd dressed with more flair than I did. Not that the photo showed much of her clothes, but the edge of the scarf around her neck brought back the whole outfit. Neat, well-fitted khaki pants and a crisp beige blouse. The only hint of color was the scarf, in tones of beige, white, and spring green. She'd even known how to tie the damned thing. My rare attempts to accessorize with scarves always ended badly, looking like a dress rehearsal for suicide by hanging or an attempt to cover up a bulky neck cast. Her scarf looked crisp and chic.

I might have disliked her, if I'd met her, but the fixed stare of those blue eyes washed away petty dislikes. She'd been alive, and someone had taken that away. I felt a cold wave of anger. I had to do something.

Which was silly, since I didn't even know who she was.

I dropped the photo back on the desk and headed for the house.

Chapter Eight

I went the long way around—through the front door—to eavesdrop on Chief Burke, though I didn't learn much.

"The area's not that big, damn it!" I heard him growl.

"Yes, but we could miss vital evidence in the dark," Sammy said. "And besides, parts of those woods are dangerous—there could be more old mine shafts around."

Now they tell us.

"True," the chief said. "I want someone on guard out there—Sammy, set up shifts. We'll pick up in the morning. At daybreak."

A ragged chorus of assents followed, and officers began spilling into the hall. I pretended to be doing something with the boxes of papers that lined one wall—the papers a female professor from UVa should have picked up hours ago. I called Kevin again.

"Still working on it," he said. Pam had definitely

failed to teach him that something along the lines of "hello" was a more customary way to answer the phone.

"One more thing. Can you find a photo of someone?"

"I can try," he said. In the background, I heard the telltale rattle of a keyboard. "Who?"

"Helen Carmichael. Professor of history at UVa."

"What's she done?" he said over more key rattling.

"Nothing, except she never called to tell me that she couldn't make it here after all. Which doesn't prove she's our unknown murder victim, but . . ."

"Cool. Hang on a sec."

Intense key rattling. I had to remind myself to breathe. Would the satisfaction of being the first to learn Jane Doe's identity make up for how mad the chief would be if he thought I'd withheld information? I honestly hadn't thought about the professor until I'd seen the boxes again.

"Piece of cake," he said. "History department has faculty profiles. Some of them have photos. Hers does."

"Is she blond?"

"Brunette, and graying."

"She could have dyed it. Does she—"

"Hang on, I'll send you a copy."

"I'm not at the computer."

"I'm sending it to your cell phone. Take a look."

I pulled the phone away from my ear and looked. A photo filled the screen. Helen Carmichael had a round, cheerful face, short graying dark hair, and, best I could tell on so tiny a photo, dark eyes. She'd need not just a dye job but major plastic surgery to resemble Jane Doe.

"It's not her," I said, feeling relief wash over me. "Not the dead woman, I mean."

"Rats."

"It's okay," I said. "It was just a wild idea."

Besides, I liked the idea that Jane Doe was a perfect stranger who had nothing to do with me or anyone I knew. Which probably wouldn't turn out to be the case, but it was nice while it lasted.

"I'll keep working on the real estate scam," Kevin said. "Bye."

I tried calling Professor Carmichael's number. No answer. I put away the phone and headed for the parlor to see what mischief my remaining guests were causing.

I found Dad deep in conversation with Mrs. Pruitt.

"I'm glad you see my point," Mrs. Pruitt was saying. "Lucius has no understanding at all. Keeps making jokes about my trips to dig up my ancestors, as if I were some kind of grave robber."

Several of the Shiffleys lounging across the room snorted with laughter. Evidently, they saw Lucius Pruitt's point of view. Mrs. Pruitt ignored them.

"I certainly understand the passion to learn about one's family history," Dad said. "I've been researching mine for years."

"How splendid," Mrs. Pruitt said. "How far back have you gotten?"

She smiled graciously, no doubt thinking she'd found a kindred spirit. Dad would set her straight.

"No further than when I started, alas," Dad said.

"How far is that?" Mrs. Pruitt said in the slightly cooler tone she saved for people whose ancestors had left no traces of themselves in the county property-tax rolls.

"I was a foundling," Dad said. "Abandoned at birth."

"How awful," Mrs. Pruitt said, drawing away slightly. "They never found your parents?"

"No," Dad said. "The police tried. So did the librarians, of course, and if they had no luck, I suppose I should have known it was a lost cause."

"The librarians," Mrs. Pruitt repeated.

"Yes," Dad said. "That's where I was found—in the fiction section of the public library, teething on a copy of *The Hound of the Baskervilles.* Which I always thought was a nice omen, don't you think?"

"Very nice," Mrs. Pruitt said. She didn't look as if she thought it nice at all. How remiss of me not to have sicced Dad on her sooner. Quite apart from the entertainment potential, it might have spared me her presence this weekend.

"Yes," Dad said. "Early childhood influences are so important—I think that explains my passion for murder!"

"Only on paper," I added quickly. Mrs. Pruitt didn't look reassured.

"Look at the time!" she said, "I really must be going. Meg, dear, thank you so much for . . . everything."

With that, she hurried out.

The various Shiffleys rose as if on cue. Four of them headed for the door, while the other two ambled over to me.

"Going to Cousin Fred's for dinner," one of them said. Randall, who seemed to be the foreman, or at least the one who liked giving orders. "Won't be back too late."

"Back?" I walked out onto the porch with them.

"Chief wanted us around, in case he had more questions," Randall said. "We figured on sleeping here anyway, if work went late, so we brought the campers."

"Maybe he'll let us get on with it in the morning," the other one said. "If not—"

"Lacie!" Mrs. Pruitt's voice boomed from the end of the driveway. "We're leaving now."

The two Shiffleys glared in Mrs. Pruitt's direction. No love lost there. If Jane turned out to be a Pruitt . . .

Lacie shot past, limping slightly, no doubt because she was wearing one shoe and carrying the other.

"Coming, Henrietta! Coming!" she called.

Halfway down the driveway, she finally stopped to put on her second shoe, though she shouldn't have tried to do it standing up. And why didn't she set down the bundles slung over both shoulders? Not just her own gear but also Mrs. Pruitt's and Mrs. Wentworth's croquet equipment, minus the mallets, which had gone to the crime lab in Richmond with the other confiscated mallets and the sledgehammers.

"They coming back tomorrow?" Randall asked, jerking his thumb at where Mrs. Pruitt and Mrs. Wentworth were stolidly watching Lacie's efforts from their car.

"God, I hope not," I muttered. And then, aloud, I said, "Depends on whether the chief lets us resume the tournament tomorrow."

"Good," Randall said, "Can't wait to hear more 'bout the Battle of Pruitt's Ridge. Night."

"Night," the other Shiffley said. The two of them set off down the lane with a long-legged gait that looked relaxed but covered ground with surprising speed. I could hear them chuckling until they reached their truck.

"What's the joke?" Dad asked, joining me.

"Beats me," I said. "Was Mrs. Pruitt telling you about the Battle of Pruitt's Ridge?"

"Yes," he said. "Fascinating story—that was when Colonel Jedidiah Pruitt won his medal from the Confederacy, you know. Must be wonderful to have ancestors like that."

"I'm sure we do," I said. "I can't imagine that our ancestors would be . . . boring."

The word *normal* almost slipped out, but I caught myself in time.

"Thanks," he said. "But it's not the same as knowing all about them, is it? Ah, here's your mother," he added as Mother stepped out onto the porch.

"We'll see you tomorrow, dear," Mother said, giving me a quick kiss on the cheek.

"I'm sure I'll see everyone tomorrow," I said. "Once word about the murder gets out. Police and

FBI agents and reporters and everyone in town with nothing better to do."

"I'll come over early to help, dear," Mother called over her shoulder as they strolled down the front walk. An oddly comforting offer. Mother didn't cook or clean, like other people's mothers— she rarely did anything like other people's mothers—but if I could get her to tackle a task, she'd get it done. If I asked her to help get Mrs. Pruitt and Mrs. Wentworth out of my life . . .

More immediate comfort had arrived. Michael's convertible sputtered into silence out on the road. I heard him exchange good nights with Mother and Dad, and a few seconds later, he strolled up the front walk.

"Is that a pizza box?" I asked. I suddenly realized I was starving.

"You notice the pizza box and not the brown paper bag from the Wine Cellar," Michael said, shaking his head. "Sometimes I wonder about your priorities."

"I was getting to the brown paper bag," I said. "Not to give anyone a swelled head or anything, but the first thing I noticed was the hunk carrying the wine and pizza."

"This isn't a hunk," he said with a faint smile. "It's a tired bureaucrat who's had a long day of meetings. I forfeited my eligibility for hunkdom when I agreed to be on the Academic Community Enrichment Committee."

"What does that do?"

"Plans the departmental spring picnic," he said,

wrapping the arm with the bottle around me. "And the fall picnic, and the holiday party, unless I can weasel out over the summer."

"Cheer up," I said as we headed for the barn. "At least there's food involved."

"I knew faculty life wouldn't all be like Indiana Jones, wearing a corduroy jacket with leather elbow patches and lecturing to adoring coeds," he said.

"Better not be."

"But the bureaucracy gets worse every year. Besides—what was Chief Burke doing here?"

He pointed. The chief and several deputies were strolling down the walk. Leaving, thank goodness.

"I was saving that for later, when you felt more cheerful," I said. "We had a murder."

"I knew eXtreme croquet was a bad idea," he said. "From your calm demeanor, I assume it's no one we know."

"No one anyone knows, supposedly," I said. "Someone's lying, though. I don't know who, but I'm sure someone is."

We adjourned to our bedroom stall and I filled him in while we demolished the pizza and a bottle of shiraz.

"Okay, I was wrong," Michael said when I'd finished. "I thought I'd had a rotten day, but yours tops it."

"Wonder if Chief Burke will let the Shiffleys work on the house tomorrow," I said.

"I could go to town and buy more sledgehammers."

"What if he decides we can't work on the house until he's solved the murder?"

"The sooner she's identified, the better, then," Michael said. "Has he considered publishing her photo in the newspaper?"

"I suspect that's a last resort," I said. "Tough on her friends and relatives, seeing her photo in the paper with a caption that says 'Do you know this stiff?'"

"True," he said.

"Anyway, maybe we should worry more about the possibility of a giant mall in our backyard. Join forces with Mrs. Pruitt to battle it or something."

"You're sure it's not a wild rumor?" Michael asked.

"Good point," I said. "Kevin's doing some cyber-sleuthing. Let's see what he's found."

I decided to check my e-mail rather than calling. Avoid annoying Kevin if he was still working. I strolled into the office and turned on my computer. Michael trailed behind, swirling the last of the shiraz in his glass.

"If it's not one thing . . ." he said under his breath. He looked discouraged. I felt suddenly guilty about dumping bad news on him when he'd had such a tough day. Then he glanced up, smiled, and I found myself wondering if the students could be relied on to stay at Luigi's for another hour or so, or if they'd come barging in—

The computer played the chord that told me it was ready for action, and I clicked the icon to open my mail.

"Five messages from Kevin," I said as I scanned my e-mail. "All full of links and attachments. Yes, I'd say the mall project's definitely more than a rumor. I'll read it all tomorrow. Right now— Michael? What's wrong?"

He was staring at my desk, looking at my contraband photo of the murder victim, which really wasn't gory enough to account for the slightly ill expression on his face.

"This is the murder victim?" he asked, his voice sounding shaky.

"Yes," I said. "You know her, don't you?"

He nodded.

"Her name's Lindsay Tyler," he said. "We were . . . um, involved."

Chapter Nine

" 'Involved,' " I echoed. I thought I kept my voice neutral, but Michael's head shot up.

"Not recently," he said. "My first year here in Caerphilly. I haven't seen her since she left the college. Almost five years ago. Before we met."

"Okay," I said. I was embarrassed to realize that I did feel relieved.

"We were thrown together, being practically the only new faces on the faculty that year," he said. "Plus the coincidence of both having done our graduate work at William and Mary, though in different departments and at different times. We hit it off at first, but it had more or less fizzled out by the time she left. In fact, long before she left, though I didn't take any formal steps to break up for a while, because I didn't think she needed to get dumped on top of everything else that was happening to her. The laugh was on me when I found out—ah, well . . ."

His voice trailed off and he seemed lost in thought.

" 'Everything else that was happening'?" I prompted after a few seconds. "Like what?"

"She didn't leave voluntarily," he said.

"They fired her?"

"Not technically. She was an instructor, on a one-year contract. They just didn't renew her contract."

"Doesn't that amount to the same thing?" I said. "She was out of a job."

"Not just out of a job. They'd all but promised her a tenure-track position, and here she was, out on the street."

I nodded. I knew what that meant. In theory, the fact that Caerphilly hadn't kept her on shouldn't have mattered, but in the real world, it had made her a lot less attractive to other colleges. Many departments would rather start over with a newly minted Ph.D. than take castoffs from some other school's faculty. A fact I sometimes fretted over when I thought about Michael's career. In a sane world, his teaching skills and publishing credits should have made him a shoo-in for the tenure-track position he'd pursued for the last six years. But Caerphilly College didn't operate in a sane world, and if he didn't get tenure here . . .

"She had a hard time finding another faculty job?" I asked, forcing my mind back to the problem at hand.

He nodded.

"Took her over a year, from what I heard, and all she found was some tiny little college out west. In Wyoming or Montana, or someplace. Which she would have hated; she thought Caerphilly was dull and way too far from the city."

"Why did they fire—sorry, fail to renew her contract?" I asked.

"Officially, they were cutting department staff," he said. "The real reason: She ticked too many people off."

"It's those all-important people skills that get you every time."

"It's not that she completely lacked people skills," he said. "Lindsay could manipulate people with the best of them."

"I'd call that a character flaw, not a people skill."

"That's one of the things I like most about you," he said, glancing up with a quick smile that flooded me with relief. "Yeah, she enjoyed manipulating people. That was what did her in."

"You think someone she was manipulating murdered her?"

Michael winced.

"Sorry, I meant did her career in," he said. "Now that you mention it, odds are, if you knew who she'd been playing mind games on recently, you could find the killer. I should go find Chief Burke and tell him all about this, right?"

"Definitely," I said. "As soon as you finish telling me. Do you think it's possible that anyone she ticked off back then might still hold a grudge?"

"Oh yes," he said. "Not only possible but probable."

"For example?"

"Most of the history department, for starters," he said. "I'm sure she ticked off people in other departments, too, but your own department's always the one where you make the most friends and enemies."

"She was a history instructor?" I asked. Something wasn't tracking here.

"Specializing in Virginia history, too, which any reasonable person could have parlayed into a neat berth at a history-mad place like Caerphilly."

"Was Marcus Wentworth chair of the department back then?"

"He's been chair for twenty years."

"Then would you find it surprising to learn that Mrs. Wentworth couldn't identify Lindsay's body?"

Michael blinked.

"Very surprising indeed," he said. "Downright suspicious. I'd think she, of all people, would recognize Lindsay."

"They knew each other well?"

"Not that well, but wouldn't a woman tend to remember someone who had an affair with her husband?"

"Under the circumstances, I think her name and face would be indelibly engraved on my memory."

"Precisely. May I add that I plan never to give you any reason to engrave any names or faces on your memory."

"Good plan," I said. "Because I'm not sure I'd be as forbearing as Mrs. Wentworth."

"Forbearing? You didn't see her reaction."

"She's not actually a widow."

"Good point," he said, smiling. "On the other hand, I suspect she knew who was to blame, and Lindsay's dead now. Although the time gap makes her less of a suspect."

"Not necessarily," I said. "Revenge is a dish best

served cold, you know. Look, are we talking about the same Wentworths here? I mean Claire, the skinny golf-playing one who's married to Marcus, the chairman of the history department, the one who looks like an albino telephone pole."

"I've always thought of him as a walking cadaver, but yes, those Wentworths," Michael said. "Getting back to the forbearing thing—did I mention that she broke an antique Delft chamber pot over his head?"

"Ouch! Please tell me it was full at the time."

"Yes, but only of sticky-sweet green punch that no one was drinking anyway, because everyone else found it slightly off-putting to serve punch in a chamber pot, however thoroughly sanitized."

"Yuck," I said. "I agree. She did this in public?"

"At one of their pretentious garden parties," Michael said. "To which I don't get invited anymore, thank goodness. History department only. Or maybe she didn't find my behavior suitable."

"What did you do?" I asked, though I wasn't altogether sure I wanted to know.

"Nothing at first. I mean, what are you supposed to do when the woman you've escorted to a party is found in flagrente delicto with the host? Punch someone's lights out? Slink home and brood for a few centuries? After Claire did her number with the chamber pot—I couldn't help it—I started laughing."

"Not very dignified."

"Yeah, but you should have seen it," he said, grinning at the memory. "There was Claire standing there with the broken chamber pot's handle in her hand,

and Marcus sitting on the floor covered with fizzy green slime, like some extra from *The Exorcist*—well, it was funny."

He laughed, and I joined him. Less at the thought of the Wentworths in such an uncharacteristically embarrassing situation than at the relief I felt. No motive for murder here—not for Michael anyway; once his sense of humor kicked in, he didn't hold a grudge, I'd found. Which gave me even less reason for jealousy.

"I take it the thing with Wentworth wasn't true love?"

"More like a last-ditch attempt to hang on to her job."

"And that was the end of it?" I asked.

"With Marcus, probably. With me, definitely. She did come over the next day to apologize. To explain that it wasn't personal; she only wanted to save her career. I think that was supposed to make me feel better."

"And did it?"

"Didn't matter by that time. I was relieved to have grounds for breaking up. But you can't expect Mrs. Wentworth to take as philosophical a view."

"No," I said. "If you ask me, Claire Wentworth has motive for murder. Possibly Marcus Wentworth, too, but he wasn't hanging around here all day like Claire."

"She was hanging around here? Why?"

He didn't sound thrilled.

"Playing eXtreme croquet," I said. "She's on Henrietta Pruitt's team."

"Here I thought croquet was a nice ladylike sport that would help you find some genteel, respectable associates," Michael said. "Instead, I find you consorting with the likes of Claire Wentworth and Henrietta Pruitt."

"If it makes you feel any better, they were well on their way to ignominious defeat at the hands of my team when Chief Burke interrupted the game."

"Well, that's something," Michael said. "So maybe I should go talk to Chief Burke."

"Talk to me about what?"

Chapter Ten

We both started. The chief was standing in the door of the tack room, frowning down at us.

"I can identify your victim," Michael said, holding up the photo. "Her name is Lindsay Tyler. She used to be on the Caerphilly College faculty, so they can give you more information."

"Sammy!" the chief called over his shoulder, his eyes fixed on Michael. A few seconds later, Sammy appeared at his shoulder. "Get hold of the personnel director at the college."

"They're probably closed now, Chief," Sammy said.

"I'm sure they are," the chief said. "If you can't get hold of the personnel director, call President Hayes. You can find his number, I'm sure. Tell him we want the file on a former faculty member named Lindsay Tyler. Pronto."

"Yes, sir," Sammy said, and disappeared.

"While we're waiting for what the college can tell us, suppose you tell me what you know," the chief said to Michael.

Michael nodded.

"You can close the door on your way out," the chief said, glancing at me.

I did so with exaggerated care.

At least Michael's beastly all-day faculty meeting had one unexpected benefit: He'd have an alibi.

I realized that I was trying not to breathe in my efforts to overhear what Michael and the chief were saying in the tack room. Better to remove the temptation to eavesdrop. Also the suspicion.

I took a shower. We'd installed a working bathroom in the barn to make living there tolerable for the summer. Later on, it would be handy for cleaning up after gardening or a particularly messy workday in my forge. Remembering all the poison ivy I'd seen during the day, I didn't skimp on the soap or hot water.

I could still hear voices from the tack room when I finished, so I headed for the house.

"Hello!" a voice called when I was halfway there. One of the students fell into step beside me. Not Tony, the tall redheaded one who kept trying to pick me up, though from just "Hello" I couldn't tell which of the other two this was. Graham spoke with an English accent, and Bill, the other, hardly said anything.

"You're back," I said, trying to make it a statement of fact rather than a complaint.

"I never left, actually," he said. Aha. Graham, the Englishman. "I wasn't up for a lot of bother, so I just ate leftovers from lunch and had a bit of nap in the back of the van. I'm not as keen on pub crawling as Tony and Bill."

"Sensible of you," I said. "Especially if the chief does let us resume the tournament tomorrow."

"Hope he does," Graham said. "Long drive from West Virginia just to sit around being suspects."

Aha. So they were the West Virginia team.

"How did you end up at a college in West Virginia, anyway?" I asked, genuinely curious.

"It's rather a joke on me," he said. "You see, I've always been keen on the American West. Cowboys and Indians. The gold rush. Dodge City. Deadwood. *Bonanza.* That sort of thing. So when it came time to go to university, I thought it would be a super idea to apply to some schools in the frontier states."

"I see," I said. "You ended up in West Virginia."

"I'm afraid I did a rather bad job of research."

"Right place, wrong century," I said with a shrug. "Back in Colonial days, the only period of history that really matters in large parts of the Old Dominion, West Virginia *was* the frontier."

"How kind of you to say so," he murmured, and his face lighted up with an expression of abject gratitude and devotion that would have made a deep impression on me during my undergraduate days. Now, it just made me nervous—how many times did I need to introduce these kids to Michael, anyway?

Possibly the time for such subtle measures had passed.

"Does the soulful, lonely exile act work on the girls back in West Virginia?" I asked.

He blinked.

"Not particularly," he said in a more normal tone of voice. "I've been assuming it was because the girls in Pineville think I'm a perfect dolt for coming to West Virginia in the first place."

"Maybe it's more that you make it pretty obvious that you think you're a perfect dolt for going there," I suggested. "Could lead them to assume you think they're dolts for not leaving."

"You could be right," he said. "So I've totally blown my chances of ever getting . . . a date in Pineville?"

"Not necessarily," I said. "Why not just concentrate on being more positive when you meet new people?"

"What new people?" he said with a sigh. "Total enrollment's only five hundred—we all rather know one another by now. For that matter, the population of Wyoming County can't be much over twenty-five thousand. Coming from Bristol, with over half a million people—"

"The population of where?"

"Bristol," he said. "It's where I grew up; a city on the—"

"I know where Bristol is," I said. "Did you say Wyoming County?"

"Yes. How was I supposed to know it was in the middle of Appalachia instead of the Rockies?"

"There's a county in West Virginia called Wyoming?"

"Yes," he said, looking puzzled. "That's where Pineville College is located. Wyoming County.

Southwest West Virginia. Any farther southwest and it'd be part of Kentucky, or so I'm told. In a place that small, how am I supposed to meet—"

"Let's talk about this later," I said. "I just realized I have to run and do something."

I was about to dash back to the barn to use my desktop computer, when I realized that Michael and the chief were still in the tack room. Was it too late to call Kevin? No, only nine o'clock.

"You got all the stuff?" he said when he picked up.

"Yes, and I'm still working through it. I owe you big time. Look, can you do one more quick search for me?"

"Sure, what?"

"Can you see if Pineville College in West Virginia has a Web site?"

"You could just Google that yourself," he said.

"I could, if the police weren't interrogating Michael in my office."

"Oh, cool," he said. Keys rattled. "Yeah . . . lot of Pinevilles in the country. Most of them have colleges. Here it is. Pineville College, Pineville, West Virginia."

"Do they have a faculty directory, like UVa?"

"Not as slick as UVa's. No photos."

"Do you see a Lindsay Tyler there? Try the history department."

More typing.

"No Lindsay."

Damn.

"There is a Tyler, though. L. Blake Tyler. Instructor in the history department. Female; says *she* received her Ph.D. from William and Mary."

"Thanks," I said. "That's exactly what I was looking for. By the way, while you're looking, could you tell me what you can find out about a Civil War battle?"

"Which one?"

"The Battle of Pruitt's Ridge. Took place in or around Caerphilly—possibly near our house—sometime during the Civil War. And Colonel Jedidiah Pruitt, the hero thereof." I spelled the names for him.

"Roger," he said. "Any date on the battle?"

"Sorry, no," I said. "Not yet anyway, but if I get any more specifics, I'll call or e-mail you."

"That would help, but we can work around it. I'll check with Joss, too," he added, referring to his older sister, Jocelyn, whose passion for history matched Dad's enthusiasm for mysteries, or Kevin's for computers.

"Thanks," I said. "I owe you."

I thought of going back and tackling Graham about his failure to identify Lindsay. Then I saw Chief Burke stride by in the direction of the house. I headed for the barn to see how Michael had fared.

Assuming I could find Michael. He wasn't in the tack room or the bedroom stall. Which irritated me but wasn't exactly Michael's fault, so I focused on my irritation with the students.

"Damn," I said aloud.

Chapter Eleven

"What's wrong?"

I started at Michael's voice and turned, to see him poking his head out of a stall at the other end of the barn, which he'd been using as a reading carrel. He was holding a book with his finger between the pages as a bookmark.

"Lindsay got her Ph.D. at William and Mary, right?"

"Right. Why?"

"Those miserable liars," I muttered.

"Which ones this time?"

"The students," I said. "Those bald-faced lying Morris men. What are the odds someone could spend over half a school year on campus with an enrollment of only five hundred students and not know one of the faculty members by sight, even if he didn't have a class with her?"

"Long odds, I imagine," Michael said. "Although gender equity has made enormous strides on the college campus, I suspect your use of a feminine pronoun for the faculty member means we're talking about Lindsay?"

"We are," I said.

"Makes the odds even longer, then," Michael said. "I hope you won't take it the wrong way if I suggest that Lindsay is—was anyway—the sort of woman men tend to notice."

"I got that impression from our brief acquaintance," I said. "And two of these students have demonstrated that they're perfectly capable of appreciating the charms of an older woman. Older by their definition, at any rate."

"Really?" Michael said. He stepped out of the stall, shoving a slip of paper in the book as he did. "Which two?"

"The smarter two," I said. "Don't interrupt me when I'm venting. We're not talking about just one blatant liar, either. Odds are, all three are lying. She was on the faculty of their college—it's a tiny college in a tiny, isolated town—impossible that not one of them recognized her."

"Wait a minute," Michael said. "I thought they drove in from West Virginia."

"Wyoming County, West Virginia," I said. "I'm pretty sure that's where Lindsay landed."

"Amazing," Michael said, sounding thoughtful. "All this time and she was only one state away."

"A six-hour drive," I said. "According to the students. They probably drove like maniacs."

"True," he said. "Still, when I thought about her, which wasn't all that often, I always found it comforting to think that there was half a continent between us. A six-hour drive isn't much. After all, those students thought nothing of coming that far just to play eXtreme croquet."

"Or did they?" I asked. "Doesn't that seem too far-fetched a coincidence? They're playing in an eXtreme croquet match several hundred miles from home and she just happens to get killed less than a mile away?"

"Probably not a coincidence at all," he said. "By the way, the chief came out here looking for you, not me. Had something he wanted to ask you."

"Roger," I said. "I should go and see him."

Michael nodded and reopened his book—*Treasure Island,* I noted with dismay. Not that I had anything against the book, but I knew that one of Michael's stress-coping mechanisms was rereading children's books.

I hurried up to the house. Things had calmed down considerably. The living room was empty except for Minerva Burke, who sat on lawn chair in one corner, knitting.

"How are you holding up, hon?" she asked.

"I've been better," I said. "Michael said the chief was looking for me."

She rolled her eyes.

"If that fool man would stay put so people could find him, instead of running around biting everyone's head off. It'll be a miracle if both of us survive till the cast comes off."

"Maybe I should stay put and wait for him."

She nodded. I sat down on the floor, leaned against the wall, and closed my eyes. Rude of me not to make conversation, but it was late. Mrs. Burke was tired, too. Normally, she knitted at breakneck speed, but tonight she was moving slowly, and stopping every so often to frown and stare at her needles as if she thought she might have made a mistake.

"There you are." Chief Burke's voice jolted me out of a doze. "I was looking for you." Actually, at the moment, he was looking at his cast and trying to insert something between it and his skin.

"I haven't gone anywhere," I said. "And— What are you doing? If you want to make a break for freedom, I'll lend you a hacksaw. That's my best flat bastard file you're manhandling.

"The blamed thing itches like the very devil," the chief said. "Doesn't work anyway," he said, handing me the file. "Anything small enough to fit in there breaks off."

"Oh, wonderful," I said. "So now you've got random bits of broken-off stuff stuck up inside your cast, compounding the itching problem."

I heard a splutter of suppressed laughter from Minerva Burke. The chief glowered at me.

"Why didn't you tell Dad about this when he was here?" I went on. "He might prescribe or recommend something."

"You think so?"

"Call him now," I said.

"I might do that." He didn't reach for his phone, though.

"Or don't call, if you want to be stubborn," I said with a shrug. "Just don't wait till it gets really unbearable in the middle of the night. He usually goes to bed around midnight. In case you're curious, I know where Lindsay Tyler is living. Was living, that is."

"Do you really?" the chief said, lifting one eyebrow.

"In or around Pineville, West Virginia."

The chief narrowed his eyes.

"Just how did you figure that out?" he asked. From the sharp tone of his voice, I suspected I was right.

I explained about Graham and Wyoming County.

"But he and the other students had already said they didn't know her," Chief Burke said, frowning.

"Yeah, but we already know one person was lying about knowing her. Michael told you she had an affair with Claire Wentworth's husband, right? I have a hard time believing some of the others never met her in the year she was here. I bet most of them are lying, so why should the students be any different?"

"In other words, you suspected them because they had no reason to lie," the chief said with a sigh.

"I know it sounds crazy—"

"Right now, it makes as much sense as anything else," the chief said. "I found out her location through more pedestrian methods. Seth Early reported an SUV with West Virginia plates parked down by the old tobacco barn on his property. When we ran the tag numbers, her name and address came up."

"Good for Mr. Early," I said.

"Course, he's still not happy," the chief said, sighing again. "Seems he's missing some sheep. Thought the SUV had something to do with it."

"Wouldn't actual sheep thieves bring a slightly larger vehicle?" I asked.

"You could fit a couple of sheep in a big SUV like that," the chief said. "Not the half dozen he's missing, though. Not without leaving traces."

"Tell me about it," I said. Farmer Early's sheep had developed an inexplicable fondness for escaping their pasture and lounging around in our front yard. Small tufts of greasy gray wool were the least obnoxious of the traces they left. "So the missing sheep are still at large."

"I'm having a dickens of a time convincing Seth Early that the SUV's owner didn't have much time for sheep rustling before she was killed."

"She was involved in many things, but I doubt if the black sheep market was one of them," I said.

"Hmph," the chief said. "Anyway, we know about Pineville. If you run across any sheep—"

"We know the way to Mr. Early's pasture, thanks."

I headed back to the barn. The chief was pulling out his cell phone as I left, and just as I hit the back door, I heard him speak.

"Dr. Langslow? Sorry to bother you so late, but Meg suggested I call."

I left. Maybe, if the students weren't back yet, I'd see if I could do a better job than Robert Louis Stevenson of cheering up Michael.

Chapter Twelve

The Ghost of Christmas Past was sitting on my chest, forcing me to relive the horrible Christmas when I was twelve and Dad decided to run up and down the roof in the middle of the night, waving a string of sleigh bells and shouting, "Ho, ho, ho!" Which wouldn't have been so horrible if he hadn't terrified Rob, who ran shrieking out into the night, startling Dad into falling off the roof and breaking his arm. Mother and I spent the night in the emergency room with Dad; Pam and several dozen neighbors were up till dawn looking for Rob; and while we were out, the three weimaraners we were dog-sitting ate the half-thawed turkey. I've disliked sleigh bells ever since.

My mood didn't improve when I woke to find that this jingling was actually the Mountain Morris Mallet Men arming themselves for the day. They were trying to be quiet, tiptoeing and shushing one another. I hate it when people do that. They usually take twice as long and make almost as much noise as if they'd just gone ahead and done whatever they had to do in their usual fashion.

I glanced at the travel alarm. Nine-thirty. I deduced we weren't playing croquet this morning, or someone would have come to badger me a lot earlier.

Michael was already up. Getting an early start on the day, or driven out by the tintinabulation of the bells?

I'd find out later. For now, I closed my eyes again. The general idea was to get a little more sleep, but the worrying part of my brain kicked into gear. Naturally, instead of worrying about the interrupted construction, which really was my problem, or the interrupted croquet match, which Mrs. Fenniman would try to make my problem, or the threat of the outlet mall, which would be a humongous problem if true, I worried about the murder.

Mrs. Wentworth had lied about knowing Lindsay. The students had almost certainly lied. What if they weren't the only ones?

Mrs. Pruitt. The more I thought about it, the odder it seemed that she'd fallen behind me in the croquet game. I could have sworn she'd taken an annoying early lead and spent the first half of the game rubbing it in whenever she talked on the radio. Yet just before I found Lindsay's body, she'd suddenly turned up behind me. What if she'd taken a detour to kill Lindsay and rejoined the game in progress? She could even have deliberately come up behind me so she could roquet my ball into the brier patch, thus making sure I'd find the body. Didn't the police always suspect the person who found the body? Or was this another notion I'd gotten from Dad and his mystery books?

Of course, Mrs. Pruitt as the culprit would be more plausible if I could think of a motive for her to kill Lindsay.

Lindsay was a history instructor—had spent a year in the history department at Caerphilly College. Mrs. Pruitt ran the Caerphilly Historical Society. Was it realistic to think they'd never met?

That depended on whether Mrs. Pruitt had been involved in the historical society six years ago, when Lindsay was here. All I had to do was find a tactful way to ask.

Then again . . . I ambled into the office and searched my in basket. Yes, there it was—the fund-raising letter we'd recently gotten from the society. Which included a promotional booklet— an expensive-looking little thing, its cover made of thick textured paper and decorated with a discreet gold embossed logo. Inside, a color picture of Henrietta Pruitt, more formidable than usual in a hooped skirt that looked as if it were six feet in diameter.

There it was, in the second paragraph. "Since assuming the presidency of the society in 1989 . . ." She'd run the historical society the whole time Lindsay was in Caerphilly. What were the odds they'd never met?

Even if they had, I didn't know what she could possibly have against Lindsay. About the only slightly odd thing I'd noticed was how funny the Shiffleys found her description of the Battle of Pruitt's Ridge. Was there something fishy there?

I checked the time. Past ten. Late enough to call Kevin. More than an even chance I'd wake him, but I wouldn't have to feel too guilty about it.

"Yeah," he said, sounding more cranky than sleepy. I decided flattery was in order before I interrogated him.

"The information you sent was fantastic! We owe you big time!"

A pause.

"Do you mean that literally?" he asked.

"Why? What's up?"

"Do you want the detailed technical explanation, or should I just mention that last night I had an expensive piece of computer equipment crash and I can't afford to replace it and—"

"How expensive?"

Yes, he knew the definition of expensive all right. I did a quick calculation and decided my MasterCard could handle it. After a few minutes of negotiation, he had new hardware—well, would have it in a few days, assuming he'd provide me with sufficiently detailed information so I could order his pricey little toy—and I had the promise of unlimited guru services for the next six months. Even if Chief Burke had solved the murder long before then, there was always the battle against the outlet mall, not to mention setting up our computers once we moved back into the house. Michael envisioned equipping our new digs with a state-of-the-art wireless computer and multimedia system. I'd be satisfied if we just got both our computers working normally again, and even for that we'd need Kevin.

"I guess this has kept you from working on the Battle of Pruitt's Ridge?" I asked.

"No, though I haven't found anything," he said. "But Joss is working on it now, so we should have something soon."

"Great," I said. "Oh, if you come across any more information about Lindsay Tyler—that's the Professor L. Blake Tyler you found last night—especially anything that shows she knew any of the people who claimed they didn't recognize her . . ."

"Got it," he said with a snicker, and hung up.

I turned my attention to the stack of information Kevin had sent about the outlet-mall project. No sense letting my long-standing dislike of Mrs. Pruitt distract me from my newfound loathing for Evan Briggs. Much as I liked the idea of Mrs. Pruitt as a cunning, ruthless killer, Michael and I had much more to gain if Briggs turned out to be guilty.

Nothing Kevin had found specifically identified Mr. Shiffley's farm as the proposed site for the mall, but Minerva Burke was right. If you knew enough about the neighborhood, you could guess where the only place large and flat enough for the outlet mall was.

I had to get up three times and pace around the room to calm down. I wasn't sure whom I was maddest at, Evan Briggs for what he was planning to do to our backyard—and, for that matter, the whole peaceful, beautiful little town of Caerphilly—or Mrs. Pruitt, who must have known for several weeks where Briggs was planning to put his mall, and hadn't enlisted us in her campaign against it, or even told us what was up.

Normally, in a mood like this, I'd have fired up my forge and worked my temper out. I couldn't do fine detail work in a temper, but it was great for anything that required heavy hammering. But even if I'd wanted to move the students' stuff out of the way, the chief had all my big hammers.

I was still fuming when Chief Burke stuck his head in the tack room's door.

"Mind if I talk to you?"

"Fine," I said. "By the way, did you know that Mrs. Pruitt has been president of the historical society since 1989?"

"That's quite a long time," he said, frowning slightly.

"Which means she was president of it when Lindsay Tyler was here. How likely is it that they didn't know each other? The historical society and the history department are like that," I said, holding up my hand with the forefinger and middle finger pressed tightly together.

"We'll look into her possible relationships with everyone who was here yesterday."

"Good," I said. "Because they're all liars. Every one of them. All but Michael, of course."

And me, the one local resident I knew for sure had never met Lindsay, but pointing that out would sound too much like saying "I told you so."

"Yes," the chief said. "Speaking of which—you say you'd never met the deceased before?"

I shook my head.

"You're positive?"

"I never even heard the name before," I said. "I

didn't recognize her. Why should I? By the time I met Michael, she was long gone—from his life and from Caerphilly."

"You'd have no reason to communicate with her?"

"None whatsoever."

"That's interesting," the chief said. "Then I suppose it would surprise you to learn that according to the telephone company, you two have been chatting back and forth quite regularly."

Chapter Thirteen

The chief sat back with a small, smug smile on his face.

"Yes, it would surprise me enormously," I said.

He paused, doing his usual waiting number. I waited, too, with an expression of eager helpfulness on my face. After a few moments, the chief sighed and handed me a sheet of paper. Something faxed over from Lindsay's cell-phone carrier, I deduced from the look of it.

"Her cell-phone records?" I asked. He nodded slightly. "Yeah, this one's my number."

"Well?" he said, one eyebrow raised.

I flipped over to the next page.

"You don't need to study the whole thing," he said, reaching for the paper. "I just wanted to show you that your number does appear there."

"I'm looking at the times of the calls," I said. "Trying to make sense out of this. Because I think I'd have noticed if some woman called up and said, 'Hi, I'm your fiancé's ex-girlfriend. Mind if I come over to get murdered in your backyard?' So maybe someone I do know was using Lindsay's phone to call me. Which would mean someone here knows her a lot better than they're letting on."

He frowned, but he let me keep the sheets.

"Doesn't have to be someone here," he said. "Could be anyone who's been calling you regularly over the last few days."

"Yes, but almost everyone I've talked to in the last few days is here," I said. "The Shiffleys and the eXtreme croquet players. Her number does look familiar."

"Not surprising, since you've called it or gotten calls from it eleven times over the last week and a half," he said. "Right up to last night, after she was dead—this was you calling her, of course."

"Of course," I said. "No cell phones in the afterlife; I hear it's the ultimate dead zone. Hang on." I reached into my pocket and pulled out the notebook that tells me when to breathe, as I called my giant spiral-bound "To Do" list. I flipped it open at the paper clip that served as a bookmarker for the most recent entries, then turned back one page.

"Yes, that's Helen Carmichael," I said.

"Beg pardon."

"That's what she was calling herself. Not Lindsay Tyler."

"Just why were you talking to her under any name?"

"She claimed to be a history professor from UVa who wanted some old papers Michael and I were trying to find a home for," I said. "There is a history professor at UVa called Helen Carmichael—I checked to make sure she was legit. I blew that, didn't I?"

The chief frowned.

"Was there some reason you didn't want to give them to the history department here at Caerphilly?" he asked. "I assume you know them—some of them anyway."

"No reason at all," I said. "Except that I tried for six months to get them even to come out and look at the stuff and finally got tired of being ignored. So I got mad one day, e-mailed the UVa history department, and a couple of weeks later this Helen Carmichael called to say she was interested in the papers and could we arrange a time for her to come and pick them up."

"Had you arranged anything?"

"We had arranged yesterday, between noon and five," I said. "She never showed—which makes sense if Helen Carmichael was really Lindsay Tyler; she was off getting killed about the time she'd promised to show up here. I forgot all about it, with the murder and everything. Didn't remember till sometime in the evening. I called her number to ask what had happened, but I didn't get an answer. Obviously."

"We were trying to identify a dead woman, and a woman you'd never met failed to show up for a meeting, and you never mentioned this?"

"I figured that before I bothered you with it, I should make sure I wasn't crying wolf—so I checked the photo of Professor Carmichael on the UVa Web site, and it definitely wasn't her. Take a look for yourself if you like. How was I supposed to know that the Helen Carmichael I was talking to was a fake all along?"

The chief scribbled a few notes.

"So Lindsay Tyler was calling you, pretending to be Helen Carmichael."

"Yes. From that number. Wait, I'll show you."

I pulled out my cell phone and fiddled with it until I activated the speaker-phone feature. Then I dialed my voice-message service and played her last message back for the chief. Since I had six more recent messages still on the system, he got to hear bits of those, too, until I found the right message. He looked annoyed, but I figured by the time we reached the mystery woman's message, I'd made my point about how busy my cell phone had been.

"This is Helen Carmichael," a woman's voice said. "I got your message. Tomorrow works for me. I'll get there as close to noon as possible and should be out of your way long before five. Thanks."

The voice sounded much as I remembered it—crisp, businesslike. She sounded like a professor—which she was, though not at UVa. No clue from her voice that she and Michael had once—

"To repeat this message, press one," the phone company's recorded voice said. "To save it, press two. To delete it, press three. To send a copy—"

"Save it," the chief said.

"Yes, sir," I said, pressing two.

"So what's in these boxes you were giving her?" he asked.

"Papers," I said. "Letters. Old newspaper and

magazine clippings. Photos. Documents. Most of it from the 1800s and early 1900s. It's all stuff we found in the house. The previous owners' heirs didn't want it, and we had no use for it. We didn't want to throw it away—not without letting someone more knowledgeable look through it to see if any of it was potentially valuable."

"Show me," he said.

"No problem," I said. I meant it—I felt downright cheerful about the possibility that he'd seize the boxes as evidence and finally get them out of the house. I led him to the front hall and pointed to the twenty-three copier-paper boxes stacked neatly in one corner of the foyer.

"All these?" he said.

I nodded.

"Good Lord," he said.

He lifted the lid of one box and examined the top few papers. A small bundle of letters tied with a faded ribbon lay on top. A program from the town's 1871 May Day band concert. A sepia-toned photo of a dozen men in stiff collars who scowled into the cameras as if they really didn't trust such a newfangled contraption not to explode in their faces. The chief glanced up at me.

"You really think something in one of these boxes was worth killing her over?"

"I don't even know if anything in any of those boxes was worth the trouble of picking up the boxes and shoving them in a car," I said. "Certainly no one from the Caerphilly history department thought so, and I warned the woman before she came all the way from Charlottesville that it might just be a pile of useless junk."

"All the way from the other side of West Virginia, actually."

"True," I said. "Not that I knew about West Virginia until last night. I thought it was Charlottesville."

The chief nodded absently. He stared at the boxes for a few minutes.

"My people are pretty tied up with the search," he said with a sigh. "The state crime lab's swamped with all those mallets and hammers."

"You don't want to impound the boxes so your people can go through them when they're finished searching?"

Obviously I didn't hide my disappointment well enough.

"I think we'll leave them here for now," he said. "I don't want anyone touching them."

"Right," I said.

"They're off-limits."

"Understood."

"And I darn well want to see anything you find in them that could have a bearing on this murder!" he barked.

"Anything we find while not touching the off-limits boxes," I said. "Got it."

He looked at me over his glasses, shook his head, and returned to the kitchen.

"I'm locking them up!" I said. "So no one will mess with them."

"Good," he called back over his shoulder.

Chapter Fourteen

I deduced from the chief's manner that he didn't think the twenty-three boxes were of any importance. My first impulse was to sit down and go through every scrap of paper until I could prove him wrong. That impulse lasted about ten seconds.

I liked my second impulse better—to lock them in the shed. In addition to the house and the barn, we still had seven other structures on the property, of various sizes and in various stages of disrepair, any of which would ordinarily qualify for the name shed, but we'd officially bestowed that title on one of the better-preserved outbuildings. It had once housed some kind of livestock, to judge from the small pen outside its door. We'd fitted the shed with a padlock; I'd made decorative but functional grates to secure the windows; and we used it to keep poisonous house and garden chemicals out of the hands of visiting children and Christmas presents away from the prying eyes of visiting relatives. It could keep the boxes secure for now.

I went in search of labor, following the sound of

the bells until I located the students in the front yard. They were attempting to teach some dance steps to two of the Shiffleys. All the better.

"Can you guys help me with something?" I asked.

"Be happy to," Graham said.

"Anything for you," Tony added.

Bill and the Shiffleys simply nodded and fell into step behind them, and Michael joined in when he saw the first load heading for the shed. Moving the boxes went quickly—almost too quickly for my purposes.

"What's in the boxes, anyway?" someone finally asked while I was counting the boxes to make sure they'd all arrived.

"Twenty-three. Good," I said. "No idea—old papers and photographs and stuff. They're something the dead woman was coming to pick up, so they could be evidence. The chief wants them locked up."

They eyed the boxes with greater interest, though I couldn't tell if anyone's interest was particularly guilty. They all drifted off while I was securing the padlock. All but Michael, who watched uneasily as I tested to make sure the lock was secure.

"If one of them is the killer, didn't you just paint a big target on the side of the shed?" he asked.

"Hope so," I said.

"So should I stick around and keep my eye on the shed?" he asked.

"Let's let Spike do it," I said.

Long experience helped me avoid getting bitten while transferring Spike from his usual pen by the barn to the pen outside the shed. Michael carried his water and food bowls over while I relocated his bed to a corner where it would be protected from rain and sun by the roof overhang. Then I tossed Spike a couple of his favorite liver treats to reconcile him to the new scenery. He paced up and down his new domain a few times before curling up to nap on the shed's doorsill, as if he understood that he was supposed to play guard dog.

"Doesn't he look cute?" Michael said.

"Positively angelic," I said. "Heaven help anyone who tries to get past him."

"Yeah, you know he's in a cranky mood when he looks that cute."

"You think we should try another dog trainer when we have time?" I asked. "Since it doesn't look as if he's leaving anytime soon." While Michael's mother hadn't formally renounced ownership of Spike, she seemed in no hurry to end the trial separation, whose original purpose was to see if his fur exacerbated her allergies. We'd already had de facto custody for months. Felt like years.

"We could try," Michael said. "Might be hard to find one anywhere nearby who hasn't already heard about Spike."

"Even if they'd heard about him, you'd think they'd welcome a professional challenge."

"I think twelve stitches is more than a professional challenge."

"That guy was overconfident," I said. "We told him exactly what to expect in the letter."

"Thank heavens your mother's lawyer cousin

suggested that letter," Michael said. "Maybe we should just let Spike be himself."

Tony, the redheaded student, came over to lean on the fence. Spike stood up and stalked toward the fence, growling.

"Yeah, sometimes he's pretty useful the way he is," I said.

"I just came to let you know that lunch is almost ready," Tony said, backing away from the fence.

"Not for you, Spike," I said.

For some reason, this made Tony nervous.

"You two go on," I said. "I want to make a phone call."

Tony left, looking over his shoulder at Spike.

"Top secret?" Michael asked.

"Only from Tony," I said. "And Chief Burke, who probably wouldn't appreciate my snooping, even by phone."

"Snoop away," Michael said. "I'll save you a place."

Since I was feeling paranoid, I retreated to the house to do my snooping in greater privacy, though privacy wasn't easy to come by. In the living room, several Shiffleys were arguing about whether the existing floor was really structurally sound, and stomping around on various parts of it in their heavy work boots to prove or disprove their arguments. In the kitchen, Mother was supervising part of the lunch preparations. The dark, unheated basement, I had all to myself.

I thought of calling Kevin, then decided to see

what I could learn on my own first. Luck was with me. Directory assistance found two H. Carmichaels in Charlottesville. It had been years since my college days there, but I still had a general grasp of the town's geography. One H. Carmichael had an address that I recognized as one of the dorms, but the other street address sounded familiar. I was fairly sure it lay in one of the quiet back streets off Rugby Road or Preston Avenue, far enough away from the fraternities to be livable on weekends, yet close enough to the campus to be desirable. The sort of place an ambitious young professor might choose.

Someone picked up the phone in the middle of the fourth ring and a woman's voice said hello.

"Hello," I said. "I'm trying to reach Helen Carmichael from the UVa history department?"

"Speaking," she said, her clipped tone suggesting that she wasn't entirely thrilled to be bothered at home.

"My name's Meg Langslow," I said. I paused for a few moments to see if she reacted. Nothing, so I continued. "I called your department a couple of weeks ago about some documents I'd found."

"What kind of documents?" she said, sounding warmer. Evidently saying "documents" to an historian was like saying "craft fair" to me. Or "homicide" to Dad.

"Twenty-three boxes of stuff that belonged to the former owner of our house," I said. "Assorted letters, photographs, and papers belonging to people living in the town of Caerphilly between the Civil War and World War One."

"Oh, right," she said. "I remember seeing a message about that. Not my period—I'm working mostly on the Colonial era. But I saw a note about your call on the bulletin board, and when no one snatched it away after a week or so, I passed your information along to a colleague at another college who might be interested."

"Lindsay Tyler?"

"That's right. Did she ever get in touch with you?"

"Yes," I said. "Do you mind my asking how you know her?"

"From graduate school," she said. "Look, is there some problem? I know she can be—well, not the easiest person to get along with, but . . ."

Her voice trailed off. I waited to see what she'd say next, but she was doing the same thing.

"She called me all right," I said finally. "Only she pretended to be you."

"She what?"

"Identified herself as Helen Carmichael of the UVa history department, and set up an appointment to come by and pick up the papers."

"That's . . . incredible," the real Helen Carmichael said.

"I gather the impersonation wasn't your idea, then. Any idea why she did it?"

"No!" she exclaimed. "Unless—well, she's not exactly happy about her exile in Pineville. Her word, not mine. I tried reminding her once how few Ph.D.'s get hired anywhere in their field, that just being employed is a badge of honor, and she snapped my head off. That was maybe five years ago, when she first moved there, but I doubt if she's learned to love the place. Maybe she thought she'd have a better chance of getting the material if you thought she was from a better-known university."

"Or maybe she did some research and found out UVa was my alma mater," I suggested.

"Very likely," Helen said. "Or maybe she thinks she's so notorious in Caerphilly that you wouldn't have anything to do with her."

"Was she?" I asked. "Notorious, that is."

She snorted.

"What happened, anyway?" I had Michael's version, but Helen Carmichael might know more about Lindsay's point of view.

"Typical Lindsay stunt," she said. "I don't remember the details—not that she didn't tell me about them ad nauseum. All I remember is that she uncovered some data that tarnished someone's halo a bit—an ancestor of one of the snootier local families."

"Probably the Pruitts," I said.

"Could be. As I said, I don't remember details. Anyway, her find was completely overshadowed by the battle that followed. Never occurred to her that the local bigwigs would mind her trashing their ancestors. Or that they might have some clout over at the college. They sent her packing."

"And she still holds a grudge?"

A pause.

"She's a bit unbalanced on the subject," Helen said finally. "I think she'd do anything to cause trouble for Caerphilly."

"The town, or the college?"

"Either. Both. Look, why are you asking all this, anyway? Did something happen when she came to collect the papers?"

"She never showed up to collect the papers," I said. "Someone killed her first."

"Oh God," Helen muttered. "They were right."

Chapter Fifteen

"Who was right?" I asked.

"When we were in grad school, a couple of the students put out a gag yearbook," she said. "Tasteless, but funny. They named Lindsay most likely to be a justifiable homicide. Of course, that was fifteen years ago, but she hadn't changed much."

I waited for a bit to see if the news of Lindsay's murder would shake loose any more information, but I was disappointed.

"Should I get in touch with the local authorities?" Helen asked after a bit, her voice sounding much more formal. "I assume even though she was impersonating me, they know it's her."

"Our local police chief would probably like to hear from you, yes," I said. I gave her Chief Burke's number.

"Thank you for notifying me," she said. "I'm sorry for . . . Putting her in touch with you seemed like a good idea at the time. I'm sorry for how it worked out."

"Thanks," I said. "Look, did she ever mention

any names of people in Caerphilly? People she particularly hated or anything like that?"

Helen thought about it for a few moments.

"She liked to make jokes about some guy she went out with," she said. "Nasty jokes about how she'd like to go back and get even with him. What was his name? Martin? No, that's not it. Something with an *M*."

Not Michael, I thought with a pang. I wanted to believe she'd long ago gotten over Michael and forgotten him.

"Marcus!" Helen said. "That's it."

"Marcus," I said, feeling a flood of relief. "That's possible. You're sure that was it?"

"Definitely Marcus. 'Marvelous Miniscule Marcus.' That's what she used to call him. If someone knocked him off, I'd tell you to look at Lindsay as a suspect. Maybe it was mutual."

"You might want to mention that to the chief, then," I suggested. "Along with anything else you can think of that might help him."

"I'll do that," she said. "I should tell him that this definitely wasn't like her normal trips to Caerphilly."

"Her normal trips?" I said. "She came here a lot? How do you know?"

"Every few months, yes," she said. "A lot more often recently. I know because she usually stayed with me on the way down or back. Sometimes both. It's a five- or six-hour drive. So she'd call me up and say, 'Heading down to Toad Bottom—can I still use your couch?' "

"Toad Bottom?"

"It's what she called Caerphilly when she wanted to be insulting. No idea why. Anyway, she didn't call me this time. So it definitely wasn't a normal trip."

"Unless she planned to call on her way back," I said. "Did she usually give you much notice?"

"No, she didn't," Helen said. "You could be right. Maybe she was killed before she could call. I suppose we'll never know. I'd better go call your police chief now."

She hung up.

Interesting. Far from moving on, Lindsay had still been angry at Caerphilly, and this hadn't been by any means her first trip back since she was fired. Even if Helen Carmichael was overstating how often Lindsay stayed with her—which was possible; some people like to exaggerate their ties to anyone who appears in the news, as doubtless Lindsay would— she must have been back here often. But why?

"There you are, dear," Mother said, when I reappeared from the basement. "Perhaps you could see what your cousin Horace is doing, and whether he has to do it right now, when we're trying to have a nice picnic?"

It wasn't really a question. I went outside to look for Horace. I didn't have to look far. As soon as I stepped out of the kitchen, I almost fell into the hole he was digging.

He and Sammy were both digging holes. They were about ten feet apart, and at first glance they seemed unaware of each other, as if some instinct to burrow had simultaneously seized both of them and they'd happened, by an astounding coincidence, to choose the same end of our yard. After watching them for a minute or so, I realized that they were very much aware of each other. Given the lethal glances traveling up and down the turf, I decided perhaps I should stay around to make sure neither of them ended up at the bottom of the other's hole. Or to find out what it was all about.

"So, getting ready to bury the bodies?" I asked.

"What bodies?" Sammy said, glancing up with an anxious expression.

"She's kidding," Horace said, sounding slightly condescending. "She forgets that you don't know our family well enough to understand our sense of humor."

"Or maybe he appreciates what calamity magnets we are," I said.

"I appreciate your family's sense of humor a lot," Sammy said in his most earnest tones. "I appreciate everything about your family."

Horace snorted.

"Almost everything," Sammy muttered, casting a baleful glance at Horace.

They both resumed digging. Obviously, something had kicked their rivalry over Rose Noire into full gear. Yet despite their dislike for each other, they were grudgingly cooperating on . . . whatever.

"So what *are* you doing?" I asked.

Both paused, still bent over their shovels, and glanced up at me, as if this were a difficult or incriminating question.

"Digging," Horace said finally.

After this accurate but profoundly uninformative

answer, they returned to work. I pondered my next question. I suspected that if I asked, "What are you digging?" they would answer either "holes" or "dirt." Tempting to resort to sarcasm—"Are you looking for buried treasure?"—but not useful.

Perhaps I should have paid more attention in Philosophy 101 when the professor was expounding on the Socratic method. Or studied Chief Burke's interrogation methods more carefully.

"Why are you digging?" I asked finally.

"Your father asked us to," Sammy said, as if this explained everything. It usually did in our family, but I was one of the rebels.

They kept digging. Horace, I noticed, was going in for depth—he'd gone nearly two feet deep—and accuracy. His hole was a tidy, precise square, and he was piling the dirt neatly nearby. But he'd excavated only about two square yards of ground. Sammy, on the other hand, had dug down a mere foot, and his hole didn't have the clean edges of Horace's, but he'd covered about six square yards of surface.

I tried again.

"For what purpose did Dad ask you to excavate this precise portion of our yard on this particular day?"

"Gardening," Horace said. He glanced at his hole with satisfaction and began digging up the next foot-wide strip, making his first spade cuts with surgical precision.

"Gardening," I repeated.

Sammy nodded. I felt slightly gratified to see that his slipshod work habits were causing him problems. He'd piled up the dirt too high and too close to

the edge of his hole and a small landslide had un-
done his last ten or fifteen minutes' work.

"That's nice," I said. "But this isn't where
Michael and I want the garden. We want it it over
there," I said, pointing to the yard beyond the barn.

They both looked over at where I was pointing,
then back at me.

"Nice spot," Sammy said.

"We can dig that up, too," Horace said.

Too, not instead. They weren't getting the point.

"Thanks," I said. "But we just planned to get one
of the Shiffleys in with a Rototiller. Next year. We're
too busy to garden this year."

"This isn't for your garden," Sammy said. I
wanted to ask who else had decided to garden in our
yard, but I stopped myself. I'd learned that much
from Chief Burke's interrogations.

"It's for Rose Noire," Horace said eventually.
"Your dad thought this would be the perfect place
for her herb garden."

I should have known Rose Noire would be involved. Dad was quite capable of deciding, unilater-
ally, that we'd be happy to donate space for a family
member's pet agricultural project, but Sammy and
Horace wouldn't have both volunteered to help for
anyone else. The only thing the two had in common
was their shared infatuation with Rose Noire.

"Does she know you and Dad are planning her
herb garden here?" I asked.

They looked sheepish. Evidently not.

"What if she doesn't think this spot has the right
vibes or feng shui or whatever gardens are supposed

to have?" I said. "You could be completely wasting your time! Besides, I think that's where the Shiffleys were planning on piling the construction materials," I added, pointing to where Sammy was digging.

Sammy's face fell, and Horace smirked slightly.

"I know that's where they'll have to put the scaffolding," I went on, pointing to Horace's excavations, which were much nearer the house. Now Horace looked downcast, too. I had no idea where the Shiffleys planned to put the construction materials, or if they even needed scaffolding, but it sounded good.

"You couldn't talk them into working someplace else?" Horace asked.

Sammy looked scornful, probably because he knew the Shiffleys well enough to understand how difficult it was to change their plans once they'd made them.

"Maybe," I said. "Even if I did, no power on earth could prevent people from walking all over this patch of ground and trampling anything Rose Noire planted here. Even if the Shiffleys got the message, we'll have subcontractors and truck drivers delivering materials and such."

Actually, I hoped our renovation project wouldn't be quite that invasive. I was depressing myself just talking about it.

"Why don't you let me talk to Rose Noire and Dad?" I said. "I'll explain about the construction, and how enthusiastic you both are about digging the garden when the time is right. I'll let you know what we come up with."

They both brightened at that. Why not? After all, this way they'd get credit with Rose Noire for the digging without doing any more actual backbreaking work. "We could have had it all dug by now," they could say, "if Meg hadn't stopped us."

They both ambled off—not precisely side by side, which would have implied some degree of togtherness. Instead, they were on parallel courses to where they thought they could find Rose Noire.

I strolled out toward the main part of the lawn and stopped in surprise. Perhaps I should have guessed from the chaos in the kitchen that today's lunch had mutated from a simple picnic for the competitors into something else.

"Good grief," I muttered. "Who are all these people and what are they doing here?"

Chapter Sixteen

Once I'd recovered from the initial shock and taken a look around, I realized that I could answer my own question. Of the hundred or so people milling about the lawn, about a third were Mother's relatives, whom I didn't remember inviting. Another third orbited Mrs. Pruitt the way my family orbited Mother, so I deduced they were members of the Caerphilly Historical Society or the Caerphilly Garden Club—or both. The membership was overlapping and possibly inbred: Most of the members drew their last or middle names from the same two dozen WASP surnames you saw on generations of tombstones in the cemeteries behind the town's Episcopal and Presbyterian churches. I also didn't remember inviting any but the three croquet-playing Dames, as the Historical Society crew called themselves.

The rest of the guests were probably Shiffleys. I deduced this from the way they and the Historical Society crowd avoided one another. Mrs. Pruitt and her minions had occupied the end of the lawn near the house, while the Shiffleys were entrenched down by the barn. Between them lay a no-man's-land that would have been blatantly unoccupied if not for my family, who milled about, seemingly oblivious of the social conflict around them. I felt a sudden surge of affection for my family, who couldn't tell a Pruitt from a Shiffley and wouldn't care anyway.

And who had assumed they were coming to a potluck lunch. As had the Dames and the Shiffleys, of course. The tables we'd set out were completely covered with plates and bowls of food, and people were wandering around with covered dishes in their hands, looking for table space.

"We'll need more tables," Michael said.

"See if the Shiffleys can contribute their saw-horses and a few sheets of plywood," I suggested.

Michael nodded and strode off.

I looked around and shook my head. If this many people showed up for a picnic in March, I didn't want to think about what would happen come summer.

I noticed Minerva Burke chatting with Mother. Was she here socially, or did her presence mean the chief was still around? No doubt I'd find out soon enough.

Mrs. Briggs and the clones had arrived. So had Mr. Briggs. He didn't look particularly cheerful or relaxed. Perhaps coming was his wife's idea. I read Briggs as a driven entrepreneur who didn't see much use in social gatherings. Why bother to make friends in a town you were diligently trying to bull-doze down and pave over?

Odd how much he'd been around recently. He'd driven his wife out yesterday, and hung around the whole day while she played croquet. We were only ten miles outside Caerphilly. Easy enough for him to drop her off and come back later. Why was he hanging around yesterday and again today?

I spotted Dad getting a head start on the dessert table and strolled over to talk to him.

"Dad, did you see Mr. Briggs yesterday?" I asked.

"Yes," he said through a mouthful of brownie.

"When?"

"Well, he was here for breakfast," Dad said. "Drove his wife out. We talked at lunch, too, so I assume he stayed to see her play. He was here when Chief Burke gathered us all to identify the victim, so he must have been here all day."

"Did you see him, apart from mealtimes?"

"No, but I wouldn't, you know," Dad said. "I didn't get to see the games, of course, since I stayed up here to keep an eye on the construction."

The construction and the duck pond.

"You didn't miss all that much," I said. "It's not much of a spectator sport."

Dad glanced around to make sure no one was nearby.

"Do you suspect him?" he asked in a stage whisper.

"I suspect everyone," I said. "Just checking. I'll keep you posted."

"Ah," Dad said.

But perhaps I suspected Mr. Briggs more than most. Unlike the boggy cow pasture, the hilly sheep pasture that formed our other eXtreme croquet field wasn't wooded. Friday morning, when our team had played Mrs. Briggs and the clones, I could see most of the other players most of the time. I remembered seeing Mr. Briggs from time to time, leaning over the fence at the end of the field closest to the house, but I couldn't swear he was there the whole time. I'd have had no chance to see him in the afternoon—he'd have gone back to Mr. Early's sheep pasture, where his wife was playing, not down to the bog with my team and the Dames.

But why had he been hanging around all day? Had he really been that interested in watching his wife play croquet? Or had he been gloating over his coming triumph?

Or maybe bumping off Lindsay Tyler?

For all I knew, he could have gotten bored and taken off during the afternoon game. Gone back to his office to do some business that would give him an alibi for the time of Lindsay's death. But he'd returned by the time the police arrived.

I made a note to keep my eyes open for a chance to talk to Mr. Briggs. Perhaps later in the picnic. At the moment, despite the fact that I hadn't invited three-fourths of the people thronging our lawn, Mother would expect me to make some effort to play the gracious hostess.

Not to mention playing shepherdess before too long. I could see a couple of Mr. Early's sheep mingling with the crowd. When we'd first moved into the house, we'd been responsible, in Mr. Early's eyes, for damaging the fence around his pasture and allowing several hundred of his sheep to escape. Since then, we'd learned that the Great Sheep Escape, although dramatic, had not been unprecedented. Mr. Early's fences leaked sheep all the time at a slow but fairly constant rate. Most of the locals cast aspersions on Mr. Early's fence-mending ability, but now that I'd come to know his sheep rather better than I liked, I blamed the sheep. Mr. Early's sheep were not only larger and woollier than your average sheep, they were also more agile and enterprising. In addition to rounding them up regularly from our yard and shooing them out of the downstairs rooms, we'd found stray sheep lying against the outside of our bedroom door on a cold morning—to take advantage of the warmth from our space heater leaking out under the door—frolicking in the wading pool we set up for some visiting junior relatives, and, to Michael's dismay, giving birth in the passenger seat of his convertible.

At least today's sheep were on their best behavior.

I noticed that Mrs. Burke and several of the chief's deputies were circulating through the crowd in what they thought was a subtle fashion. If they wanted to overhear gossip about the murder, they were doomed to disappointment. Most of the guests were talking about eXtreme croquet, not murder.

Mrs. Pruitt and Mrs. Fenniman were already bickering over the logistics of restarting the tournament.

"Easier just to start the game over," Rob suggested.

"Nonsense," Mrs. Pruitt said. "I'm sure we all remember where we were when the police notified us. We can just pick up from there."

From which I deduced that she thought her team had been ahead when Chief Burke interrupted the game and she didn't want to risk losing that advantage.

"Let me consult the rules on that," Mrs. Fenniman said. Which suggested that she wasn't entirely sure who'd been ahead and wanted time to figure it out before deciding whether to agree to resume the previous game or dig in her heels and insist on a "do-over."

"There's the issue of poor Meg's ball," Mrs. Pruitt said, bestowing a suspiciously genial smile on me.

"What about my ball?" I asked.

"It hasn't been found, has it?" Mrs. Pruitt said.

"Yes, it has," Sammy piped up. "We found it last night."

"Where is it, then?" Mrs. Fenniman snapped. "You haven't gone and lost it, have you?"

"Of course not," Sammy said. "We took it to the crime lab with the mallets."

"Down in Richmond? Dear me!" Mrs. Pruitt said, shaking her head with a sadness that was almost believable. "You'll need a few strokes to get back on course from there, won't you?"

She wasn't really suggesting that I resume playing the ball from the crime lab, was she?

"I think we can call that an out-of-bounds ball," Mrs. Fenniman said.

"Are we sure?" Mrs. Pruitt asked.

"I'll check with the board of regents," Mrs. Fenniman said, as if that settled it. Which it probably did; the eXtreme croquet board of regents generally backed Mrs. Fenniman's interpretation of the rules.

I had no idea whether that was because they agreed with her or because they'd guessed her capacity for making their lives miserable by phone and e-mail if they contradicted her.

"What if one of the players turns out to be the killer?" Mrs. Pruitt asked. "I don't suppose that's covered under the rules?"

"Already asked them about that last night," Mrs. Fenniman replied. "They recommend that the affected team be allowed to field a substitute. Unless murders during our games happen frequently, in which case local custom should prevail."

Mrs. Fenniman was particularly fond of the line about local custom prevailing, since she considered herself, as the pioneer who'd introduced eXtreme croquet to Caerphilly, entitled to decide what was and wasn't local custom.

"It would be different if the victim had been a player," Mrs. Fenniman said. "Grounds for immediate expulsion."

"But spectators are fair game, naturally," I added.

"Hmph," Mrs. Pruitt said, but she didn't argue— only sailed off with her head held higher than usual.

"So when you start the tournament up again, which field will you use?" Tony, the redheaded student, was asking Mrs. Fenniman.

"The cow pasture, of course," Mrs. Fenniman said.

"If Chief Burke lets us," I added.

"Oh, I hope he does," Rose Noire said, frowning in distress. "The cow pasture's a much better field."

"Much more interesting terrain," Mrs. Fenniman agreed nodding.

"I prefer cows to sheep," Rose Noire said. "The sheep are impossible to hit."

"To hit?" I echoed, my mouth open. Here I'd been carefully concealing my accidental ricochet off the cow from her, because I thought she'd be appalled—and she was using the sheep for target practice?

"As walking wickets," she said. "Most of them have wool so long, it drags on the ground. No way to get a ball through their legs. With the cows, it's almost too easy."

"Yes," Mrs. Fenniman said. "If someone sheared them, the sheep would be much more interesting than cows. Doable, but not too easy."

"You're right!" Rose Noire exclaimed. "Let's talk to Mr. Early!"

They hurried off.

Chapter Seventeen

I noticed that Tony, like me, was watching Rose Noire and Mrs. Fenniman with openmouthed astonishment.

"So how long have you been playing eXtreme croquet?" I asked.

"About a month now," he said.

"Oh, really? For some reason, I thought it was longer. How did you get interested?"

"Bill saw a notice somewhere about your tournament and thought it would be a gas to get up a team," he said. "Before that, we just mostly did the Morris dancing."

Interesting. Bill, who of the three students seemed least interested in the game. Or, for that matter, in food, drink, and their beloved Morris dancing.

"Is he okay?" I asked. "He seems a little . . . quiet."

"He's been moody lately," Tony said. "For the last week or so."

A week. Which meant we couldn't take his moodiness as a sign of guilt. Unless he'd been premeditating the murder for a week. Seemed farfetched, but I filed it away for later consideration.

Not that I couldn't keep an eye on the moody Bill in the meantime, so I took my plate and sat down at the students' table, opposite him and Graham. Tony followed me, and, thank goodness, Michael.

"So how is everyone this morning?" I asked.

"Brilliant," Graham said, beaming at me.

"You have a very comfortable barn," Tony said.

Bill glanced up and made an inarticulate noise before returning to the fascinating chore of rearranging the food on his plate.

"Chief Burke's happier today," Michael said. "Though I don't think it has anything to do with the case."

"Nothing to do with the case," I said. "I suspect Dad gave him something for the itching."

"Perhaps we ought to talk to him," Tony said to Graham. "Meg's father, I mean."

"Perhaps we ought," Graham said, squirming in his seat and reaching down to scratch his shin. "It's not getting any better."

"What's not getting any better?" I asked. "Show me."

Graham pulled down his long white sock to reveal a large patch of irritated red skin with a few telltale white blisters forming in the center.

"Yuck," I said, fighting the impulse to draw back in revulsion. After all, the stuff wasn't contagious, and I'd had worse-looking cases myself. "Yes, you've got poison ivy all right. Did you take a shower last night?"

"I'm sorry," he said. "I took one this morning, but we've done quite a bit of rehearsing this morning. Morris dancing gets rather vigorous and—"

"I'm not complaining about how you smell," I said. "I'm trying to find out if you're still walking around with urushiol all over your shins, or, worse, on your hands."

"Urushiol?" Graham repeated.

"It's an oil contained in poison ivy, which is almost certainly what caused your rash," I said.

"Poison ivy?" Tony said. "Oh, man, I get that stuff bad."

"What should we do?" Graham said. "It's not, uh, potentially fatal, is it?"

"No," I said. "You'll only wish it was."

Tony was inspecting his shins now, which looked worse than Graham's.

"Isn't there anything we can do?" Graham asked.

I closed my eyes. I was perfectly capable of explaining all about poison ivy—how to identify it, how to make sure you washed the urushiol off if you thought you'd touched it, and the limited ways to treat the rash that resulted if you didn't wash well or soon enough. The idea made me tired.

Besides, why deprive Dad of the chance? He'd actually enjoy it.

"Go see my dad," I said, pointing to the buffet table, where Dad was explaining something to Lacie Butler—something that required much gesticulating. "Do everything he tells you. In the meantime, don't touch the rash."

They raced off. Correction: Tony raced. Graham walked slowly and carefully, as if afraid his legs would break off if he ran.

"What about you?" I said to Bill, the quiet one.

"Stuff doesn't bother me," he said with a shrug.

"Lucky you. If you want to keep it that way, try not to bother it. Immunity to poison ivy can wear off at any time."

He shrugged again. I wasn't sure whether he didn't believe me or just didn't care.

As we ate, we watched the drama on the other side of the yard. Dad shooed Tony and Graham into the barn—for long showers with plenty of Fels-Naptha soap. Dad reappeared with plastic garbage bags protecting his hands, carrying all their clothes into the house for washing. Eventually, Tony and Graham emerged, wrapped in bath sheets, awaiting the arrival of clean, urushiol-free clothes as Dad applied cold Domeboro compresses to their shins and scrutinized the remaining visible skin for signs of inflammation.

Rose Noire's herbal studies must have uncovered a remedy for poison ivy, for, as we watched, she appeared and handed Tony and Graham steaming mugs of something. Something unusually nasty-tasting, from the expressions on their faces when they sipped. Unfortunately, while my cousin's herbal concoctions often seemed remarkably effective, she had no idea how to make them palatable. No idea or perhaps no intention—was it a New Age concept or an old wives' tale, that anything really good for you ought to taste slightly foul?

"Quite a production," Bill said after a while.

"Dr. Langslow has extensive experience with poison ivy," Michael told him.

"Especially since my brother, Rob, comes down

with a case every year in spite of all Dad's lessons on how to identify the stuff," I added.

"Langslow?" Bill repeated.

"That's our last name, yes," I said.

"Your brother's Rob Langslow? *The* Rob Langslow?"

"You must be a computer gamer," I said. "Yes, he's the CEO of Mutant Wizards."

"Wow," Bill said. "That's awesome!"

I wondered how awesome he'd find it if I revealed how little Rob knew about either business or computer programming—so little that his senior staff encouraged him to do anything he liked as long as it didn't involve showing up at the office until summoned. Things ran better that way. They knew that if they needed him to sign checks, impress clients, or participate in a brainstorming session, they could always track him down with a phone call. Unfortunately, given Rob's incompetence with cell phones, they'd gotten into the habit of making that call to me.

I knew better than to say anything like that. Besides, it was heartening to see some actual enthusiasm from the previously morose Bill. He even did his Morris dancing with a grim, deadpan face, as if under duress—which was the only way you could get me to participate in Morris dancing, but he was supposed to be an enthusiast.

"Lawyers from Hell is still my all-time favorite," Bill was saying. "And Ninja Accountant Ducks totally rocks!"

"I'm sure he'd love to hear that," I said. He probably would. Ninja Accountant Ducks was definitely Rob's brainchild; I could tell from the title alone. For that matter, as long as the company's brainstorming sessions included Rob, they continued to produce a steady stream of offbeat ideas for successful products. Whether these ideas came from Rob's brain or whether his presence merely stimulated in others the kind of freewheeling, outside-the-box thinking that could produce them, I hadn't figured out. Like most of my family, I was just happy to see Rob gainfully employed. Even the money we'd begun to earn on our Mutant Wizards stock paled beside that.

"I'm a computer-science major," he said. I knew what was coming. The eager rundown on his qualifications, followed by the impassioned plea for me to convey his résumé to Rob.

"Give Rob your résumé, then," I said, in the hope of cutting short the usual rigmarole.

"Just give it to him?" Bill said. He looked daunted at the thought.

"Better yet, give it to Mother. She's chairman of the board. Works closely with the personnel department."

Actually, Mother was the personnel department, for all practical purposes, vetting the résumés the company received and performing most of the initial interviewing. She'd started doing this after Mutant Wizards went through what we in the family referred to as "a bad patch," which I thought was a nice euphemism for having several employees arrested for assorted crimes, up to and including murder. I had to admit, things had run much more smoothly since Mother took over the hiring, and it had the added advantage of keeping her too busy to launch the interior-decorating business she'd been talking about for several years.

"Okay," Bill said. "I can see why you don't want a creative genius like him wasting his time on routine administrative stuff."

I resisted the impulse to point out that without people to do the routine administrative stuff, Rob's so-called creative genius wouldn't have gotten him anywhere.

"What about Tony and Graham?" I said. "Are they computer majors, too?"

"Tony is," Bill said, sounding a bit surly, as if he begrudged the idea of sharing Rob with his friends. "Not sure what Graham's majoring in. Engineering or computer science, probably, but he's only a freshman."

"Not humanities, then?"

Bill shook his head.

"So I guess it's understandable why none of you knew Lindsay Tyler," I said.

Bill's face froze.

"I mean, I guess none of you takes many history courses. That's what she taught, right?"

"I guess," he said. "I pretty much stick to the computer-science building."

"Never saw her around campus?"

He shrugged. I let the silence drag on.

"Now that they told us who she is, yeah, I sort of recognize her," he said finally. "But it's not as if any of us would have any reason to know her that well. And I guess it's right that people look different when they're dead."

I nodded as noncommittally as possible.

"I should see how Tony and Graham are doing," he said. He got up and hurried over to where they were still sitting with their legs propped up so the cold compresses wouldn't fall off their shins. They weren't sipping their mugs of herbal tea, though. Cousin Horace and Deputy Sammy had each appropriated a mug and were sipping away, faces tense with the effort of smiling after each swallow. Rose Noire appeared oblivious to their heroic efforts. She was showing Dad one of her herb jars—presumably the one from which the tea had come—and gesticulating enthusiastically. Dad was nodding and beaming. Evidently, he approved of Rose Noire's concoction. A good thing there were only a few remaining shreds of dried weed left in the jar, or Dad would have ordered a round for the house, on general principles. If Rose Noire ever found someplace where she could grow herbs in quantity, we were all in trouble.

Missing from this touching tableau was Bill, who had forgotten his stated intention of checking on Tony and Graham and had gone straight into the barn.

"Touching, isn't it, how concerned he is about his buddies?" Michael said.

"Yeah," I said. "Something fishy there."

"Definitely."

"I can't see how it fits in with the outlet-mall thing, though."

"Maybe it doesn't," Michael said. "Looking at

the crew we have here, I can imagine more than one of them's up to something shady, can't you?"

"All too well," I said.

Just then, Dad came bounding up.

"Meg!" he exclaimed, "I have a great idea!"

Chapter Eighteen

Dad's great ideas always made me nevous. I braced myself for an argument—probably over the proposed herb garden—but Dad's enthusiasm had moved on.

"I'm going to train Spike tó do something about the sheep!"

"Do what about them?" I asked, following Dad to Spike's pen. "Chase them around until they have the ovine equivalent of a nervous breakdown?"

"Chase them back to Mr. Early's fields," Dad said.

"He'd be good at the chasing part," Michael said. "It's the 'back to Mr. Early's fields' concept he'd have trouble grasping."

"Or he could at least keep them out of your yard," Dad suggested, on a more practical note.

"Oh, great idea," I said. "Turn him into a sheep-chasing dog. Wasn't that a recurring plot device on *Lassie*—they want to put Lassie down because they suspect her of chasing sheep?"

"Killing sheep, actually, but yes," Michael said.

"Farmers don't much like the idea of a dog messing around with their sheep."

"But look at him," Dad argued, leaning on the fence of the pen. "Would any sane farmer suspect him of killing a sheep?"

We looked at Spike, who yawned sarcastically.

"Definitely," I said.

"It might take him time to figure out how, but yes, I can see it," Michael agreed. "He's got that sociopathic gleam in his eyes."

"You're just prejudiced against Spike," Dad announced, climbing over the fence. "You'll see."

He bent over to pick up Spike, who, surprisingly, didn't bite him.

"Leave him here for now," I said. "He's already working as a guard dog, remember."

"Oh, that's right," Dad said, standing up again. "Well, I'll see if your brother can fill in for a while."

"Fill in guarding the shed or herding sheep?" Michael asked.

Dad climbed nimbly over the fence again and trotted away.

"I'll borrow a few sheep from Mr. Early to get started," he called over his shoulder.

"Why bother?" I called back. "We had half a dozen of them a little while ago. If they've gone home, I'm sure a few more volunteers will show up before the day is out."

"I don't think he heard you," Michael said.

"Oh, he heard me, but he's pretending he didn't. This is a recipe for disaster."

"Cheer up," Michael said. "There's a silver lining. What happens if the local farmers show up thirsting for Spike's blood?"

"You're not suggesting we give him to them!" I exclaimed.

"Of course not. But we can pack him back to Mom. Explain that he's just not cut out to be a farm dog. That we can't guarantee his safety."

"You may have something there," I said. "Just the same, let's keep an eye on what he and Dad are up to."

Just then, my cell phone rang, and I scrambled to pull it out. Kevin.

"Hello, Kevin," I said, determined to set a good example of telephone etiquette. "How are you?"

"Not having much luck on this battle thing," he said.

Maybe good examples were wasted on Kevin. At least he got to the point, which was rare in my family. Rare, and possibly worth encouraging.

"Found anything at all?" I asked.

"First of all, there's no record of a Colonel Jedidiah Pruitt. There was a lieutenant by that name with the Thirteenth Virginia Cavalry, but no colonel."

"So Mrs. Pruitt inflated her ancestor's rank."

"Hard to prove it—Civil War records aren't perfect. But yeah, probably."

"So was Lieutenant Pruitt the gallant hero of the Battle of Pruitt's Ridge? Or did Mrs. Pruitt inflate his gallantry along with his title?"

"Beats me," he said.

"What do you mean? What did you find on the battle?"

"Nothing."

"Nothing at all?"

"Yeah, and that's weird."

"Not necessarily," I said. "I figure we'd have heard about it by now if it was a major battle."

"Yeah, and Joss would have made us go there sometime, with it only an hour away," he said, "Remember I said if I had trouble, I'd ask Joss?"

"Good idea."

"Yeah, except Joss can't find anything about it in any of her books, either. She tried a lot of variant spellings of Pruitt and Jedidiah. Tried all the spellings we could think of for Shiffleys, too. No go. She says she needs more information. Like when it happened and if it was part of another, larger battle. 'Cause the only thing she can think of is maybe the locals call it something different from what the history books do."

"The way Yankees say the Battle of Antietam for what Southerners call Sharpsburg?"

"Joss used that example, too, only she said this would be like ignoring both names and calling it the Battle of Miller's Cornfield, after a place where part of it happened. Which would be pretty stupid."

"Unless you were one of the Millers," I said. "Tell Joss I'm sorry I put her through all that."

"She's having a blast," Kevin said. "She wants to come and visit you next weekend to interview the locals about it. Do some oral history stuff. Write a paper for one of her classes, or maybe even an article. So if you could start getting some leads, that would be great."

I was tempted to suggest that if Joss really was planning a career as a historian, she should do her own research, but then—realized that wasn't fair. She'd just turned her life inside out for hours, looking for information for me; the least I could do was ask around at bit for her. It would be months before I could afford any more expensive bribes to nieces and nephews, and I might need her help.

Especially if the undocumented Battle of Pruitt's Ridge played a role in the upcoming Battle to Prevent the Outlet Mall. Besides, I still needed someone to take the twenty-three boxes off my hands. Maybe Joss.

"I'll see what I can turn up," I said. "Talk to you later."

As I hung up, I realized I knew exactly whom to ask about the Battle of Pruitt's Ridge. Someone I'd have consulted before now if Kevin and the Internet weren't so temptingly available at the touch of a few buttons. Ms. Ellie, the town librarian.

"I'm going to town for a bit," I said.

Just then, Dad came bounding up.

"Meg!" he exclaimed. "Can I use your computer?"

"What for?" I asked.

"I want to print out some pictures of poison ivy to show the boys," he said.

"I'll help," Michael offered, standing up. Help, in this case, meant doing it himself, to prevent Dad from completely fouling up the computer as he had the last time he'd used it. "You go on to town."

"Going to do some digging?" Dad asked.

"Don't let Chief Burke catch you," Michael warned.

"I just realized that we have library books due," I said with great dignity. "I'm going to return them today, since we're not playing croquet for the time being."

"Ah, I get it," Dad said, putting his finger to his lips. "Mum's the word."

He dashed off toward the garage.

"Good thought," Michael said. "What Ms. Ellie can't dig up isn't worth finding."

Chapter Nineteen

Eventually, I'd learn to call first, instead of assuming that everyone in a small town like Caerphilly would automatically be where I expected to find them whenever I felt like dropping in on them. Ms. Ellie was out of town at a library conference, according to Jessica, the teenage library aide. Unfortunately, Jessica couldn't tell me how long the conference would last. All day? All weekend? All summer?

"Maybe I can help you?" she asked.

"I'm looking for information about the Battle of Pruitt's Ridge."

A blank look.

"Something about town history? Around the time of the Civil War?"

"Well," Jessica said, "there's Mrs. Pruitt's book. . . . We have a copy in the reference section."

"Perfect."

Actually, it was far from perfect. I suspected Mrs. Pruitt had gotten a discount on a large consignment of stale adverbs and adjectives and was trying to use them up as quickly as possible. But it had a chapter about the Battle of Pruitt's Ridge.

Col. Jedidiah Pruitt's long-suffering wife had just given birth to the fourteenth of their eventual seventeen children and he'd gone home to inspect the new arrival, accompanied by a small party of aides or adjutants, or whatever colonels drag around with them when they travel. Just east of Caerphilly, they surprised a numerically superior party of Union soldiers looting nearby farms. The colonel led his party in a strategic retreat, then rallied the townsmen— presumably in June 1862, when this took place, the war hadn't yet claimed every able-bodied male over twelve and there were still townsmen to rally. Colonel Pruitt and his impromptu force caught up with the invaders in a wooded area and achieved a resounding victory for the Confederate cause—Mrs. Pruitt's words, not mine. To me, it sounded as if the colonel had chased off a few chicken thieves and called it a battle, but my niece Joss had often told me that I had no appreciation for the finer points of military history and strategy. Someone had agreed with Mrs. Pruitt, since they awarded the colonel the Distinguished Medal of Valor, whatever that was.

I studied the photographs accompanying the text. A 1954 photograph of the battleground, covered with grazing black-and-white cows. Was it our eXtreme croquet field? Possibly. Or perhaps one of a hundred other local cow pastures.

I flipped the page and came to a much older photo: a man with more beard than face, standing beside a petite woman in voluminous skirts, who was holding a baby so bundled up, you could only see a small part of his face. *Her* face; the caption told me these were Colonel and Mrs. Pruitt and Victoria Virginia Pruitt, the infant whose birth had brought the colonel home to achieve his glorious hometown victory. Mrs. Pruitt's face looked vaguely familiar, so I supposed a few of the seventeen children had survived to help populate the town.

I leafed slowly through the rest of the photos. Several were of bearded men in uniform, staring grimly at the camera, holding guns and swords. One was of two soldiers; the man on the left was holding, incongruously, an accordion, the other something that looked like a cross between a guitar and a ukelele. Most of them looked like any other Civil War–era photograph—the poses stiff and formal, the picture randomly splotched or faded. I couldn't help lingering over one postbattle shot that showed several forlorn bodies lying beneath a tree. I couldn't tell whether they were Union or Confederate, but evidently the colonel's victory hadn't been completely bloodless. Another, less graphic but equally heartrending, showed a tattered scrap of fabric—part of a sleeve, to judge from the remnants of a chevron—hanging from a rusting barbed-wire fence. I couldn't be sure, since the photo was in black and white, but the dark stain on the fabric scrap looked like blood.

And a map.

"Yes!" I hissed. Jessica glowered at me for breaking silence, but she had a long way to go before she could replace Ms. Ellie.

I studied the map. I located the small road to town, which hadn't changed its course in the intervening fifty years—it had been almost that long since the county last paved it. Mr. Early's and Mr. Shiffley's farms. Between them, the Sprocket house—which locals would still call the Sprocket house even if Michael and I lived there fifty years. The Battle of Pruitt's Ridge had taken place along a rocky ridge between Mr. Shiffley's farmhouse and the Sprocket house.

On our croquet field.

Chapter Twenty

I used up most of my change making copies of the relevant pages of Mrs. Pruitt's book on the library's ancient copy machine.

I tried not to gloat prematurely. After all, it was a very small battle. Virginia was pocked with battlefields. This wouldn't automatically kill Briggs's outlet mall.

But it was promising. With a little more research and documentation . . .

At least Mrs. Pruitt had been reasonably conscientious about citing her sources. *The* source, in the case of the chapter on the battle—it had all come from a 1954 issue of the *Caerphilly Clarion*.

Wonder of wonders, the library had back issues of the *Clarion* on microfiche. I had to surrender my library card to use the microfiche reader, but after that, Jessica was happy to hunt down the proper roll for me. I found the original article—a center spread with lots of pictures.

Mrs. Pruitt had left out half the information in the article—the more interesting half, if you asked me.

The colonel received his Distinguished Medal of Valor not from the Confederacy but from the Caerphilly town council, which had invented the decoration on the spot, just for him. The paper showed a nice photo of his brother, Mayor Virgil Pruitt, pinning it on his chest. Nothing succeeds like nepotism.

Mrs. Pruitt had also omitted any mention of the three-day bash the colonel had thrown to celebrate his victory, complete with several pit-roasted hogs. Sometime during the evening of the second day, a group of marauders had looted and burned the Shiffley Brothers Distillery. Excerpts from the 1862 *Clarion* (not, alas, available on microfiche) left it up in the air whether the marauders were the defeated Yankees taking their revenge or the colonel's own troops, reprovisioning the victory celebration. As a final footnote to the affair, on returning to his command, the colonel himself was court-martialed and reduced in rank for going AWOL and missing the whole of the Seven Days' Battle. Another thing Mrs. Pruitt had glossed over in her version.

I used up the rest of my change making copies of the article. Then I tortured my eyes looking through fifty more years' worth of microfiche for follow-up stories. There weren't any. Which was odd, since, according to the article, the town had contacted the Park Service about the possibility of funding an archaeological dig at the battle site, and several prominent Civil War historians were coming to study the cache of old documents that had been found in a trunk in someone's attic—presumably moved there from the ruins of a family farmhouse.

I did find one useful bit of information—proof that Lindsay Tyler hadn't been a total stranger to the Caerphilly Historical Society. I found four different articles in the social columns that listed her as an attendee at the society's meetings. Better yet, a photo, showing her, Mrs. Pruitt, Mrs. Wentworth, and half a dozen other ladies, all smiling at the camera as the newly elected officers of the society. Lindsay had been vice president and historian. I made copies of those, too.

No follow-up on the battle, though, and no clue where the old documents had ended up—not in the Caerphilly Town Library, though. I made sure of that, to the great discomfort of the poor library aide. To my dismay, she broke down in tears.

"I don't know where it is," she wailed. "It's not my fault. I can't be expected to know what everyone is doing with the computer."

"I was using the microfiche reader, not the computer," I said.

"They probably still think it was me!" she wailed.

"Think what was you?" I asked, fishing in my purse for a tissue. "Here, use this."

I handed her a wad of paper napkins from Luigi's. The top one wasn't entirely clean, I noticed, wincing, but perhaps she found the familiar smell of pizza sauce comforting.

"Someone used the library computer to hack into a bunch of places," she said. "And they accused me of doing it because it always happened on weekends, when I was here."

"That's awful," I said.

"They'd totally have arrested me if my computer-science teacher hadn't stood up for me and told them there was no way I could possibly have figured out how to do it," she said, lifting her chin, as if her teacher had vouched for her character rather than her technological shortcomings.

"They never found out who did it?"

"No, but now I have to keep a log of who uses the computer when," she said. "Or any of the machines. Every time I turn around, there's something else I have to do."

"Tough job," I said, trying to sound sincere.

"Yeah, but you know, it's been really useful," she said, interrupting herself to blow her nose with one of the napkins. "I mean, for figuring out what I want to do with my life."

"You were thinking of becoming a librarian?" I said. I must have sounded dubious.

"Not anymore!"

I breathed a silent sigh of relief.

"Well, I'm not going to accuse you of anything, don't worry," I said. "Just tell Ms. Ellie I was here and that I'll drop by to see her sometime soon."

"Yes, ma'am," she said, sounding sullen. I had a feeling she wanted me to stay and hear all the reasons why she'd given up the idea of a career in library science. She'd still complain about the crazy woman who had insisted on turning the building inside out while looking for some missing papers, but Ms. Ellie would know I wanted to talk to her.

Back at the house, the picnic lunch had turned into one of those sprawling, loosely organized all-day parties that generated spontaneously whenever you put a critical mass of my relatives in close proximity to a good supply of food. The Shiffleys seemed equally at home. The number of enormous pickup trucks parked along the side of the road had doubled in my absence. The buffet tables looked fuller than ever, though the overflowing trash cans (and the half a dozen black plastic trash bags nearby) suggested that we'd already produced legendary quantities of corncobs, chicken bones, potato peelings, watermelon and lemon rinds, well-gnawed ribs, and other picnic debris. A small group of Shiffleys was providing a musical accompaniment—ably assisted, I was pleased to see, by a couple of my relatives.

I strolled through the crowd, looking for one face in particular: Henrietta Pruitt's. Now that I knew the story—well, not the whole story, but some of the less heroic details—about the Battle of Pruitt's Ridge, I wanted to talk to her.

I found her in the kitchen, packing up to leave. Actually, Lacie Butler was scurrying around, gathering up Mrs. Pruitt's wraps and the dishes on which she'd brought her contributions to the feast, while Mrs. Pruitt sipped a cup of tea and looked on with an air of long-suffering patience.

How is that so different from what your own mother does? my contrary side asked.

Mother would at least be polite. And Mother did the occasional bit of work. Right now, she was fixing more tea.

"Going so soon?" I asked Mrs. Pruitt.

"Well, it's gotten rather . . . lively for me," Mrs. Pruitt said with an unconvincing smile. "Too much noise just destroys my nerves."

Mother was pointedly tapping her toes to the music and ignoring Mrs. Pruitt, other than occasionally refilling her teacup. If I'd been Mrs. Pruitt, I would have had someone else taste the tea first.

Just then the musicians outside reached the end of a set of reels, and loud applause and cheers erupted from the yard. Mrs. Pruitt shuddered delicately.

"On top of yesterday's shock," I said. "Seeing a dead body."

"Yes," she said, shuddering more dramatically. "Although I didn't actually see the dead body, of course," she added quickly. "Just the photo. Still— the very idea . . ."

She sipped again and closed her eyes as if stoically enduring unspeakable tortures.

"Yes, the photo," I said. "I guess that's why you didn't recognize her. Only seeing the photo."

"I beg your pardon?" she said.

"I mean, I'd assume you'd recognize her, since she was a member of the historical society when she was here."

"She may have attended a few meetings," Mrs. Pruitt said.

"Enough meetings to get elected vice president and historian." I pulled out one of my photocopies— the one with the photo of the society's new officers.

Mrs. Pruitt studied it for a few moments.

"Oh, yes," she said, handing back the photocopy. "I remember her now. Not a particularly satisfactory officer, I must say. We never saw that much of her. You can see why I didn't recognize her, of course. The years weren't exactly been kind to her, were they?"

Kind? If you asked me, the years had been downright lavish with their generosity. Lindsay had looked better at forty than many women did at half that age. But Mrs. Pruitt looked happier now that she'd found an excuse for her failure to identify the victim. Damn.

I changed the subject.

"By the way, I ran into a copy of your book at the library," I said. "Fascinating stuff. Mind if I ask you a few questions about it?"

"Certainly," she said. "Except—my goodness, look at the time! Lacie, how much longer are you going to take?"

"I'm sorry, Henrietta," Lacie said. "Everything's nearly ready."

An optimistic estimate, since it took her twenty-five minutes to finish whatever it was she was doing. She might have done it faster if Mrs. Pruitt had continued to ignore her instead of micromanaging the process. Or was I merely miffed because Mrs. Pruitt's nonstop harangue at Lacie effectively prevented me from continuing to quiz her about her history book?

Strange. Most authors I'd met were more than willing to talk about their brainchildren, whether you wanted them to or not.

Mrs. Pruitt finally bid Mother and me an effusive good-bye and exited, with Lacie trailing after, carrying so much stuff that Eric went to help her, unasked. Silence reigned in the kitchen at last. For a few moments.

"What a ghastly woman," Mother said.

Chapter Twenty-one

"You see why Michael and I haven't jumped at the chance to join the country club," I said. "Or the historical society, or the garden club."

"Quite understandable. The way she treats poor Lucy Butler!"

"Lacie," I said.

"Whose only fault is that she really needs to speak up for herself more," Mother continued. "Learn to say no. Someone should take her in hand."

"I think Mrs. Pruitt already has," I said, wincing. I could see Lacie's life being made a living hell, caught between the devil of her habitual servitude to Mrs. Pruitt and the deep blue sea of Mother's demand that she grow a backbone.

"And why wouldn't she talk to you about her book?" Mother asked. "Most of the time, you can't shut her up about her insufferable family's history."

"Because she suspects I want to interrogate her about the Battle of Pruitt's Ridge," I said. "Which probably wasn't the glorious Confederate victory Mrs. Pruitt's book makes it seem. Even I figured that much out, so you can imagine what a real historian would say."

"Oh dear," Mother said. Conflicting emotions fought for control of her face—her dislike of Mrs. Pruitt warring with her sympathy for anyone betrayed by the harsh reality of history. She had forgiven Dad for proving that Isaiah Hollingworth, the ancestor who had gotten her and countless cousins into the DAR, had actually been an infamous Tory, rather than a patriot. Forgiveness came easier, since Dad made his genealogical revelation about the time she'd grown completely bored with the local DAR, thus giving her the perfect escape hatch. She'd spent weeks crafting her resignation speech—and practicing the look of dignified sorrow and resignation with which she'd deliver it.

On the other hand, she still hadn't forgiven the historians who revealed, to her horror, that the subtle, muted, tasteful Williamsburg colors she was so found of using in her decorating schemes were only subtle, muted, and tasteful because they'd faded in the two centuries since our misguided Colonial forebears had painted their drawing rooms with electric blues, lush scarlets, and garish eggplant purples. I'd made the mistake of taking her to Mount Vernon after they'd repainted the dining room in a verdigris green so vivid, most people stopped to blink when they entered. I thought it was cool. Mother had spent the rest of the afternoon lying down in a darkened room with a cold compress over her forehead, sipping weak tea and muttering things about the father of our country that would have gladdened the heart of George III.

"Still, she doesn't have to be rude about it," Mother said, as if that settled everything. Mother could forgive anything but rudeness. She'd always had a soft spot for distinguished gentlemanly crooks like Cary Grant's character in *To Catch a Thief*. Several years ago, when she and Dad had a burglary, she complained far less about the loss of their new television set than the fact that the ill-mannered intruder had failed to wipe his feet and left muddy footprints all over her Oriental rug.

Just then, Lacie dashed back in.

"Forgot something," she said with a nervous giggle. "So silly of me."

Her own purse.

"Lacie, dear," Mother said.

I grabbed a glass of lemonade and beat a retreat. Maybe Lacie needed rescuing after all.

Outside, I found that Dad had appropriated two of Farmer Early's sheep and was trying to teach Spike the rudiments of herding them. At least I assumed that was why Dad was on his hands and knees, yipping like a small dog and pretending to nip at the heels of the sheep. The sheep ignored him. Spike sat with his head cocked to one side, clearly fascinated, but he didn't seem interested in joining the fray.

"So how's it going?" I asked.

"Slowly," Dad said.

"I keep telling him it's not the barking," Horace said. "It's all in the eyes."

Dad sat back, pulled a handkerchief out of his pocket, and mopped his forehead.

"Is that lemonade?" he asked.

"Here." I handed him the glass. "You need this more than I do."

"Thanks," he said. He gulped half the lemonade without stopping, then sat back again to mop more slowly and frown at the sheep.

"Yes, going slowly," he said. Then, as if afraid he'd sounded too discouraged, he straightened his spine. "Repetition is the key," he added.

"All in the eyes," Horace said.

"Repetition," Dad repeated, with a small frown at Horace. "Repetition and patience."

And a working sense of humor, I'd have added. One of the sheep contributed some manure to the lawn, a few inches from Dad's foot. Dad sighed and gazed at it for a few moments, then stood up and tugged at the sheep. It resisted at first, then allowed itself to be led, one grudging step at a time, until they were about six feet away from the manure pile. Dad repeated the process with the second sheep, then drained the lemonade glass.

"Thanks," he said. "Tell you what. I'll do another demonstration. Then you pick Spike up and put him right beside me. While I'm still herding. Let him get the idea that he's supposed to do it, too."

"Oh, I get to pick him up," I said. "What have I ever done to you?"

But Spike was enjoying his lesson, or so I deduced from his perfunctory attempt to bite me. I took him closer, where he could get a good look at what Dad was doing, and Dad once again yipped, bared his teeth, and snapped at the heels of the oblivious sheep.

"Sheep, Spike," I said in deliberate imitation of the command Rob used to set him in motion against cows. When I set him at Dad's side, he sat down and curled his lip, as if protesting the smell.

"Rowrrrrrr!" Dad growled, and bent toward the sheeps' legs again.

One of the sheep kicked him in the head.

It wasn't a forceful kick; only the tip of the hoof grazed his forehead. But as Dad was so fond of pointing out, the skin of the face and scalp has a rich blood supply, causing cuts to the head to bleed more profusely than cuts anywhere else on the body.

"Oh my God!" Horace said. "Should we call a doctor?"

"I *am* a doctor," Dad said. "Stay calm."

Which was precisely what I'd heard him say a hundred times over the years while dealing with the minor injuries his children and grandchildren inflicted on themselves and one another. But usually by the time he said this, he was already staunching the bleeding with something, and now he was just sitting there with blood running down his face.

"Get some ice," I said, grabbing the handkerchief Dad was holding and pressing it to the cut. "And some dish towels or something."

Horace ran off.

"What's wrong?" Rob said. He appeared at my elbow and abruptly disappeared. I heard the small thump as he hit the ground—Rob usually fainted at the sight of blood.

"Dad, can you hear me?"

"Of course I can hear you," he said. "Stop shouting."

"Dish towels," Horace said, dumping several of them in my lap.

"I actually meant clean ones," I muttered.

"What's going on?" Mother had come trailing out of the kitchen after Horace.

"Do you remember what happened to you?" I asked Dad.

"Of course I remember," Dad said. "The sheep kicked me."

"One of *those* sheep?" asked Mother. I glanced up and saw that she had put her hands on her hips and was glaring at the sheep. The sheep, as if sensing the presence of danger, suddenly left off grazing and scampered in the direction of their pasture.

"See? It's all in the eyes," Horace said.

"Meg, do something," Mother ordered.

"I am doing something," I said. "I'm doing the same thing Dad usually does when someone gets hit in the head. He's not unconscious, and he doesn't appear to have any short-term amnesia, and his pupils and pulse seem normal, so he probably doesn't have a serious concussion."

"She's right," Dad said, "That's exactly what I'd say."

"But it wouldn't be a bad thing if you took him in to the ER to make sure," I added.

"I'll drive," Horace said.

"Let's take my truck," Randall Shiffley suggested. "That way, he can lie down till we get there."

"No, no," Dad said. "It's only a flesh wound. I'll be fine. I'll just sit here quietly for a while. No sense going to the ER on a Saturday night."

The Shiffleys kept trying to convince Dad to go, but my family knew better. Horace and Randall eased him into an Adirondack chair at the edge of the lawn and Horace bandaged the wound.

"I'll keep an eye on him," Horace announced.

"You see?" Dad said. "What do we need the ER for?"

Well, Horace did have a certain amount of medical knowledge. Most of it gleaned from examining dead bodies at crime scenes, but as long as Dad was happy.

I was relieved to see that in all the fuss over Dad, Rob hadn't been completely forgotten. Michael was checking on him.

"Your brother's all right," Michael said.

"That's a matter of opinion," I said.

"Ha, ha," Rob murmured.

Michael returned to what he'd been doing—tending one of the many grills that dotted the yard. Possibly one abandoned by the Shiffleys, who were still hovering, offering rides to the ER.

"Burger?" he asked.

While I was eating, I glanced around the yard and fretted.

"A penny for them," Michael said.

"Mrs. Pruitt is looking guiltier and guiltier," I said.

"Wouldn't 'more and more guilty' sound better?" he asked.

"I like guiltier," I said.

"So what's the problem?"

"The problem is that for now, she's on the side of the angels, fighting Mr. Briggs's outlet mall."

"So you'd rather Briggs turned out to be the killer."

"I'd love it if they turned out to be accomplices, but fat chance of that," I said. "Still, we shouldn't overlook Briggs."

I noticed then that Mr. Briggs was strolling about near the edge of the yard.

"I think I'll have a chat with him," I said.

"A chat about what?" Michael asked.

"His plans for the neighborhood. His whereabouts Friday afternoon. Stuff like that."

"Meg—"

"Don't worry," I said. "I'll be tactful and subtle."

"Meg, wait," Michael called. Evidently, he didn't have much confidence in my tact and subtlety.

Chapter Twenty-two

I caught up with Evan Briggs near the edge of the yard, where the ground dropped off rapidly. He was gazing over the landscape, turning his head slowly. I could tell he noticed my arrival, but he didn't speak.

"Nice view," I said.

He nodded.

"Beautiful," I continued. "Unspoiled."

He didn't say anything, but I noticed he was watching me out of the corner of his eye, a small frown on his face. It was much the way people watched Spike, once they'd come to know him.

Subtlety wasn't working, and it wasn't my forte anyway.

"So do you really want to build the world's largest outlet mall there?" I asked. "Or is that just a nasty rumor?"

"I'm afraid I can't talk about our corporate plans," he said.

"True, then," I said.

"I didn't say that."

"No, but if it was false, you'd say so, to get me

off your back. If you had any guts, you'd just come out and say it was true. But no, you just say you can't talk about it. Do you really think everyone who wants to stop you is going to wait around until you're ready to announce it?"

I was trying to keep my voice calm and civil. He was better at it. Not surprising. I'd seen him at the county board meetings during the squabble over his town house development. People had hurled insults at him and made wild, improbable threats, all of which he'd ignored, as if he hadn't heard a thing.

"You can't stop progress, you know," he said.

"Not everyone considers *development* and *progress* synonyms."

"You can't stop development, either."

"Maybe not, but you can damn well try," I said. "You can fight it with everything you've got."

"You can try."

"I will."

To the casual onlooker, perhaps it looked as if we were having a friendly conversation. We were both smiling, or at least baring our teeth at each other. Mother, whose antennae were more finely tuned to social nuances than most humans, suddenly appeared at my side.

"Meg, dear," she said. "Are you making Mr. Briggs feel at home?"

"I hope not," I said. "By the way," I added, turning back to him. "I don't suppose you'd be nice enough to tell me who else is against this horrible outlet-mall plan?"

He pursed his lips and glared at me.

"Oh, well," I said. "I can find out anyway. I mean, I'm sure Mrs. Pruitt is gearing up to fight you, and I could always join forces with her if I had to. I was just hoping for an alternative. She's not exactly my favorite person in the world, but under the circumstances—"

"Now, Meg," Mother said in her most soothing tones. "I'm sure Mr. Briggs isn't up to anything terrible. If you just sit down and talk about things, I'm sure you can reach some mutually satisfactory agreement."

Briggs startled us both by uttering several words Mother usually pretended not to know.

"I beg your—" Mother began, drawing herself up.

"I don't know what you people think you're trying to do," he snapped. "You're not going to get away with it. I don't care what you think you know or who you show it to. Just leave me alone."

He stomped away.

"What an utter barbarian," Mother said in her iciest tone. If we were living in the kingdom of Etiquette, where Mother had the power of high and low justice, Evan Briggs would just have forfeited his head. He and the sheep.

"A barbarian, definitely," I said. "Can you see him as a murderer?"

"Easily," Mother said. "He chews with his mouth open. Do you think he is?"

"I have no idea."

"I'm sure you'll figure out, dear." She patted my shoulder encouragingly before returning to the lawn—presumably so she could cast withering glances at Mr. Briggs from closer range and with a larger audience. And hover near Dad.

"That was dramatic," Michael said. I started slightly. I hadn't realized he'd followed me and heard part of our conversation with Briggs.

"He's defensive about something."

"No kidding," he said. We both stood gazing, not at the landscape, but at Mr. Evan Briggs.

"Something Mother said set him off," I said. But why? To me, she sounded like the soul of reason and conciliation. Which ticked me off, but only because she was being reasonable and conciliatory to the man who wanted to turn our rural retreat into a concrete jungle. Why would Briggs react so savagely?

"Maybe it was an accident," Michael said. "Some phrase that hit him wrong."

" 'I'm sure you can reach some mutually satisfactory agreement,' " I repeated. "That's what she said."

"Why would that annoy anyone?"

"Well, it annoys me because I know she means 'Stop being rude to your guests or you'll be sorry later,' " I said. "I have no idea why it would annoy Briggs."

" 'I don't care what you think you know or who you show it to,' " Michael said, echoing Briggs's words. "What does that sound like to you?"

"Like someone telling a would-be blackmailer to publish or be damned. Can you imagine Lindsay blackmailing someone?"

The fact that he thought about it for ten or fifteen seconds before speaking almost answered the question for him.

"Not for money," he said finally. "But to accomplish something she felt she had to accomplish . . ."

His voice trailed off and he shrugged.

"To save her job, for example," I said.

"Yes, if she wasn't blackmailing Wentworth, she was certainly planning to."

"How did she feel about development?"

"Anti," he said. "Which was pretty ironic for someone who considered a town without a major mall beyond the pale of civilization, but we all have our inconsistencies. So yeah, if she were still in town, she'd oppose it. But I can't imagine she would have cared that much after she left. And what could she possibly have had on Briggs?"

"I have no idea," I said. "But I intend to keep my eye on him. He's up to something."

"Speaking of up to something, here come the sheep again," Michael said, pointing.

Someone had profited from Dad's lessons. Two sheep—possibly the two Dad had been using as teaching tools—were scurrying back into the yard, with Duck in hot pursuit, snapping at their heels with her beak and quacking loudly as she came. She chased them to the far side of the yard and down the hill toward the cow pasture, then halted almost precisely at our property line before marching back in the direction she'd come—toward Mr. Early's pasture.

"Shouldn't she chase them the other way?" I asked. "Wonder if this has anything to do with Mr. Early's missing sheep?"

"Do you suppose she's nesting up in his pasture now?" Michael asked.

"We can take a look tomorrow," I said. "I have another project in mind for tonight."

"A project. Dare I hope it's one that involves champagne, caviar, and perhaps a hot tub?"

"The boxes," I said. "Let's go look at them."

Michael followed me out to the shed. Spike leaped up, growling fiercely, when I reached to open the gate of his temporary pen. When he recognized us, he retreated to his corner to sulk at being deprived of a chance to bite someone. Not that he wouldn't have bitten us as willingly as an intruder, but he knew we were already wise to most of his tricks.

"It's getting dark," I said. "We should take him inside with us before the owls come out."

Once he finished the treat we used to lure him in, Spike curled up in one corner of the shed with his back to us and we turned to the boxes.

"Still there, all twenty-three of them," Michael said.

"How can you count that fast?" I asked.

"I don't have to count," he said. "I can see that there are still four stacks of five boxes each, plus the three extras."

"Ah," I said, nodding. "Higher math. I'm impressed. Yes, still there, all twenty-three of them. We'd better get started going through them."

"Whatever for?"

"For more information on this."

I reached into my purse and pulled out the sheaf of photocopies and microfiche copies I'd made at the library.

"Wonderful," he said as he began leafing through them. "We can use this to help stop the outlet mall."

"Exactly. But it would be better if we had the original source material, which isn't in the library."

"You're thinking it might be here?"

"Could be," I said. "Or maybe we'll find something related. So we're going to look through these boxes and see what's here."

"You didn't look through them when you packed them?"

"Not really," I said. "Whenever I found any old papers or photos, I put them in a copier box for the Sprockets. I didn't inventory them or anything. It was last summer, when I had no idea we'd need to document how critical the Battle of Pruitt's Ridge was to the outcome of the Civil War."

"Right," he said. "You also think these might have something to do with Lindsay's murder."

"It's possible."

"And that's why we have to do it tonight."

"Before Chief Burke figures out the same thing and appropriates them," I said. "Why, was there something else you'd rather do?"

Just then, we heard fiddle music start up, accompanied, after a few seconds, by the jingling of bells. We both cocked our heads to listen.

"Are the bells getting louder, or am I just getting really tired of hearing them?" Michael said after a few moments.

I peeked out the shed door.

"Not louder," I said. "More numerous."

Outside, the Morris Mallet Men had recovered

sufficiently from their poison ivy to give lessons. Apparently, they'd brought plenty of extra bells—enough to equip most of my visiting relatives and the Shiffleys, too.

"Maybe if we fake a power outage," Michael suggested. He was rubbing his temples as if his head hurt. "I could creep into the basement and flip all the circuits. Shut down their CD or tape player or whatever."

"No, let them have their fun," I said. "Besides, I don't think cutting the power would do any good."

"The music's battery-powered?"

"Shiffley-powered. Remember, they were playing all afternoon."

"That's right," Michael said. "Just when I was getting to like them."

I did like the Shiffleys' musical performance—or I would have, if not for all the accompanying bells.

"I suppose the bells are essential," Michael said, echoing my thoughts. "No possibility we could sell them on the concept of stealth Morris dancing."

"I like that idea," I said. "Let's work on it tomorrow. After we've done the boxes."

"Right." Michael looked back and forth between the door and the stack of boxes, as if trying to decide which was worse, beginning Morris dancers or rummaging through the boxes.

"Let's get started," he said, grabbing a box. "What do you want to bet that if we find anything at all interesting, it will be in box twenty-three?"

Chapter Twenty-three

It wasn't quite that bad. We hit pay dirt in box nine-teen. Not that we didn't find a great many strange and interesting things in the first eighteen boxes. Hundreds of old photos, the kind where everyone begins to look alike because they're all frowning from the effort of sitting still long enough. Hundreds of old letters that we didn't read—half of them were cross-written, to save paper, and most were in fading ink on fragile paper. Newspapers we didn't dare open for fear they'd crumble. We weren't looking for contents yet, just dates. Anything from during or shortly after the Civil War we studied carefully and put aside in a special stack—a small stack. Most of the stuff was from the late 1800s through the 1920s.

"Hey, that's still pretty old," Michael said when I complained about this. "Probably a great research project here. I recognize most of the last names— old Caerphilly families. And all the newspapers and documents are local."

"Fodder for a real history of Caerphilly," I said.

"Something a lot more accurate than Mrs. Pruitt's version."

"You thinking of writing it?" he asked.

"Not on your life. "That's a job for a real historian. But I have changed my mind about giving them to someone from UVa or Caerphilly. Caerphilly didn't care, and UVa sicced Lindsay on me, though I suppose that's Helen Carmichael's fault, not UVa's."

"Then what are you going to do with it all?" Michael asked, eyeing the stack of boxes.

"Give it to Joss, if she wants it," I said. "If she's serious about studying American history, well, here's a motherlode of original source material she can cut her teeth on."

"Keep it in the family," Michael said, nodding. "Good plan."

I'd hit a dull patch in box nineteen—a bunch of documents from the mid 1950s and early 1960s, which made them about a century too new to be useful at the moment. Still, I kept on methodically. After all, I'd made no effort to arrange things by date, only to gather all the papers of possible historical interest in the boxes.

At the bottom of the box I'd begun to call the "Eisenhower archive," I found it—a nondescript manila file folder, but when I opened it, I discovered the original photograph of Col. Jedidiah Pruitt and his wife and daughter.

I opened my mouth, but before I could tell Michael, I became transfixed by the photo. Not so much by the contents—though it was easier, in the original, to get some idea of their personalities. The colonel looked smug and self-satisfied, less interested in his wife or the new addition to his family than in preening for the photographer. At first glance, his wife looked demure, with her lace bonnet and downcast eyes. Demure, and surprisingly young for someone who'd had fourteen children. Doubtless she'd started having them at an age when modern girls aren't even allowed to baby-sit. After studying her for a few minutes, I decided her eyes weren't downcast after all. She was glaring sideways at the colonel's hand, which lay on her shoulder with such a casual, proprietary air, and I didn't think her gaze looked particularly affectionate.

"So I'm voting for her as most likely to become a self-made widow," Michael said, looking over my shoulder.

"Do you blame her? That's baby number fourteen she's holding."

"Justifiable homicide, then," he said. "I take it that's the heroic Colonel Pruitt?"

"Or not. The jury's still out on whether the battle was much of a victory."

"Still—fascinating."

I agreed. Michael perused the folder's contents— the rest of the photos, the fragile clipping from the 1862 *Clarion*, and the equally fragile letter that mentioned the burning of the Shiffley distillery. I lapsed back into my fascination with the photo of the colonel and his wife. I realized I didn't know anything else of their history. I didn't know if the colonel had survived the Civil War, though odds were he had, since she went on to have three more children. Had his wife lived to a ripe old age or died in childbirth with the seventeenth child? What was her name, anyway? It bothered me, not having anything to call her but Mrs. Pruitt. The more I looked at her, the more annoyed I became with how little I knew about her. Mrs. Pruitt, wife of the colonel, who gave birth to seventeen children—surely there was more to her life than that?

And while the colonel looked like a Pruitt— round-faced and already running to jowls beneath the bushy beard—I couldn't remember seeing an echo of her features in any of the modern Pruitts I knew. I figured I should check the family genealogy, though, because her strong, sharp features looked familiar. Probably many old local families were descended from the determined-looking colonel's lady.

"What's wrong?" Michael asked.

"Nothing's wrong. It's just amazing to think that they could have held these very photos over a hundred and forty years ago. We're touching pieces of history."

"We've been touching pieces of history for several hours now," Michael said, yawning. "You only just noticed? About half a ton of history by now. I've got little crumbly bits of history all over my hands and clothes. Or does it only count as history if someone's put it in a book?"

"It counts, but I don't get excited right now unless it's history we can use to fend off the outlet mall," I said, putting the manila folder carefully aside.

"Well, let's hurry and search the rest of the history for more useful bits," Michael said, reaching for another box. "You realize that these photos, fascinating as they are, don't to a thing to prove or disprove Mrs. Pruitt's story of the battle."

"What do you mean?"

"There's only one photo of the battle—the aftermath, anyway. We might prove it's Mr. Shiffley's pasture those bodies are lying in, but even that would be hard. We have no idea if it really was taken in July 1862. Could have been anytime during the Civil War, and some Pruitt assumed it was their pet battle and labeled it decades after the fact."

"You're right," I said, nodding. "Furthermore, we know Jedidiah Pruitt existed, but not his rank, or even that he was in the Confederate army—he's wearing civilian clothes in the photo. Naming his daughter Victoria Virginia could have been a generic patriotic act rather than a commemoration of a particular battle."

"In short, something happened on that field during the Civil War, but we have only the Pruitts' version."

"We also have the *Clarion*'s version," I said. "From 1862 and 1954. Which has some details that aren't exactly flattering to the colonel, so I believe it more than Mrs. Pruitt's account."

"Yes, but who knows what unflattering details they omitted," Michael said. "After all, the Pruitts used to own the *Clarion*."

"They did? In 1862 or 1954?"

"Both. They founded it just before the Civil War and didn't give it up till one of them ran it into bankruptcy in the sixties. So maybe they published a few negative details that they didn't dare leave out, because everyone already knew them—but who knows what they suppressed?"

"We need to find more source material," I said, nodding.

"Which means back to the boxes," Michael said with a sigh.

I glanced at the photos again before I dug back in. Now that we'd raised so many questions about the real story behind them, I found it easier to resist their pull. Especially the melodramatic one with the scrap of cloth fluttering on the wire. Something about that bothered me. Maybe it was a famous Civil War photo of some other battle. I could ask Joss later.

The Morris dancers ceased and desisted around 11:30, and we finished the last box shortly thereafter. Apart from the folder that I felt sure was the original source material for the *Caerphilly Clarion*'s article on the Battle of Pruitt's Ridge, we didn't find anything else relevant.

"Of course, how do we know what's relevant?" Michael said. "Not being Lindsay, we can't really guess what she was looking for."

We both contemplated the boxes in silence for a few moments.

"Tell me—" I began, then stopped myself.

"Tell you what?" Michael said after a second.

"I was about to ask you to tell me about Lindsay. But it sounds like I'm prying into your past, and I'm not. Just wondering what she was like."

"And why someone would have wanted to kill her," he said. "I understand."

"Do you mean you understand what I'm asking, or you understand why someone would want to kill her?"

"Maybe both," he said. He looked nostalgic—no, that wasn't the word for it. More a cross between wistful and rueful, if there was such a thing. He frowned and thought. I waited.

"When I first met her," he said finally, "I admired her fierceness."

"Fierceness?" Perhaps I'd just discovered the secret of his ability to tolerate Spike.

"About causes. Against injustice. She was always marching into battle about something—writing letters to the editor, carrying around petitions, organizing demonstrations, telling people off. I remember saying to someone who found her irritating that the world was filled with people who never stood up for anything, except maybe their own self-interest, and she wasn't afraid to speak out."

"Sounds admirable," I said. I meant it. I wouldn't have minded meeting the woman he was describing. I wouldn't have minded it if someone described me that way.

"Yeah," he said. "Trouble was, I was seeing her the way I wanted to see her, not the way she was. It wasn't really about the cause to her. It was all about the battle. She went around looking for things to get mad about. And she always found something. If I believe in something, I try to stand up for it, even if not everyone approves, but there's big difference between that and reveling in the number of new enemies you create every time you do anything. If you disagreed with her cause, you were a fascist, or an idiot, or a Neanderthal. If you agreed with her cause but not with her methods, you were a wimp or a coward. If you agreed with her on everything, she could still find a way to tick you off."

"Sounds uncomfortable."

"It was," he said. "Uncomfortable to be around, at any rate, though she thrived on it. Ultimately self-destructive. I remember when she told me that the history department had decided to get rid of her. She wasn't upset; she was jubilant. Another big battle she could fight."

"Were they? Trying to get rid of her, I mean. Or was she just paranoid?"

"Nothing paranoid about it," he said. "They definitely had it in for her. They weren't even subtle about it. She'd have had a great case against them—in the press anyway. Outspoken radical professor ousted by reactionary administration. Chauvinists punish uppity female. Except by the time it happened, she not only didn't have any allies; she'd have had leave town to find more than a handful of people who weren't already enemies."

"Damn," I said.

"What's wrong?"

"I wanted to dislike her," I said. "Out of—I don't know. Retroactive jealousy, I guess."

"She wasn't hard to dislike," Michael said with a sigh.

"She made people unhappy, herself most of all, I

suspect," I said. "But she didn't deserve to be killed like that."

"The problem was, once she got cornered—once it started to look like she was going to lose—she got . . . Well, she changed. She started thinking in terms of what she could get on people, and how she could use it against them. The affair with Marcus Wentworth—as I said, I think she wanted to use it to blackmail him into saving her job."

"Do you think he was the only one? Or do you think she tried with other people?"

"I don't know," he said. "I wasn't seeing much of her by then. And, hell yes, she probably was blackmailing people. Not for money, but to save her job. The last time I saw her before she headed out of town, she was even madder, and talking about getting back at people. Making them pay, making them sorry, ruining their lives. I warned a couple of the people I figured she had it in for. Kept an eye open for any sign that she was doing something like that. After a while, I figured . . . well, not that she'd calmed down—she was a marathon grudge holder—more that putting her life back together would keep her busy when she first left, and by the time she'd been gone a year or so, I figured she had newer enemies to torment. To tell the truth, maybe I was just relieved that she hadn't decided I was one of her enemies."

"What if something made her decide to come back after her old enemies after all?" I said. "Or what if she'd been harassing or blackmailing some of them all along?"

And, not that I was going to upset Michael by mentioning this, what if her turning up practically in our backyard wasn't a coincidence, but part of some plot to cause him trouble?

"I'm beat," Michael said after a short pause. "Let's knock off."

"As soon as we pick everything up," I said.

"We're going to lock up, aren't we?"

"Yes, but we're leaving him here to guard," I said, pointing to Spike. "We don't want to leave anything on the floor, where he could shred it or pee on it. For that matter, we should get those boxes up off the floor. He could do serious damage if he decided to pee on them."

"You really think he'd do that?"

Spike chose that moment to lift his head, look over at us, and heave a deep sigh, as if hurt by our distrust. Then he curled up again into a tighter ball.

"You're right," Michael said. "We definitely need to get all the boxes out of his reach."

Luckily, we happened to have a supply of cinder blocks in a nearby shed. In fact, we happened to have quite a lot of miscellaneous building materials left over from various construction and repair projects the previous owners had undertaken and usually left unfinished. We eventually decided that a base of three cinder blocks put the boxes high enough that Spike would have a hard time doing any damage to them.

As soon as we opened the door to leave, Spike switched from looking aloof and disdainful to looking pitiful and abandoned.

"Why does he do that when he knows we won't fall for it?" Michael said as we strolled toward the barn.

"Because he knows we'll still feel guilty enough to give him extra liver treats," I said. "At least I did."

"If it's confession time, so did I," Michael admitted. "If we have kids, we'll have to work harder on not letting them play one of us off against the other."

I made a noncommittal noise. Not that I was opposed, in theory, to the notion of children, but I didn't really want to think about taking on any more long-term projects until we had the house fit to live in again.

"Of course, most children aren't as devious as Spike," Michael said.

"You really haven't paid enough attention to my nieces and nephews, have you?"

"I have," he protested. "They try, but they don't quite match Spike. Though what they lack in deviousness, they make up for with vocabulary and opposable thumbs."

"And many children grow up to be college students," I added. By March, Michael was usually feeling somewhat jaundiced about the intelligence and sanity of each year's crop of students.

"With luck, they outgrow that, too," he said.

Our resident collection of college students were all asleep when we crept past them to our bedroom stall. At least they were asleep until Michael tripped over a large stack of bells they'd left lying around, but that was their own fault.

As I drifted toward sleep, I found myself thinking about the photos. My little bits of history. I didn't want to trust them to the shed, so I'd brought the manila folder with me and hidden it in plain sight, along with several dozen similar folders holding paint samples, brochures about different brands of windows, appliance warranties, and other detritus of the house remodeling. I was looking forward to pitching the whole collection out—well, all except for the warranties—when the house was finished. But Mrs. Sprocket, from whom we'd bought the house, wouldn't have pitched out anything. She'd have shoved the whole collection into a twenty-fourth copier-paper box, and perhaps in a hundred years some historian might find it a fascinating resource on early-twentieth-century domestic architecture. How much of our collection was just as random—stuff saved simply because it had been gathered? Or worse, stuff left in Mrs. Sprocket's house because no one else had any use for it?

Not something I needed to know, but that didn't stop my brain from fretting about it for an annoyingly long time before I finally dropped off. I'd been asleep no more than half an hour when Spike's barking woke us.

Chapter Twenty-four

The whole idea of putting Spike and the boxes in the shed together was to catch anyone who went after the boxes. I kept reminding myself of that when the barking began and I rummaged around for my shoes.

"Wake up!" I hissed to Michael. "Spike's barking."

"Wha?" he muttered.

"Someone's after the boxes!"

"S'three," Michael said. He had one eye open and was looking at the clock.

"Yes, three A.M.," I said. "That's when burglars strike."

Through Spike's barking, I could hear another sound, one that didn't quite register. I ran to the barn door, stepped out—

Straight into the path of a stampede of naked sheep.

Okay, they weren't all naked. Only half a dozen of them. Two or three more had been partially sheared, and the remaining dozen or so still had their wool. Most were trotting briskly back in the direction of Mr. Early's pasture—probably a subterfuge, as Mr. Early's sheep never went home of their own accord—but a few were already peeling off in various directions. Going to pay a call on Mr. Shiffley's cows, perhaps, or down to the creek to skinny-dip.

The small pen outside the shed, where Spike spent the day quietly snoozing, now contained several large piles of sheared wool, along with a remarkable amount of sheep manure.

Inside the shed, Spike was still barking fiercely, and I could see his head popping into view every few seconds—the windows were too high for him to look out, so he was jumping up, hoping to catch a glimpse of what was happening outside.

But I was seeing the back of his head. He was trying to see out of the window at the back of the shed.

I ran around the shed. No one there, but I found a screwdriver lying below the window, and I could see signs that someone had tried to pry out the iron grille I'd put over the window. Fat chance making much progress on that before morning. I'd done a solid job on the installation.

"Good boy, Spike," I said. I repeated it several times, in the hope he'd get the notion that "good boy," in this context, meant "All right; you warned us about the burglar; so shut up already."

"What's going on?" Michael asked from the front of the shed.

I strolled around to join him.

"Spike detected an intruder."

"It took him this long to let us know about it?" Michael said, gesturing to the piles of wool.

"Whoever did the shearing was someone Spike

didn't consider an intruder," I said. "He didn't bark until someone tried to break in through one of the back windows."

"Thereby startling not only Spike but also the sheep thieves?"

"I don't think they were stealing the sheep," I said with a sigh. "I don't even think they planned to steal the wool. They—"

"What the hell are you doing to my sheep?"

Mr. Early had appeared. He had obviously dressed hastily. His plaid shirt was unbuttoned. He hadn't bothered to tie the high-topped tennis shoes he was wearing instead of the usual work boots. And was that a glimpse of leopard-print boxer shorts I was seeing above the waist of the hastily donned jeans? I tried not to stare. Luckily, he was without the shotgun he sometimes carried when alarmed over the fate of his flock. In his disheveled condition, he looked less intimidating than usual, and I was surprised to realize that he wasn't really an old codger. He wasn't much older than Michael. Mid-forties at most.

"We just got here ourselves," I said. "Your guess is as good as mine."

"What the hell?" Mr. Early said. He walked up to the fence around the pen and stared at the piles of wool, then over at the several naked sheep, which, true to form, had drifted back into our yard and were grazing peacefully a few feet away.

"I thought it was the perp who returned to the scene of the crime, not the victims," Michael murmured.

"Well, that's a new one," Mr. Early said finally. "Usually they just take the whole sheep."

"What's wrong? Meg, Michael, are you all right?"

Rose Noire crossed the yard at a dead run. Rose Noire, who had driven back to town several hours ago, along with Mrs. Fenniman, who was staying at her apartment.

"We're fine," I called. "Go back to sleep."

"Is everyone all right?" she called. She hardly stopped to look at us before clamoring over the fence, lifting up an armful of the wool, and gazing at it in wonder, as if only by touching it could she even begin to fathom the sudden miracle of its presence. Even if Mr. Early noticed the little bits of wool clinging to her clothes when she arrived, he'd have a hard time proving she hadn't just acquired them.

"What happened here?" she said, letting the wool sift out of her arms.

"Someone sheared Mr. Early's sheep without permission," I said.

"And did a damn careless job of it," Mr. Early grumbled.

" 'Careless'?" Rose Noire repeated. "Oh, surely not. They're not hurt, are they?"

"I don't see any blood," I said. "So I imagine the sheep are fine."

"Well, that's all that really matters, isn't it?" she said. "As long as the sheep are happy. And oh! Look!"

We all turned to see what she was pointing at. Just another naked sheep, as far as I could see.

"What's wrong?" Mr. Early said, frowning and squinting. He patted his shirt pocket then pursed his lips and squinted harder. I suddenly suspected that he usually wore contacts, hadn't had time to put them in before dashing out of the house, and for some reason didn't want to put on the glasses I could see sticking out of his shirt pocket.

"Look at him!" Rose Noire exclaimed, clasping her hands with enthusiasm.

"Her," Mr. Early said. "That's a ewe."

"You don't usually get to see the shape of their bodies with all the wool," Rose Noire said. "The wool's beautiful, of course—but look at her! What a noble animal!"

The sheep in question raised her head just then and looked at us, as if acknowledging Rose Noire's praise. To me, she looked distinctly odd and scrawny, but I could see Mr. Early's face take on a gleam of pride.

"They're Lincolns," he said. "Largest breed in the world. Longest wool, too."

"Magnificent!" Rose Noire said. She scrambled deftly back over the fence and drifted over to admire the sheep.

"About those fleeces," Mr. Early said. He was looking at Rose Noire, not the piles of wool.

"Why don't you let us clean up?" I said. "We'll gather up the fleeces and drop them off at your place in the morning."

Mr. Early nodded and stumbled off after Rose Noire.

Enter Mrs. Fenniman.

"What's going on?"

"Help us gather up the fleeces," I said.

"Why?" she asked.

"So you, too, will have an excuse for being covered with little tufts of wool," I said. "Hurry, while Rose Noire is distracting Mr. Early."

"Hmph," she said. "Those sheep are filthy. Ought to be a law."

"There is," I said. "It's called larceny. He sells the wool, you know, and can get a lot more for it if it's cut off properly instead of hacked off by amateurs."

"I may never look at another piece of gabardine," she said, but she helped us pick up the fleeces. Rose Noire, in the meantime, helped Farmer Early collect his sheep and went off to help him take them home, still chattering nonstop.

Michael fetched a tarp and we gathered up the fleeces and loaded them in the back of the pickup. We still said "the pickup" instead of "his pickup" or "our pickup," because we were still maintaining the fiction that the battered ten-year-old truck we'd recently acquired was something we'd be getting rid of when we finished the construction. I'd already figured out that, while he'd never give up his convertible, Michael got almost as much pleasure out of hauling things around in the pickup—including things that would have fit quite nicely into the convertible's almost nonexistent trunk.

"One of us can drive the stuff over in the morning," Michael said, though obviously he was dying to do it. Hauling actual farm paraphernalia in the pickup!

"Fine," I said, turning to Mrs. Fenniman. "Do you need a place to stay, or will you be heading back to town now?"

"Hmph," she said. "Rosie'll be needing a ride."

"She'll charm Mr. Early into giving her one," I

said. "Or if she doesn't, we'll look after her when she turns up."

"Hmph," she said again getting into her car. "That old codger."

Evidently, Mr. Early's impersonation of a grizzled curmudgeon had fooled most people.

"Hide the rest of the evidence," I said.

" 'Rest of the evidence'?"

"Whatever you used to do that," I said, gesturing to the fleeces.

"Already did. Under your hedge."

"I'll get them," Michael said, heading for the hedge.

"You didn't happen to notice anyone else when you were fleeing, did you?" I asked.

"Like who?"

"Like whoever set Spike off."

She shook her head and started the car.

"No one else there," she said. "We just made too much noise and woke him."

She drove off.

She sounded so definite that I found myself checking to make sure the screwdriver was still tucked securely in my back pocket.

"Found them," Michael said. When we got back to the barn, I found out that "them" included not only a pair of battery-operated home hair-cutting tools but also two sets of nifty night-vision goggles, which we couldn't resist testing.

"Cool," Michael whispered. "These would be really useful for . . . doing chores at night. Stuff like that. We should get a set."

"We just did," I said. "Two sets. They were abandoned by the unknown intruders who viciously denuded Mr. Early's sheep, remember?"

"Very cool," Michael said. He was tilting his head and looking at the ceiling, fascinated by some effect he saw.

I put on my set. Yes, I could see fairly well, though all the colors vanished into a luminous gray-green tone. I crept out of the stall and peered down the barn at sleeping students. They appeared to be sleeping quite soundly. So soundly that they'd missed the entire ruckus with the sheep? I hadn't thought to check on them when I'd dashed out, and now I'd never know whether they'd slept through the whole thing or used the diversion created by the sheep to steal back into the barn and feign sleep.

Michael tired of playing with the goggles quickly—after all, it was almost four o'clock in the morning—and we went back to sleep. I made sure my goggles and my shoes were handy, though. Spike was quiet now, and I doubted that whoever had tried to break into the shed would do it again tonight, but just in case.

Chapter Twenty-five

Sunday morning dawned bright and clear. Normally, I'd have taken the weatherman's word for it, but I got to observe it firsthand, thanks to the Shiffleys, who began talking, laughing, and rattling pots and pans outside at 6:00 A.M. Only the fact that they were producing the most heavenly smells—of bacon, sausage, eggs, and, above all, coffee—saved me from demonstrating what an ungracious hostess I was, and even then it was touch-and-go.

Michael brought me some coffee and wisely left me alone until the caffeine could take effect.

If only everyone were that considerate.

"I've got the new mallets," Mrs. Fenniman said, bursting into the stall when I was halfway through my mug. I looked up blearily. Yes, she was flourishing a pair of croquet mallets. How remiss of me, not spotting their usefulness as weapons before.

"That's nice," I said. "Who knows when we'll get a chance to use them, though."

"This afternoon," she said. "Didn't you get my message?"

"Message?"

"The chief said last night that he'd probably allow us to use the course this afternoon," she said. She leaned one mallet against the side of the stall—mine, I deduced—and began taking practice swings with the other.

"Afternoon is six hours away," I pointed out. "And didn't he say 'probably'?"

"Need to start working on our form," she said, lining up an imaginary shot. Or maybe not so imaginary—was she about to roquet my travel alarm out of the barn?

"My form will be better if I get more sleep," I said. "Or didn't you hear what an exciting night we had? Someone kidnapped and shaved several of poor Mr. Early's sheep. No telling what he'll do if he ever finds out who's responsible."

"Hmph," she said, abandoning her attack on my alarm clock. "You'll thank me next time we tackle those walking wickets!"

"I thought we were going to finish the game on the cow pasture first," I said. "Or replay it, if that's what the rules require."

"Probably replay it," she said. "Unless the chief gets on the ball and arrests one of the Dames. You think that's a possibility? I could drag my feet on getting the tournament started if there's a good chance one of them will land in jail and they'd have to forfeit."

"It's possible," I said. "No idea how likely. But you said there was no penalty for murder."

"Yeah, but there is for not showing up."

Of course. I closed my eyes, lay back as if returning to sleep, and hoped she'd take the hint. This was
more family togetherness than I wanted before I'd
finished my coffee.

"I'm rooting for Claire Wentworth as the culprit,"
she said.

"Her rather than Mrs. Pruitt?" I asked, opening
my eyes again in surprise.

"You think Mrs. Pruitt is more likely?"

"They're both equally likely, as far as I can tell," I
said. "It's just that most people find Mrs. Pruitt more
annoying."

"That's only because most people see more of
Mrs. Pruitt," Mrs. Fenniman said. "Believe me, if
you'd spent the whole afternoon hiking around a
bog with Claire at your heels, you'd find her just as
annoying."

"No doubt," I said. Then what she'd just said hit me.

"Wait a minute," I said. "What do you mean the
whole afternoon? Were you and Mrs. Wentworth together that long?"

"From the second wicket, when she broke her
mallet," Mrs. Fenniman said. "That's right, you'd
forged ahead, you and Henrietta, and the rest of us
were stuck on the second wicket. Now there's a diabolical wicket, if I do say so myself."

She beamed with pride. I didn't argue with her.
She'd placed the wicket on a small island in the
middle of what would be, come summer, a babbling
brook. This early in the spring, though, the brook
was a mean gush of ice water, interrupted not only
by hundreds of rocks but also by the exposed roots

of a large oak tree that would topple when the running water had eroded another foot or so of the stream bank out from under it. I'd nearly broken my own mallet there.

"Diabolical," I agreed. "So Mrs. Wentworth broke her mallet there? Didn't she have a spare?"

"No, Lacie was a wicket or two ahead by that time, and it was her job to tote the Dames' spare equipment around," Mrs. Fenniman said. "She had that huge pack, remember? Ridiculous, expecting one person to schlep around the gear for a whole team. Next time, I'm going to make it a rule: You carry your own crap or hire a sherpa."

"Are you allowed to make your own rules?" I asked. "Don't you have to consult the board of regents?"

"I'll talk 'em into it," she said. "Anyway, you should have heard the way Claire Wentworth lighted into Lacie when we found out she'd forgotten to pack the spare mallets."

"Typical," I muttered.

"So Rose Noire said Claire could share her mallet. Only she started falling behind by the next wicket, and I said the hell with it, Claire could share mine."

"That was nice of you," I said.

"The hell it was," Mrs. Fenniman said. "I didn't want to stop the game long enough to send someone back to the house for another mallet, and I damn well didn't want to listen to Claire ragging on Lacie anymore."

"Okay, it was selfish and cunning of you," I said. Mrs. Fenniman basked in the praise.

"See what I got for it," she said. "An uninterrupted afternoon of Claire Wentworth's company."

"Completely uninterrupted?" I asked. "Do you know what that means?"

"Means I know what hell will be like," Mrs. Fenniman grumbled.

"It means she has an alibi for the murder."

"Damnation," Mrs. Fenniman said after a moment's thought.

"If it's any comfort, you have one, too."

"I'd take my chances if it meant she might swing for it."

"Unfortunately, if your afternoon in her company was completely uninterrupted—"

"I'd have remembered an interruption," Mrs. Fenniman said with a sigh. "It would have stood out like a small island of serenity in a hellish afternoon. Why do you think I kept nagging everyone to keep the game moving briskly?"

Her fondness for ordering people around, I'd assumed, but I only shrugged.

"No way she could have done it during the morning game?" she asked. "No one but those feckless students around to keep an eye on her all morning."

"I don't know what the medical examiner said about time of death," I said. "But Horace thought she couldn't have been dead more than an hour."

"Horace would know," she said. "Damn. Here I was getting my hopes up about the chief arresting Claire, seeing as how she has such a good reason to dislike the victim. Ah well. You can't have everything, can you?"

She shouldered her mallet and strode out of the barn.

By this time, I was awake enough that I decided I might as well get up and see what was happening.

The Shiffleys had started a fire in the barbecue pit and set up half a dozen grills nearby.

"Did you hear the news?" Tony asked. "We're free to go whenever we want."

"That's great," I said. Then, in case I had sounded too enthusiastic about their impending absence, I added, "I assume that means you're no longer suspects."

"Oh, it could just mean he knows where to find us if he wants us," Tony said. "Pineville's a pretty small town."

"Still, it must be a relief," I said. "Knowing you can go home anytime you want. After breakfast, if you feel like it." Not that I was hinting.

"Yeah, as soon as Bill gets back," he said. "He was feeling restless and decided to take a drive."

I could sympathize.

"Unless we're still in the tournament," Tony added. "I understand that's starting up again this afternoon."

"I thought it was a double-elimination system," I said. "You lost to the Dames Friday morning and the clones Friday afternoon. So you're eliminated, right? If not for the murder, you could have gone home Friday night. Or Saturday morning. Not that you wouldn't have been welcome to stay around for the rest of the fun," I added, in case that sounded in-hospitable. "Assuming we'd been having fun instead of sitting around being suspects, which isn't my definition of fun. But you wouldn't have had to."

"Well, it's not definite that we're eliminated," he said. "Since so many of the murder suspects are on the competing teams. I mean, if they arrest Mrs. Pruitt, or one of the real estate ladies, wouldn't they have to forfeit the rest of the tournament?"

"I suppose," I said. "That would depend on when we have the rest of the tournament." I was thinking if we have the rest of the tournament, but I knew Mrs. Fenniman too well to believe a mere murder would discourage her from completing a project. "If they're out on bail when we start up again, I assume they could play; there's nothing against homicide in the rules. Even if they are eliminated, though, does that necessarily uneliminate you?"

"I have no idea," Tony said. "Bill and Mrs. Fenniman were talking about it earlier. Studying the rules."

He pointed with his thumb at a nearby picnic bench where Mrs. Fenniman sat. Sure enough, she was hunched over a stained and battered wad of paper that I recognized as her copy of the tournament rules. I still had no idea whether Mrs. Fenniman had acquired the rules from some official source or invented them herself. If it had taken her more than a few minutes to answer this new rules question, she was still deciding what ruling would most benefit our family team.

"Roger," I said. "I guess we'll just have to wait and see what she comes up with."

"Meanwhile, we have all the more time to spend

together," he said, giving me another of those annoyingly flirtatious smiles. He even batted his eyelashes at me, which I thought was against the union rules for guys old enough to shave.

"Yes," I said. "My fiancé has been saying how nice it's been, having a chance to get to know everyone instead of having everyone troop off to the croquet field first thing in the morning."

Too subtle? Perhaps not; his smile faltered slightly.

"Oh, yes, your fiancé," he said. "Marvin."

"Michael."

"Michael," he repeated. "What is it he does again?"

"Theater."

"Much of a living in that?" Tony asked.

I looked pointedly at the house. Which wasn't entirely paid for with Michael's earnings—my blacksmithing contributed, too, to say nothing of our stock in Mutant Wizards. But Tony didn't have to know that.

"He's employed, then," Tony said. "Excellent. Must make it difficult for you, though."

"Difficult?"

"And lonely," he added. "A long-distance relationship is so hard to maintain. Where does he work, anyway? Los Angeles or New York?"

"Here in Caerphilly," I said. "He's on the faculty of the drama department."

"Ah," he said, his face brightening again. "That's nice. Those who can, do, and all that."

Implying that if Michael were teaching, rather

than acting in New York or L.A., he must not be very good.

I wanted to say that those who can't shouldn't mock those who can do well enough to teach others, but he was technically my guest, so I suppressed the urge to deflate his ego, either with a smart remark or a well-placed kick. My tight smile should have warned any reasonably savvy people watcher that he was treading dangerously close to the edge. Tony rattled on.

I found myself brooding over the news. The chief was telling everyone they could go home, and releasing the croquet field. Did that mean he'd solved the murder? Surely someone would have told me if he'd made an arrest. Unless he was still in the process of making it.

Even if he hadn't made an arrest, perhaps he thought he'd solved the crime. Which was good. That was his job. The world would be a safer place with the murderer locked up.

So why was I so peeved that I still had no idea who had done it?

"You're up," Michael said, sitting down beside me.

"Don't sound so surprised," I said.

"That was pleasure, not surprise," he said. "Did you hear? While we were shuffling through the boxes last night, Chief Burke made enough progress in his case that—"

"He's letting everyone go home and releasing the croquet field," I said. "Don't rub it in."

Michael glanced at my mug, saw that it was still a

third full, and sat back to wait for me to ingest more caffeine.

Mrs. Fenniman sauntered over.

"Well, I'm heading into town," she said.

"I thought you were spending the morning warming up," I said.

"Going to take a break. Drop into Trinity Episcopal for the ten-thirty service. See if I can rattle the competition."

She sauntered off, the croquet mallet still over one shoulder.

"The competition?" Tony murmured.

"Mrs. Pruitt and her team all attend the local Episcopal church," Michael explained. "I'm sure that's all Mrs. Fenniman means by 'the competition.' She's an Episcopalian herself."

I drained the mug.

"Come on," I said to Michael. "Let's not just sit around waiting until Chief Burke deigns to tell us what he's found. Let's do something."

"Such as?"

"Let's go inspect Mr. Early's sheep pasture," I said, standing up and stumbling in the right direction.

Chapter Twenty-six

"Will Mr. Early like that?" Michael asked, falling into step beside me.

"Possibly not, but if he complains, we'll say we're inspecting the wickets to make sure they're in place in case we play here today. Or to make sure we can find them all to take them away tomorrow. If we run into him, we can inquire about the health of his naked sheep."

"Or ask how late he and Rose Noire stayed up . . . talking," Michael said with a grin.

"Whatever works. Come on."

We strolled across the road and climbed over the fence into Mr. Early's pasture.

"What are we looking for, anyway?" Michael asked as we climbed the hillside.

"At the moment, the starting stake."

"I mean in general. What clue do we hope to uncover here?"

"Well," I said. "Remember I'm assuming Mrs. Pruitt and the other Dames are more likely suspects than the other two teams."

"And your family aren't suspects at all."

"Mrs. Fenniman channels all her homicidal instincts into eXtreme croquet these days," I said. "I doubt if Rose Noire has any. Rob might, but he can't stand blood, so if he'd offed Lindsay, we'd have found him lying nearby in a dead faint."

"That makes sense," he said. "And yes, the Morris Mallet Men and the Realtors' team would have had a harder time getting over to the bog to kill Lindsay. Not impossible."

"More possible for the students than the Realtors," I said.

"Are you impugning the Realtors' fitness?" he asked. "All three look spry enough to scamper over to the other field and back."

"Not their fitness, but their knowledge of the terrain," I said. "Remember, we'd already played a game that morning. My team played the Realtors up here in the sheep pasture, and the Dames played the students down in the bog."

"So both the Dames and the students had all morning to study the lay of the land around the crime scene?"

"Precisely," I said.

"The Realtors are local, you know," Michael pointed out.

"Yes, but do you really think Mrs. Briggs or either of the clones have ever clocked much time slogging around in Mr. Shiffley's cow pasture? Then there's Mr. Briggs, who wasn't stuck here all day playing croquet. I like him as a suspect. More than I like Mrs. Pruitt, to tell the truth, though I admit I have ulterior motives in wanting to find him guilty. Ah, here it is. The starting stake. Now look around."

"Nice," Michael said.

He was looking at the house. Even the horrors of re-modeling did little to dim Michael's fondness for the house, and I tried to keep seeing it through his eyes.

"Nice view of the house, yes," I said. "And any-one at the house would have a nice view of the game—especially anyone scampering around on the roof, ripping off old shingles and smashing up rotten boards."

"I suspect the chief has interrogated the Shif-fleys," Michael said.

"Fat chance of getting him or them to tell us any-thing," I said. "So we'll puzzle things out for our-selves. Let's find the next wicket."

"Yes, we're pretty visible up here," Michael said, waving at someone below. "Not just from the roof but from most of the yard, too."

"Not heavily wooded like the bog. That's why we made Eric referee up here. Not as demanding as refere-eeing in the other field. Most of the time, we could all see one another. Occasionally, someone would disap-pear into a gully or over a hill, but most of the time, we could have shouted back and forth to keep the turns moving. The Shiffleys could see most of us pretty much of the time, and I bet they were looking. When we played up here in the morning, every time I glanced down, I'd see one of them gawking and point-ing. I doubt if the novelty wore off by afternoon. If they'd seen anyone do anything, Chief Burke would have arrested someone by now."

"So the people who were playing on this field are off the suspect list entirely?" Michael asked.

"Not entirely," I said. "But they go way down to the bottom of the list. And I'll check with Eric to see how the game went. If one or two of them finished particularly early and returned to the house alone, we move them back up the list again."

"Or if whoever came last was a lot slower than the rest," Michael said. "I can see someone hanging behind the rest and taking a detour to the other field."

"Good point," I said. "Then there are breaks. If they had to halt the game for a bathroom break, or to replace a broken mallet, or if anyone spent a long time hunting for a ball—"

"So they're still on the list," Michael said. "Good."

"Not that good. Too many suspects."

We trudged around the rest of the wickets in companionable silence, enjoying the peace and quiet. At least Michael was enjoying it. He kept pausing at each new vantage point to gaze down with pride at our house and land. Our new home.

For me, when I looked down at them from up in the sheep pasture, they looked strangely small and fragile. I kept seeing them dwarfed by the hulking shapes of a giant mall with a divided highway where the narrow country road now ran, hearing car horns and engines at close range instead of the baaing of sheep and the lowing of cows in the distance, smelling exhaust fumes and fast food instead of the wholesome country odors of grass and manure.

I was working up a mild case of anticipatory nostalgia over the manure when I saw a familiar sight: Dad leading a pair of sheep across the road toward the pasture. He was wearing a bandage over his forehead. Either the cut was larger than I'd remembered or Dad's sense of melodrama had gotten the better of his common sense. It looked less like a working bandage and more like the oversized headband Ralph Macchio wore in *The Karate Kid.*

"I see your father's found a few more of Mr. Early's lost lambs," Michael said.

"How that man makes a living at this, I'll never know."

"Be quite a shock to the sheep, I imagine, if we can't stop this mall project," Michael mused.

"They'd cope," I said. "Better than we would, I imagine. Foraging in the food court. Riding up and down the escalators. Standing outside the better clothing stores like living advertisements for natural fiber. Lambing time in the linen department. They'd love it."

Mr. Early had showed up and helped Dad propel the sheep through the gate and now the two were leaning on the fence, talking.

"Mr. Early has some information!" Dad announced as soon as we were within earshot.

Chapter Twenty-seven

" 'Information'?" I echoed. "About the murder?"

"He was watching the game Friday afternoon," Dad informed us.

"Keeping an eye on those juvenile delinquents, mostly," Mr. Early said.

"The college students," Dad said, nodding.

"Was there some particular reason you were watching them?" Michael asked.

"Been missing some sheep," Mr. Early said. "Since Friday. Really missing, not just kidnapped and barbered."

"I doubt if the students took them," I said. "For one thing, they're staying in our barn, and I think I'd have noticed if they'd smuggled in any sheep."

Though if Mr. Early chose to assume the denuding of his sheep had been a prank perpetrated by the college students, I wouldn't try to change his mind.

"You never know," Mr. Early said. "Besides, they could have been up to some mischief. Ran into Fred Shiffley at the feed store and he said they were chasing his cows that morning. So I kept an eye on them to make sure they didn't get up to anything with my sheep."

"Very prudent," Dad said.

I winced. I suspected it wasn't the students chasing the cows, but my brother and Spike. Just as well to let Mr. Shiffley blame the students for that, too.

And if Mr. Early had been watching the students suspiciously . . .

"Were you here the whole time?" I asked.

Mr. Early nodded.

"Were they up to anything?"

"No," Mr. Early said, frowning, as if reluctant to admit the students' innocence. "Not that I could see. Can't speak to what they did after they finished playing, though."

"What time was that?"

"I don't wear a watch," Mr. Early said, holding up a sinewy, watchless wrist to emphasize his point.

"Approximately," I said.

"No place for clock-watchers out here. I get off work when the work's done."

"Could you get a rough idea from the position of the sun?" Dad asked.

"About three o'clock, or half past," Mr. Early said. "Definitely before the postman showed up, which is usually around four."

Was it how Dad asked, or the fact that he was asking? I wondered if I should let him question Mr. Early.

"So you didn't notice anything suspicious," I said.

"I didn't spot those juvenile delinquents doing anything suspicious."

"Did someone else do anything suspicious?"

"Saw Evan Briggs wandering off in the middle of the game," he said. "He was standing right here, watching his wife's team; then he just up and wandered off."

"Wandered off where?"

"Back toward your house," he said. "Then he got in his car and drove away. Left just after the game started, and didn't get back till it was nearly over."

Aha! So Mr. Briggs had sneaked away from the game.

"Thank you," I said. "That's interesting. Could even be important."

"Glad to oblige," Mr. Early said. "So how's your cousin this morning?"

"I haven't seen her. I don't think she's up yet."

"Ah," he said. "I'm sure she's exhausted. I shouldn't have kept her up so late. Helping with the sheep and all."

Michael was overcome by coughing. I had to suppress my own laughter. Probably not the time to reveal that staying up all night and sleeping till noon was Rose Noire's normal routine.

"I'll tell her you asked about her," I said. "Or you could drop by later for the picnic."

"You've planned another picnic?" Dad asked.

"No, but that won't stop everyone from having one anyway. You'll see when things start up," I added to Mr. Early.

He nodded—was he blushing?—and strode away.

"Sammy and Horace will be furious," Michael said.

"Furious about what?" Dad asked.

"Long story," I said. "I'll fill you in later." Maybe by the time later rolled around, Dad would have forgotten and I wouldn't have to explain. I was getting tired of explaining Rose Noire. I'd already had to reassure Michael that since she and Horace were at best third cousins once removed, there was nothing unsuitable about his infatuation.

Back at the house, Dad went off to minister to his poison ivy patients and Michael decided to make a run to the county dump to clear out our accumulated trash.

I found myself staring up at the roof. Where the Shiffleys had been all day Friday. Was there something I could learn up there? Something worth climbing up forty feet in the air?

No way to know till I tried it. I took the stairs up to the third floor and, after staring up at the bare rafters overhead for many long minutes, finally forced myself to take the ladder up to the roof.

Strange, how what initially looked like a perfectly ordinary ladder turned out, once I started climbing, to be not only unusually tall but afflicted with dangerously wide gaps between the rungs. Trust the Shiffleys to bring a mutant ladder designed for giants. But as long as I refrained from looking down, I could keep moving steadily up, and when I reached the end of the ladder, I crawled out onto one of the flat horizontal sheets of plywood they'd nailed down to hold supplies. After a mere ten or fifteen minutes of scolding myself to stop being such a baby, that is.

At last, I stood on the platform. Okay, I was

hunched slightly, and clutching a rafter for dear life. But I was up there, on the very top of the roof. The view was spectacular. Almost made up for the way my stomach had stayed somewhere down by the foot of the ladder.

I was facing the front of the house, and Seth Early's sheep pasture lay spread before me like a stage set. I could see sheep grazing and lambs suckling, sleeping, or gamboling. Over to my left, Mr. Early was mending yet another break in his fence—presumably the source of the sheep Dad had just returned. To my right, under a grove of trees, Rob was leaning against a tree, holding one end of a leash, seemingly oblivious to the fact that at the other end Spike was straining for escape. I frowned. Walking Spike was what Rob usually did when he was troubled about something and wanted to think it over in solitude—Spike's function being to guarantee the solitude. What was bothering Rob?

I could worry about that later. For now, I studied the panorama. As I'd thought from the ground, hard for anyone to have left the sheep pasture croquet field without one or more Shiffleys seeing them.

For that matter, hard for anyone to have reached the cow pasture without their knowledge. I shuffled slightly so I could turn around and face the other way. The rolling acres of Mr. Shiffley's farm spread out before me. On my left, I could see all the way to the trees lining Caerphilly Creek. Straight ahead was the Shiffley farmhouse, looking tiny but distinct, even to the miniature thread of smoke rising from its matchstick-size chimney and the fleet of battered tractors and other farm machinery, which looked, at this distance, like props from a flea circus. To my right, the road wound toward town, and above the trees I could even see the top of the faux Gothic college bell tower. From up here, the whole vast, impassable woods we'd stumbled through Friday afternoon looked like a small island of trees in the middle of Mr. Shiffley's large, rolling expanse of boggy pastureland.

Very boggy land. I couldn't imagine Mr. Shiffley's pasture passing the perc test you'd have to do before installing a septic field. Did you have to do a similar test before you got permission for commercial buildings? I'd have pulled out my notebook that tells me when to breathe and jotted this down as an idea to pursue, but that would have meant letting go of the rafter.

Anyway, I reminded myself that I'd crawled up here to meddle in the murder investigation. Battling the outlet mall would have to wait—possibly till we saw which of the combatants on either side escaped a murder indictment. Which meant I could scuttle down again now. I'd proven to my own satisfaction that any time the Shiffleys were up here—which meant any time between their ungodly early start at 7:00 A.M. and whatever time the chief had called them all down from the roof to be interviewed—no one could easily enter or leave the woods without one or more Shiffleys seeing them.

Which made whatever the Shiffleys had seen a

fairly important piece of evidence. Unfortunately, the one thing I hadn't learned from my Shiffley's-eye view of the countryside was how to get the Shiffleys to talk to me.

"Looking for something?"

Chapter Twenty-eight

I managed not to shriek, but I started and clutched the rafters more tightly with both hands. Randall Shiffley had appeared beside me.

"Checking out the view," I said. "Glorious view."

Randall flicked a dubious glance down at my white knuckles.

"Well, it would be glorious if I had a solid floor beneath my feet. And walls or a railing around me. I was wondering if there's still time to change the renovation plans. Build a cupola up here. Or a widow's walk."

"Plenty of time," Randall said, leaning back against a rafter and crossing his arms. "Cost money, though."

A familiar answer.

"True," I said. "Maybe Michael and I should wait to decide on any changes to the plan till we find out what's happening there."

I pried one hand off the rafters to gesture, with as casual an air as I could muster, toward Fred Shiffley's farm. Then I placed my hand back on the rafter, rather than grabbing it. At least I think I did.

"What's happening?" Randall repeated.

"Well, right now it's a spectacular view, but who'd want a widow's walk with a spectacular view of an outlet mall? For that matter, maybe we should put a hold on all the renovations until we see what happens next door."

Randall frowned but didn't say anything.

"You think the Planning Board will approve it?" I asked after a few moments.

"No telling, with that Briggs fellow involved," he said.

That Briggs fellow. He made no effort to hide the loathing in his voice.

"You don't like him?"

Randall shrugged slightly.

"I should think he'd be pretty popular in your branch of the family."

Randall looked at me as if I'd said something spectacularly stupid.

"Won't the outlet mall make your uncle Fred pretty rich?"

"Damn fool notion," Randall said. "We all understand that the farm has to go someday—times change. But not like that."

Interesting—dissention in the normally uniform ranks of the Shiffleys?

"I suppose you've tried reasoning with him?"

"Some of us have," Randall said. "All his brothers have been yelling their damned heads off at him ever since they found out. Couple of 'em took a swing at him once or twice. Hasn't worked."

Yelling and throwing punches. Not exactly what I'd call reasoning, but given my relatives' quirks, who was I to question the Shiffley family's interpersonal dynamics?

"He's pretty strong-minded," I said instead.

"Stubborn as a mule, you mean. Worse than most of us. I could have told the old goats that. All they've accomplished is getting him so riled up, he's threatening to leave his money outside the family."

"To whom?" I asked. Not that Fred Shiffley changing his will had any obvious relevance to Lindsay's murder, but you never knew.

"Farm Aid and the ASPCA," Randall said.

"Good causes."

"Yeah, but it's not like he doesn't have family could use the money," Randall said. "Stubborn old goat. If they'll just leave him alone till he cools down . . ."

He shrugged his shoulders, as if he wasn't making any bets about his father's and uncles' ability to let well enough alone.

"So Evan Briggs isn't exactly a hero to the Shiffley family right now," I mused aloud.

"If he was the one who bought it Friday, I'd worry about what my dad and his brothers were up to," Randall said. "None of us had anything against that Tyler woman, though."

"If Evan Briggs turns out to be the killer, none of you will mind much, I imagine."

"Hard to see how it could be him," Randall said. His tone sounded casual, but I detected a faint note of eager curiosity, as if he'd love to know what dirt I had on Evan Briggs but would rather chew off an arm than ask.

"He was seen leaving here shortly after the afternoon croquet games began," I said. "Drove off somewhere. What if he parked somewhere nearby, hoofed it over to your uncle Fred's pasture, and killed Ms. Tyler?"

Randall shook his head.

"Don't think so," he said. "I happen to know where he went."

"Where?"

He frowned slightly and studied a knothole in a nearby board with intense interest.

"Well, if it's a guilty family secret," I said.

He snorted slightly.

"There's some of us think Briggs is trying to pull a fast one, so we keep an eye on the bastard. When his car pulled out, Vern said, 'I bet he's going over to see Uncle Fred.' So we watched where he was going and, sure enough, when he got down the road a piece, he turned into Fred's lane."

He jerked his head in the direction of the tiny, distant farmhouse. Yes, if you knew where the road was, and happened to want to keep an eye on Evan Briggs, you could track him pretty well from up here.

"He stayed there the whole time?"

Randall nodded.

"Damn long time," he said, leaning to spit over the side of the roof, as if the idea of spending prolonged time in Evan Briggs's company left a bad taste in his mouth. "Some of us were for going over there and seeing what was up, but about the time Vern and I were getting ready to do it, we saw Briggs's car head back."

"No chance he could have come back and walked down to the murder scene in time to be the killer?" I asked.

"No," Randall said. "It was just about then your dad came up to give us the news that someone had been killed. He didn't tell us who, though, and I remember Duane saying, kind of hopeful like, that maybe Briggs had finally killed himself, driving around with one hand on his cell phone and the other on his Palm Pilot. Couple minutes later, Briggs drove up."

"Thus cruelly dashing your hopes," I said. "Damn."

Not to mention my own hopes. Frustrating that my efforts to track Briggs's whereabouts on the day of the murder had succeeded not in implicating him but in giving him a reasonably good alibi.

Randall nodded as if he understood.

"So if Briggs didn't do it, who did?" I said, just to see what he'd say.

Randall frowned.

"I couldn't say," he said. "If I were Chief Burke, I'd take a lot closer look at people who think they can get away with anything in this town."

He turned and began to climb down the ladder.

"By the way," I said.

He stopped and looked back up at me.

"The name Toad Bottom mean anything to you?"

"Toad Bottom? Why? Where'd you hear that name?"

I pondered the expression on his face. Not guilt or anxiety. More like keen interest, with a hint of amusement.

"I heard someone call Caerphilly that," I said. "Wondered why."

"It's someone who knows his history, then," Randall said. "That's what the town used to be called. Before the Pruitts waltzed in and took over. Wasn't fancy enough for them, so they got the town council to change the name."

"Many people know about it?"

"Not unless they've been digging pretty far back in the town history," Randall said.

Or talking to the Shiffleys. Which I was beginning to think might not be all that different. Was there a way to tap the Shiffleys' historical knowledge without letting them know I was doing it to fight the mall project? I'd have to work on that. Maybe sic Joss on them.

"Thanks," I said.

Randall nodded and climbed down. I followed, much more slowly, though. Randall was nice enough to steady the ladder for me. Although midway down, I suddenly felt a twinge of anxiety. If Randall was the murderer, what a perfect way to get rid of someone who was inconveniently nosy.

Nonsense, I told myself. He wouldn't try to commit a murder here in plain sight of everyone down in the yard, would he?

Not if he were sensible. Still, I breathed a lot more easily when my feet were back on a solid floor.

"You sure you want that widow's walk?" Randall asked. "You really don't seem to like heights."

"A weakness I'm trying to overcome," I said before scurrying toward the stairs. I wanted to feel solid ground again.

Of course, the first person I saw when I got outside was Evan Briggs. If Chief Burke was making an arrest, presumably it wasn't him, damn it.

Still something fishy going on, I thought, remembering how he'd lost his temper while talking to Mother and me the night before. So I decided to rescue him—he was talking to Rose Noire.

Chapter Twenty-nine

I strolled over and feigned pleasant surprise when I spotted them.

"Oh, there you are," I said to Rose Noire. "Could you go help Mother with something?"

"Right away," she said. "We'll talk again later," she said to Mr. Briggs as she scurried off.

Mother hadn't asked for Rose Noire's help, but she was never short of little tasks for representatives of my generation to perform when they fell into her clutches.

Mr. Briggs's smile looked strained. He didn't seem all that happy at being rescued from Rose Noire.

"You wanted to talk to me about something?" he asked a little brusquely. Obviously, our earlier conversation hadn't endeared me to him.

"I thought perhaps you needed a break," I said. "Rose Noire can be overwhelming if you're not used to her."

"Overwhelming," he said. "Yes, that's one word for it. She told me she was a druid in a past life."

"A druid?" I repeated "Are you sure?"

"Reasonably so."

"That's a relief, then," I said. "When she told me, I thought sure she'd said a dryad."

"Dryad?" Briggs repeated.

"You know, a tree spirit," I said. "I have to admit, that's slightly weird. A druid's a lot more . . . normal, don't you think?"

"I think that would depend on one's definition of normal."

"Your definition of normal probably includes a lot more concrete and steel than anything to do with trees anyway," I said.

He made a noncommittal noise, as if he wasn't sure he liked the direction our conversation was taking.

"Or historical battle sites, for that matter."

I could see his jaw clench. Bracing himself for another tirade from another tree-hugger, no doubt.

I decided tackling him head-on was as good as any tactic.

"Look, I'm not trying to blackmail you, but I know Lindsay Tyler was," I said. "So what was she offering, anyway? Her expertise to discredit the historical significance of the Battle of Pruitt's Ridge?"

His mouth fell open again.

"What makes you think—" he began. Then he changed gears. "I have no idea what you're talking about. Ms. Tyler had nothing to do with this project; we'd never even met."

"Only talked on the phone, then?" I said. "I saw her cell-phone records, you know."

I would have had no way of recognizing Evan

Briggs's phone number—I'd barely recognized my own on Chief Burke's printout—but he didn't have to know that.

Briggs glared at me. I smiled back as sweetly as I could but said nothing. It worked for Chief Burke. He just sat there staring at people and they started talking. Eventually, it worked on Briggs.

"Do you really want to tarnish Ms. Tyler's memory with the details of her bizarre—and, need I say, unsuccessful—attempt to extract money from me in return for her help in discrediting Mrs. Pruitt's account of the Battle of Pruitt's Ridge?" he said. "She'd look like a common blackmailer."

"I don't really give a damn about her memory," I said. "Neither do you. But I assume that even if we have quite different ideas about what to do with that land over there, we both want to see her killer brought to justice, even if only because it will clear those of us who aren't guilty."

"I fail to see what her blackmail attempt has to do with the murder," he said. "I told her I didn't give a damn what information she thought she had. Didn't matter to me. I haven't done anything illegal and I'm not planning to."

"It never occurred to you that she might have tried blackmail again with someone else? Someone who didn't take it as lightly?"

"Oh, I see," he said. Some of the hostility left his face. "Of course, since I don't know what information she wanted to sell, I have no idea who else might be a potential customer."

"Not even a guess?"

"She didn't tell me much, you know," he said. "That's the problem with selling information—you let the customer test-drive the merchandise, you blow the sale."

"No guesses?" I asked. "She didn't even drop a hint?"

He thought about it briefly.

"A couple of times she referred to the so-called Battle of Pruitt's Ridge," he said. "As if it didn't really deserve to be called a battle."

"Only a small skirmish, you mean?"

"Yeah, or maybe it was just a drunken brawl they pretended was a battle so they wouldn't look like fools. Maybe histories got the sequence mixed up, and the raid on the Shiffley distillery was what kicked everything off. Who knows?"

Or maybe she had proof that the Pruitts made the whole thing up. Not that I'd mention that to Briggs just yet. Interesting that he knew more about the battle than most of the people in town.

He had pursed his lips and was looking at me as if making a decision. Then he shook his head and spoke again.

"Even if it happened just the way the history books said, who cares?" he said. "Outside of Henrietta Pruitt and a few other stuck-up bi—biddies at the Caerphilly Historical Society. So something happened here once upon a time—people still need places to live and work. Life moves on."

"So you didn't need Lindsay's information," I said. "Who did?"

"No one."

"Come on, even I can think of someone else," I said. "If she had something that made the Pruitts look stupid, you think she wouldn't blackmail Mrs. Pruitt with it?

"Yes," he said with considerable heat. "And Lady Pruitt would definitely do anything to keep her damned family escutcheon unblotted."

"Who else?" I asked.

He shook his head.

"She's the main problem," he said. "If it weren't for her, the rest of them would lose steam pretty quickly."

I hoped he was underestimating the depth of the local opposition to the outlet mall, but I decided not to say so. He must have guessed my reaction from my face.

"Oh, they'd still be against the mall, but they'd be fighting it on sensible grounds, instead of this whole historical landmark baloney. Besides—"

Just then, we heard a shriek from near the buffet table. We both glanced up.

"Oh, damn," Briggs exclaimed. All the color drained from his face and he ran toward the buffet.

Odd, I thought as I loped along behind him. It was Lacie Butler shrieking. Why would Briggs care—

But it wasn't Lacie Butler Mr. Briggs was running toward. Mrs. Briggs had fallen to the ground and was having convulsions.

Chapter Thirty

"She's poisoned!" Lacie shrieked.

"Nonsense," Dad said. "It looks like an ordinary epileptic seizure. Briggs, has she ever had one before?"

"Yes, but we thought the medication was working. Until—Shouldn't we take her to the hospital?"

"Right now, let's just make sure she doesn't injure herself," Dad said. "Michael, could you get a pillow?"

"Right," Michael said, and ran for the barn.

"If you'd all give us some room—she needs air," Dad said, glancing up at the rest of the crowd. "Air and a little quiet."

He was frowning at Lacie, who stood with her eyes wide and her hands pressed over her mouth, making noises ranging from loud whimpers to the occasional shriek—not something likely to hasten Mrs. Briggs's recovery. It was starting to get to me.

"Lacie," I said. "Lacie!"

She didn't react. I considered administering a brisk slap to the face—a bad idea, since my iron-

work makes me stronger than most women. Before I
had the chance, Mother grabbed Lacie's arm.

"Lacie, dear," she said in an icy tone that had the
same effect my slap would have. "Let's get out of
the way and let Dr. Langslow deal with this, shall
we? Rob, help her, will you?"

Mother and Rob literally dragged Lacie to the
other side of the yard, her feet leaving small ruts in
the ground as they went.

Everyone else took Dad's hint—even Eric, who
ran to Dad's car to fetch his medical bag. Michael
delivered the pillow. Dad extracted the name of Mrs.
Briggs's doctor from her husband, and I found his
number, gave his weekend emergency service a
message, and left Dad's cell-phone number. Then I
rejoined the rest of the guests.

"Will she be all right?" one of the Suzies asked.

"Dad's taking care of her. I'm sure she'll be fine,"
I told her.

"He was afraid this would happen," the other
Suzy said.

"Yes," the first Suzy chimed in. "That's why he
had us keep an eye on her during the game."

"Had you keep an eye on her?"

"Not during the morning game," she said. "He
stayed for that—she can't drive, you know, so someone has to take her anywhere she wants to go. Since
her seizures started up again, he mostly takes her
himself. But he had an appointment in the
afternoon—he had to leave before lunch ended. He
made us promise never to let her out of our sight."

"And we didn't," the second said.

"Didn't help our game much," the first added. "Not that we had much of a chance of winning to begin with."

"Helping May was more important," Suzy two said with a firm nod.

"Do you know where he went?"

The Suzies shook their heads.

"It must have been important if he left May to do it," one of them said.

Important to him. I glanced across the yard again. An honor guard of Shiffleys was carrying Mrs. Briggs toward the driveway, with Mr. Briggs hovering anxiously over her and Dad scrambling along behind, his oversized headband/bandage askew. If the ER got much more business from our parties, they'd send the county health department over to shut us down as a public menace.

"We should go down and see if they need anything," one of the Suzies said.

The other one nodded.

"We'll see you later," the first one said. I watched as the two of them meticulously deposited their trash and recyclables in the appropriate containers before bustling off on their errand of mercy.

"You look glum," Michael said as he joined me. "What's wrong?"

"Oh, I just like it better when people stay in their pigeonholes. Mr. Briggs was a lot easier to hate when he was merely a despoiler of the countryside and not also the caring husband of a sick wife. And the clones. They're reasonably nice people. I should make an effort to learn their names or something.

Even though we're destined to end up squared off on opposite sides of the mall battle."

"Life's messy," Michael said. "Come have some brunch. The Shiffleys are pretty good cooks."

Everyone was subdued after the Briggses' sudden departure. Except for Dad, who was busy reassuring everyone that Mrs. Briggs would be fine—I deduced as much from the fact that he hadn't gone to the hospital with her—and relating anecdotes about epilepsy and other seizure disorders, which was bound to give us a lively afternoon if any of my more impressionable hypochondriac relatives were listening.

When the inevitable stray sheep showed up, we found that Spike had learned something from Dad's sheep-herding lessons after all. Not something we wanted him learning, unfortunately. He'd figured out that if you sneaked up behind the sheep and nipped their heels just right, they'd leap into the air in a fair imitation of Morris dancers before kicking at him. Unfortunately, he'd also discovered that people, currently more plentiful than sheep, reacted just as amusingly and didn't kick with such gusto. I exiled him to his pen and left a message on the answering machine of yet another dog trainer who'd been recommended to us.

Even more unsettling, Mother was up to something. She'd been sitting for an hour, talking to Lacie. If anyone came near, she lowered her voice and gestured imperiously for privacy. The one scrap of conversation I overheard wasn't encouraging.

"Your loyalty is admirable, Lacie dear, but you have yourself to consider. . . ."

That was all I'd caught, but it was enough. Mother was trying to drive a wedge between Mrs. Pruitt and her minions. Foment rebellion in the lower ranks of the Caerphilly Historical Society. I was slightly relieved when, after getting a call on her cell phone, Lacie scurried out to her car and drove off, but the damage was probably already done.

I was so busy worrying about what Mother was up to that I was caught off guard by a shift in the direction of Dad's attention.

Chapter Thirty-one

"Meg," Dad said, "what are we going to do about the Shiffleys?"

"Why? What do we need to do about them?" I asked, sitting down beside him at one of the picnic tables. "Are they causing a problem?"

"No," Dad said. "But they're here."

Which counted as a problem in my book, though I didn't want to say it. Not where any of the Shiffleys might hear me, and that could be almost anywhere. Most of them were still harmlessly occupied with their grills, fixing bacon, eggs, and grits for all comers, but earlier I'd had to break up an argument between two of them over some aspect of the suspended roof repairs. I wouldn't have bothered, no matter how loud they got or how wildly they gesticulated, if they hadn't chosen to stage their argument three stories over my head, on the framework of two-by-fours that would eventually support the new roof. Fortunately, they'd kept their balance better than their tempers.

"They don't have to be here," I said aloud. "I

suppose Chief Burke told them not to leave town, or something of the sort, but I'm sure he didn't mean that they had to stay here camped in our backyard. Not that they're not welcome to camp here if they want to," I added, for the benefit of any lurking Shiffleys. "But they don't have to be, so I don't see why we need to entertain them or anything like that."

"I wasn't talking about entertaining them," Dad said. "But even though they can't work on the house until the chief okays it, we must have plenty of things we could have them do."

And pay them for doing, of course.

"Such as?" I asked.

"Well . . . for example, what about the pond? We could ask them to find a way to make it hold water. I know you don't want to have to go up and fill it every day the way I've been doing and— Oh my God! Duck!"

I admit, I started slightly when he shouted that, and I was pleased to see that Tony and Graham hit the ground and scrambled under the picnic table as efficiently as if they'd drilled for weeks. Unnecessary, but if they planned to keep playing eXtreme croquet—or, for that matter, hang around my family for the rest of the day—it was nice to see they'd paid attention and picked up a few useful survival skills.

"At ease," I said to them. "What about Duck, Dad?"

"Where are my shoes?" he said. He scurried around, looking for them in a variety of improbable places. "I need to get up to the pond right away. With all the excitement yesterday, I forgot to fill it.

The water was low yesterday morning; it'll be nothing but mud by now. Poor Duck."

"She'll be fine," I said, handing him the shoes, which had been hidden in plain sight on one of the picnic benches. "Ducks do like swimming, but it's hardly a life-or-death issue if they can't. She can cope."

"It'll make her crankier, though," Rob said. "She's already pretty hard to live with."

"Hard to live with," Tony said. "Try vicious."

"That's only temporary," Dad said, looking up from his effort to untangle a knot in one of his shoelaces. "Because she's gone broody."

"Ah," Graham said, but Tony looked puzzled.

"It just means she's laying eggs," I explained. "Duck lays eggs all the time, so in her case, it means she's sitting on the eggs, instead of just laying them and leaving them around everywhere for people to step on.

"And she gets cranky and takes it out on anyone who comes near her nest," Rob added.

"Can you blame her?" Rose Noire said. "She's only expressing her maternal instinct and protecting her eggs from harm."

"I guess you'll have baby ducks pretty soon, then," Graham said.

"Not unless Duck has found a drake while none of us was looking," Rob said.

"So what do you do with the eggs, then?" Tony asked.

"Eat them, I should think," Graham said.

"I'm a vegetarian," Rose Noire announced. "I don't eat any eggs."

"No one in the family has the heart to eat Duck's eggs," I said. "We usually put them in the refrigerator and argue for a while about whether someone should cook them or not. Eventually, when we're pretty sure they've gone bad, someone finally gets up the nerve to throw them out."

"Would anyone get upset if someone did eat one of the eggs?" Graham asked.

"Why—would you like one?"

"No, but I think that's part of what the Shiffleys are scrambling out there on the grill."

"They're scrambling Duck's eggs?" Dad asked, looking up. "Oh dear."

"Calm down," I said. "We've said for years that someone should."

"Yes, but those weren't very fresh," Dad said. "I'm not sure they're safe to eat."

"The Shiffleys have noses, Dad. If they don't use them, it's not our fault. It's not as if we set out to poison them."

" 'Poison them'?" Graham echoed. "What would happen if you ate them?"

"That would depend on the poison," Dad said. "For example, salmonella—"

"Don't coach him, Dad. You remember what happened when you gave that talk about the bubonic plague at the last family reunion. Besides, we need to see about the pond."

I hustled Dad out of the barn before his enthusiastic and graphic descriptions of salmonella poisoning could affect the obviously impressionable minds of the two Morris Mallet Men. The minute he got outside, he dashed off at top speed toward the pond. I followed, but I didn't catch up with him until we were nearly at the pond, where the slope of the land grew steeper and slowed him down even more than me.

"Dad—about the pond," I said between pants. "I know you were trying to do the best for Duck and Eric, but I'm not sure we need quite such a large pond."

"Gives you room for expansion," he said.

"Yes, but I'm not sure we have any plans to expand our duck population." I dropped into a walk, since were almost at the top of the slope. "Besides, I'm not sure the Shiffleys are experts in pond making. I mean, they did this one, right? Which doesn't hold water. I was thinking we could ask the nearby farmers who did their ponds, then get some bids from seasoned pond makers. Determine how large a pond we can afford. Approach the whole pond project logically."

"Oh dear," Dad said. He was gazing out over the pond, no doubt digging in his heels to argue.

"I don't mean to sound negative," I said. "But if we have the Shiffleys do anything with the pond, I really think we should just have them fill in this one, and then we can start all over later."

"No, we can't fill this one in just yet," Dad said.

"Why not?" I asked.

Instead of answering, he pointed toward the pond, which had shrunk to a puddle about the size of a bathtub, surrounded by a sea of mud.

A few feet away from the puddle, the handle of a croquet mallet was sticking up out of the mud.

Chapter Thirty-two

"Don't touch it!" I called out to Dad, who was squelching through the mud toward the mallet. "I'm calling Chief Burke."

"I won't touch it," he said, stopping about two yards from it. "I'm just going to look at it."

"I think the chief would be happier if we looked at it from over here, instead of messing up the mud around it with footprints."

Dad didn't answer, but he stopped six feet away from the mallet.

"Obviously, it wasn't stuck here," he said. "Someone threw it in the pond while it was full."

"How can you be so sure?"

"Because mine are the only footprints in the mud," he said. True. The only human footprints anyway—oddly enough, I saw countless hoofprints around the outer edge of the mud circle, the parts that had probably been exposed since the day before. Sheep prints, by the size of them. Maybe our yard was only a side attraction en route to the irresistible lure of the duck pond.

"Besides, look at this," Dad called.

I paused in the middle of dialing, sighed, and squelched over to his side. The head of the mallet was embedded in the mud, and nearby was half a cinder block. Someone had stripped a vine of its leaves, tied one end to the mallet and threaded the other end through the cinder block.

"To make sure it sank, of course," Dad said, nodding. "What's that buried in the mud behind the cinder block?"

Dad leaned as far as he could to the left, and I did the same thing to the right—to avoid making any more footprints than we already had. Then I finally gave up and took a few steps. Chief Burke would be furious anyway.

"A woman's purse," I said, leaning forward as far as I could. "With things spilling out of it." I could see a wallet, and a folded newspaper.

"Here," Dad said, handing me his pocket birdwatching binoculars. I raised them to my eyes, adjusted the focus dial—

And saw Mrs. Pruitt. Not the real thing, but her picture staring out from the newspaper. I could see her face, and a frill of black lace along her cheek.

I remembered the lace—part of an ornate bonnet, festooned not only with the lace but also with ribbon, feathers, and jet beads: Mrs. Pruitt's overelaborate interpretation of what a well-dressed lady of the Confederacy would wear.

"It's a copy of the *Caerphilly Clarion*," I said. "The one from a few weeks ago with the article on what the historical society was doing for this year's Caerphilly Heritage Days."

"So if this is Lindsay Tyler's purse . . ." Dad began. "Which we'll know once we examine the wallet—"

"We won't be examining anything," I said, pulling out my phone again. "I'm calling the chief."

"I meant 'we' in a more general sense," Dad said.

"Yeah, right," I said. "Chief Burke? I think we've found something you'll want to see."

Yes, the chief wanted to see it, and he wanted to see it undisturbed. If we had found a body, I'm not sure anything in the world could have kept Dad from examining it, citing his medical skills as justification. Fortunately, I had greater expertise about croquet mallets and women's handbags. Not all that much greater, but enough to keep Dad entertained while the police rushed to the scene.

The mallet didn't keep him interested for long. I could see enough of its head to confirm that it was an ordinary mallet, rather than one of the special eXtreme croquet mallets that had a distinctive wedged face, used for lofting your ball out of bogs and sand traps. Dad, after close study, announced that the killer had used a cow hitch to attach the vine to the mallet and a mere granny knot to tie it to the purse strap.

"Fascinating," I said. "I'm sure those details will break the case for Chief Burke."

"It wasn't even tied to the cinder block," he said, shaking his head with disappointment at the killer's shoddy workmanship. "Just threaded it through the hole in the block."

"Considering how hard it would be to tie any kind of knot with a vine, I think the killer did pretty well," I said.

The purse proved more useful as a delaying tactic. I subjected it to close inspection through the binoculars, then doled out my findings one tidbit at time. By the time we finally heard sirens approaching, I was running out of tidbits.

"Either a Gucci or a Fendi," I said. "Or maybe a Coach." Not that I knew what any of those brands looked like. I hadn't shopped for purses in over a decade. Whenever my purse started wearing out, I'd hunt down the leather worker who made it—we attended the same craft shows—and have him make another one just like it. But since Dad had no idea what the various brands looked like, either, he nodded solemnly at the information.

One detail I did notice, though—about the newspaper, not the purse. I could see a mailing label stuck to the upper right-hand side. A slightly mud-specked label, but I could still read Lindsay's name. Her name, and a Pineville, West Virginia, P.O. box.

"She subscribed to the *Clarion*," I said.

"Is that significant?"

"Probably," I said. "It proves that she didn't just come back from time to time; she was actively keeping tabs on the town."

"Or someone in it," Dad said.

I nodded and handed the binoculars to Dad so he

could take a turn. The sirens were getting closer. Just for the heck of it, I pulled out my cell phone and took a few photos of our find. Still life with cinder block, croquet mallet, and designer handbag. Dad beamed his approval, so I leaned over, held the phone as close to the tableau as possible, and snapped a few more. Then the sirens stopped, and I stuck the phone back in my pocket. Dad was peering intently through the binoculars and I was looking nonchalant as Chief Burke, still puffing from the hill, joined us.

"We didn't touch anything," Dad said, beaming at the chief as if our self-restraint was something remarkable. Actually, for Dad, it was.

"I can see that," the chief said. "Why don't you wait for me down at the house?"

"Don't you want us to tell you how we found it?" Dad asked.

"Down at the house."

"Come on, Dad," I said, tugging gently at his arm.

Dad looked so despondent that even Chief Burke must have felt sorry for him.

"Unless there's something important you need to show me that can't wait," he said.

Dad's face fell slightly. Obviously, he couldn't think of anything urgent.

Maybe I could.

"There is one thing," I said.

They both looked at me.

"I realize that this is evidence, and Horace or whoever processes it will use gloves and all."

"Naturally," the chief said. He glanced at his watch, as if wondering what was taking Horace or whoever so long.

"You might want to take extra care with the vine," I said.

"The vine," the chief repeated.

"Look at it," I said, handing him Dad's little binoculars. He frowned at them; then, making it obvious that he was humoring me for now but wouldn't much longer, he lifted them to his eyes and focused on the tableau before us.

"Very nice," he said. "I can even read the fine print on the newspaper. Must be useful for birding."

He took the binoculars away from his eyes and held them out to me.

"Never mind the newspaper," I said. "Look at the vine."

The chief wielded the binoculars again. Dad didn't move his feet, but he leaned over so far that I had to grab him to keep him from falling facedown in the mud.

"Oh my God!" Dad exclaimed. "You're right! Good catch!"

"Right about what?" the chief growled.

"It's a poison ivy vine," I said.

"How can you tell without the leaves?" the chief asked.

"Those hairy little roots all up and down the vine are a dead giveaway," I told him. "The vines are just as virulent as the leaves."

"More so," Dad said, nodding. "You realize what this means."

"You don't need to worry," the chief said. "It's evidence; we'll handle it with gloves."

"The urushiol could have spread to the purse, or the cinder block," Dad said. "For that matter, be careful with the water it's soaking in."

"And the outside of any gloves you use to touch the stuff, or any boots you use to wade in and retrieve it," I added. "You're missing the more important part—what this tells us about the killer."

"The killer will have a rash on his or her hands," the chief said, nodding. "Got it. Here's Horace. Why don't you wait for me down at the house? Don't tell anyone about the poison ivy. We'll hold that back."

"But—" Dad began.

"Down at the house," the chief repeated.

"Come on, Dad," I said. "We can tell the chief more about it later. I assume I should tell Mrs. Fenniman that the croquet tournament is off again."

"It was never on again in the first place," the chief said. "I told her *maybe* you could start up again, *if* I was sure we'd finished with the crime scene."

"No argument from me," I said.

"But this means—" Dad began.

"Come on, Dad."

I grabbed Dad's arm and steered him back down the hill. He managed to keep silent until we were halfway down; then he couldn't hold it any longer.

"He's not getting it!" he exclaimed. "The killer might have a rash on his hands. But the skin on the palm of the hands and the soles of the feet isn't that sensitive. He might not react there."

"True," I said. "But the killer wasn't just touching the poison ivy; he—or she—was tying knots. I think you'd end up rubbing it all over the back of your hands if you were tying knots."

"Would you?" Dad asked.

"I'm pretty sure you would," I said. "Let's try it with some twine."

We adjourned to my office in the barn, where I pulled out the ball of twine I kept with the wrapping and mailing supplies. When Michael walked in a few minutes later, we were still sitting around tying knots and bickering.

Chapter Thirty-three

"Yes," I was saying. "So it's theoretically possible to tie a knot without touching any of the more sensitive parts of the hand, but it requires a real conscious effort. Not something a normal person would do if he doesn't know he's holding a poison ivy vine."

"I must have missed something," Michael said. "I was coming to share the glad tidings that Chief Burke has found the murder weapon and you'll all get your blunt instruments back tomorrow, and I find you plotting some kind of masochistic macramé with poison ivy vines."

"The chief didn't mention poison ivy?" I asked.

"Oh, dear, does he have it, too?"

"No, but the killer might." I explained about the vine. Yes, the chief had said not to tell anyone, but Michael wasn't a suspect, and he'd overheard half the story anyway.

"So it's possible the killer will have a poison ivy rash," Michael said as he watched Dad's demonstration of how to tie a cow hitch using only the less susceptible tips of the fingers. "Seeing how often most people wash their hands, though, isn't that one of the least likely places to get it, even if you're exposed? I mean, washing soon enough after exposure prevents inflammation, right?"

"True," Dad said. "So the killer might not have poison ivy at all."

His shoulders slumped.

"Or the killer might have poison ivy someplace he touched before washing his hands," I said.

"The students," Dad murmured. "Two of them have it all over their shins. If they touched their shins before washing their hands—"

"While putting on their damned Morris bells, for example?" I suggested.

"Last time I looked, almost everyone who played in the cow pasture had poison ivy," Michael pointed out. "The clones and Mrs. Briggs don't, but they only played in the sheep pasture. Mrs. Wentworth has a touch on one ankle, and Lacie got it on her face—probably tripped and fell in a patch."

"Meg and Rob don't have any," Dad pointed out.

"Only because you've trained us all our lives to recognize the stuff," I said.

"What if the killer's someone like me, who doesn't react to it?" Michael said. "And yes, I know that immunity to poison ivy can wear off at any time, and I don't tempt fate by picking bouquets of the stuff. But even if I recognized the vine, I'd take the chance if I had to hide the murder weapon in a hurry, needed something to tie the cinder block on with, and knew I'd never reacted before."

"Bill," I said. "The quiet one. He said poison ivy

didn't bother him. And I haven't noticed Mrs. Pruitt complaining."

"She was wearing gloves," Dad said.

"That's right," I said. "All the Dames were. Didn't protect the rest of their bodies, though."

"So the killer is someone with a poison ivy rash, someone immune to poison ivy, someone who was wearing gloves, or someone with excellent personal hygiene," Michael said. "I must say, that narrows the field nicely."

"And it seemed so promising," Dad said.

He shook his head and strolled out of the barn, looking so downcast that I'd have been upset if I hadn't known that he'd find something to be excited about in another five or ten minutes.

"So the poison ivy isn't an important clue after all," I said. "Maybe something else is."

"What?"

"I'll show you," I said, and led the way to the corner of the barn where we stacked the recyclables.

It was empty.

"Damn."

"What's wrong?" Michael asked.

"Didn't we have a whole stack of newspapers out here?"

"Yes, the ones I was supposed to take to the recycling center last weekend," Michael said. "I know. I'm sorry. It's just that taking your father and your nephew around to those farm stores Saturday—"

"Where are they?"

"Don't worry," he said. "I'm getting on top of this decluttering thing. They're gone."

"Gone? Damn."

"Why damn?"

"I needed something from one of them."

"Ah," he said. "If that's the case, they're not really as gone as all that. Not beyond recovery, that is. In fact—"

"You still have them? Where?"

"Trunk of my car."

"Show me."

The trunk of his car and the passenger seat. Naturally, the issue of the *Caerphilly Clarion* I wanted was nearly at the bottom of the stack.

"That's it," I said when I spotted the picture of Mrs. Pruitt and Mrs. Wentworth in their costumes. "The very issue."

I sat down on the ground to thumb through it while Michael packed the newspapers again—this time into the truck, which made more sense anyway.

"Did you find what you were looking for?" he asked, after a minute or two.

"I have no idea," I said. "I don't know what I'm looking for, so it's difficult to tell when I've found it."

"If you don't know what you're looking for, then why this particular issue?"

"Lindsay had a copy in her purse," I explained. "She must have brought it along for a reason. I'm just hoping I'll recognize whatever it is when I see it."

"And?"

"Let's go into town and get a pizza," I said.

"I think that's a non sequitur."

"No, it's not," I said. "I just flipped past an ad for

Luigi's and realized that I'm starving. Let's go get a pizza."

"There's enough food for an army here," he said. "With all these guests, shouldn't we stick around?"

"Play host and hostess? Tell me you're kidding."

"I was thinking more of making sure none of them burns the place down," he said.

"True," I agreed. "But I'm tired of picnicking with relatives and suspects."

"I'll fetch some food and we can eat in the barn," he said. "If anyone tries to join us, I'll chase them out. I don't know about Spike, but I was paying attention during your father's sheep-herding lessons."

"You're on. No eggs, though, okay?"

"Your wish is my command," Michael said, making a deep bow.

"While you're getting the food, I'm going to go through this paper," I said, waving it triumphantly as I retreated to our bedroom stall. "I have the feeling that the critical clue we need is somewhere within these pages."

Chapter Thirty-four

"Breakfast," Michael announced, entering the stall with a plate in each hand. "What's wrong?"

I sighed.

"So maybe the critical clue isn't as obvious as I thought it would be," I said.

I stared balefully at the rumpled sheaf of newsprint.

"No clues at all?" he asked, setting a plate beside me.

"Plenty of them. Entirely too many clues."

"Run them down for me," he said, sitting down and digging into his own plate.

"Okay. Front page—Mrs. Pruitt and Mrs. Wentworth in costume, with a long article about the historical society's plans for this year's Caerphilly Heritage Days, which we know caught Lindsay's eye."

"Because it was on the cover," he said, nodding.

"Because she marked it," I said. "See?"

I pulled out my cell phone and called up the photos I'd taken of the purse. You could just barely see it, but someone—presumably Lindsay—had scribbled several exclamation points in the margin beside the photo of Mrs. Pruitt.

"Besides, listen to this. 'The society is also exploring the possibility of staging a reenactment of the Battle of Pruitt's Ridge at the town's sesquitricentennial in 2008, according to Mrs. Wentworth.' "

"So maybe if Lindsay had a bee in her bonnet about the battle, that inspired her to come and confront someone from the society," Michael said.

"Interesting that it's Mrs. Wentworth bragging about the battle, not Mrs. Pruitt," I said.

"Isn't that an important enough clue for you?"

"I would be if there weren't so many other clues in this issue," I said. "There's also a piece in the article on the town council meeting, saying that a presentation on Mr. Evan Briggs's proposed commercial-development project had been postponed for a few months."

"The outlet mall?"

"Presumably," I said. "Here's the article about the eXtreme croquet tournament."

"Yes," Michael said. "I remember how furious Mrs. Fenniman was that they didn't put it on the sports page."

Although I didn't mention it to Michael, this issue of the *Clarion* was also the one that first officially described Michael and me as an engaged couple. Just a passing reference in an article listing "Professor Michael Waterston and his fiancée, Meg Langslow," among the attendees at a faculty dinner, but it had triggered an orgy of congratulatory calls and cards, not to mention numerous interrogations about where and when the wedding would take place—all of it reinforcing my determination to insist that we elope.

However dramatic an effect that one sentence had on my life, surely it wasn't nearly as important to Lindsay. She might not even have read it—might not even have noticed the coincidence that she was picking up the boxes of documents from her former boyfriend's fiancée.

Unless her reason for visiting had been to inspect me, not to pick up the boxes. What if she'd come out of jealousy or curiosity, and whoever killed her had assumed she was here for some other reason?

Not something I'd mention to Michael. Even if he had been her reason for coming to get the boxes, he wasn't the reason she died—that lay in the killer's motives.

"Why so thoughtful?" Michael asked.

I was searching for an answer when we heard a knock on the stall door. Unusual—most people just barged in.

A head peeked over the door.

"Ms. Ellie," Michael said. "How are you?"

"Fine, thanks," she said. "I think Dr. Langslow was looking for you just now. Wanted you to help round up some sheep."

"Not again," Michael said, but he didn't look too put out as he left the barn. It worried me sometimes, how much he enjoyed all the little agricultural tasks we were learning.

"Hello, Meg," she said, turning to give me a brisk business-like hug.

Either she'd come straight from her conference or she dressed every day as if going to work—her clothes elegant, tailored, and businesslike, except for the familiar purple running shoes, which had been my first clue that I'd like her.

"I'm disappointed," she said. "I thought you were having croquet all day."

"It's probably starting up later this afternoon," I said.

"Lovely sport."

"If you don't mind the company."

"Yes, I hear you've got the cream of Caerphilly society playing."

"I have no idea why," I said. "The game of eXtreme croquet doesn't really seem like their kind of pastime."

"Perhaps they thought you said eXtreme *crochet* and they're too embarrassed to back out," she said with a smile. "Anyway, Jessica said you asked for me."

"I did, yes. I wanted to ask you some questions. About local history. Specifically, the Battle of Pruitt's Ridge."

"The Battle of Pruitt's Ridge," she repeated. Her voice sounded odd.

"I have a million questions," I said. "For starters, do you know any other references? I only have the article from the *Caerphilly Clarion.* Mrs. Pruitt took all the information in her book from that—and left out any information that wasn't flattering to the Pruitts, which doesn't exactly surprise me. Who knows how much the *Clarion* left out, for fear of offending the Pruitts. Not to mention the fact that I have every reason to believe that the Pruitts made the battle up, or exaggerated it way out of proportion and— What's wrong?"

She had turned slightly away from me and her shoulders were shaking. Was she upset? Perhaps someone in her family had died in the battle, but that was a hundred and fifty years ago. Even in Virginia, people these days didn't react quite that personally to the Late Unpleasantness, as many preferred to call the Civil War.

"What's wrong?" I asked.

She turned back and looked at me over her glasses. "Is there somewhere private we can talk?"

"My office," I suggested, pointing to it.

She nodded, then strode off. I could barely keep up with her, which was slightly embarrassing—she was a good six inches shorter than I was and had to be around seventy-five, unless she'd gotten her master's in library science at an age when most people were still in kindergarten.

All the while, I kept wondering what I'd done to upset Ms. Ellie. Not only upset her but cause her to give me the librarian look—the one that quashed unruly patrons in an instant, and informed you without a single word that she knew perfectly well it wasn't your brother who had spilled chocolate syrup on *The Black Stallion's Return.* The look still worked on me, even though I liked Ms. Ellie and considered her a friend, damn it.

I followed her into the tack room and shut the door.

"The Battle of Pruitt's Ridge," she said. I could see that her face was twitching slightly; obviously, the very idea of the battle aroused some strong emotion. "What got you interested in that?"

"I think it might have something to do with the murder," I said. "Or with Mr. Briggs's outlet-mall project. Or both. Look, if this is a touchy subject . . ."

She burst out laughing. Not a few giggles, but a long, hearty belly laugh. After a few seconds, she plopped down in my desk chair and leaned back, the better to enjoy it.

"Oh, dear," she said finally, wiping her eyes. "I know you're serious; it's just that—"

She relapsed into chuckles. I sat down in Michael's chair to wait until she could talk again.

"I'm sorry," she said. "No, there aren't any other references. As for the original source documents— do you want to know the true story of the Battle of Pruitt's Ridge?"

I nodded.

"There wasn't a battle."

"It's a local legend?"

"It's a complete and utter fake, that's what it is."

"How do you know?"

"Because I made it up."

Chapter Thirty-five

She sat back and waited for my reaction.

"You made it up," I repeated. I probably sounded skeptical. After all, I'd seen the documents.

"Me and a couple of my friends—all gone now, bless them; it was more than fifty years ago. We were at the annual town Fourth of July celebration—July 4, 1953—waiting through all the speechifying till the fireworks began, and Mayor Pruitt—that would be Henrietta's husband's grandfather, not the Civil War–era one—was carrying on about the town's long and distinguished history, and the Pruitt's long and distinguished service to the town, and I just got fed up. I cooked up a plot to get back at all those stuffy old town fathers, and when I told my friends about it, they all jumped at the chance to help."

"So you made up the story of a fictitious battle."

"We didn't just make up a story," she said, shaking her head and smiling. "We documented it. My friend Grant immersed himself in Civil War history for weeks, finding a way to weave our fake battle plausibly into the real fabric of events. My brother Blair took the photographs—we wanted some authentic-looking photos to document the event, because everyone knows the camera doesn't lie, right?"

"Of course not," I said. I wasn't sure whether to feel embarrassed or angry as I remembered the emotion I'd felt while handling the fake photos.

"He did a superb job," Ms. Ellie said, almost as if reading my mind. "He studied Civil War–era photographic techniques, learned to re-create them—you can't imagine how many hours of research and experimentation went into making those two dozen photos. Edwina did the costumes—we needed clothes that looked as if people had gone to war in them. Normal wear and tear, gunpowder stains, things like that. And the makeup—we didn't want anyone to recognize the people in the photos. I did the documents. Writing all the letters in different period handwritings, creating the phony newspaper accounts and the official documents—and artificially aging them and the photos, so they really looked old. If we'd done it as a living-history project, we'd have gotten straight A's—you can't imagine how much we learned. Then we had Grant write up a paper about the battle for one of his classes—he was a history major at the college. Had a class with a professor who was one of Mayor Pruitt's buddies. We knew if we could fool him, he'd show it to the mayor."

I realized my mouth was hanging open. All Ms. Ellie'd ever said about her life before retirement was that she'd spent four decades in a boring government desk job. I'd heard wild rumors that she had been a CIA field operative in Latin America, a DIA expert on the Middle East, or an FBI agent who had infiltrated the Mafia, but I'd always assumed these rumors were false, and that like so many other librarians, she'd developed her fierce will and combative manner from a lifetime of defending the written word against neglect, censorship, and dwindling acquisition budgets. Now . . .

"So the prank worked?" I asked aloud.

"Too well," she said. "Grant was waiting to hear back from his professor, and the next thing we knew, there was an article on the front page of the *Clarion,* all about a fabulous new discovery in local history. From the article, you'd think the professor had done all the discovering, with a little minor legwork from Grant. They'd already invited some distinguished Civil War historian to examine the new artifacts, and contacted the Park Service about an archaeological dig to pinpoint the site of the battle. I suspect it was one of the historians who blew the whistle."

"Well, the point was to embarrass Mayor Pruitt publicly," I said.

"This got too public. We didn't realize how much the mayor would do to get back at us. Now I wonder how much he really could have done and how much was just bluster—though when you think about it, in a small town in the 1950s . . . water under the bridge anyway. We agreed to help hush it up and they dropped all the various charges and disciplinary actions. They didn't kick any of us out of college— Grant went on to become a historian, and Paul a lawyer, so I suppose they're just as happy it never came out. Edwina married a stodgy botany professor and turned respectable on me. I suspect, if they ever told anyone else about it when they were older, they were happy to pin the blame on me. Ellie the troublemaker."

"If it was all hushed up, how come Mrs. Pruitt is going around bragging about it?"

"Mayor Pruitt hushed it up a good deal too well. Never told any of his family the whole story, I suspect. So after he died, there was no one to warn Henrietta Pruitt off when she set her troops digging around in the *Clarion*'s archives and they found the original article."

"The *Clarion* never printed a disclaimer or correction?"

"They just pretended it never happened," she said with a chuckle. "I think a few people at the college remembered something. Not the whole story, just that there was some unpleasantness. Made it hard for Henrietta to get anyone in the department interested in studying it."

"So she did it herself. And blew it."

"Did it herself?" Ms. Ellie said, laughing. "Henrietta Pruitt? Of course not. She and Claire Wentworth never actually do anything. They just delegate to their underlings at the historical society—none of whom have any actual training at historical research. There was some talk five or six years ago about getting a historian to do a new, expanded edition, but I imagine she had a hard time finding anyone."

Five or six years ago—about the time Lindsay Tyler had come to town.

"I assume none of Mrs. Pruitt's underlings would have had enough training to recognize all your photos and documents as forgeries?"

"I doubt if they even saw them," Ms. Ellie said. "I certainly didn't have them, not that I'd have shared them if I had."

"Do you know what did happen to them?" I already knew, but I wondered if she did.

She shrugged.

"Smoke and ashes, if the mayor got his hands on them," she said.

"How many other people know this story?" I asked.

"Two or three people I've told over the years," she said. "Not sure why I'm telling you now— maybe because I'm getting along. Want someone to know about it. Or maybe because I'm getting tired of hearing Henrietta Pruitt bragging about her husband's fictitious heroic ancestors. They had a photo of her in her Southern belle's ball gown on the front page of the *Clarion* the other day. Humbug!"

"Did anyone ever come around asking questions, sounding as if they were onto the story?"

"Couple of people from the college, but they gave up when they found out all we had was the microfiche of the old newspapers."

"Was one of them an instructor named Lindsay Tyler? A tall blond woman with—"

"I remember Lindsay," Ms. Ellie said. Not fondly, I gathered. "She spent more time with the microfilm than most. Ruder than most, too."

"Do you think she figured out the prank?"

"No idea," Ellie said. "Never said anything to me if she did."

"Of course she wouldn't," I said. "If she guessed that the documents were faked—possibly from the same details I finally noticed—"

"What details?" Ms. Ellie asked.

I reached for the folder—the one with my photocopies, not the originals. For whatever reason, I wasn't ready for anyone—not even Ms. Ellie, their creator—to know we'd found the originals. I pulled out a couple of sheets.

"I noticed a tree with an odd-shaped branch," I said. "Here it is. The one taken in 1953 by the *Clarion*'s photographer. Looks as if the tree's crooking its finger to tell someone to come closer."

"Yes, it does," she said.

"And a hundred years earlier, it was crooking its finger the same way," I said, picking up the supposed battle site photo. "I don't know what species of tree it is, but you'd think it would have grown slightly in a hundred years, wouldn't you?"

"Not that anyone noticed that at the time," she said with a chuckle.

"I should have realized immediately what was wrong with this one," I said, holding up the photo of the tattered uniform sleeve on the barbed-wire fence.

Ms. Ellie studied it for long seconds, then shook her head.

"You've got me," she said. "Still looks fine to me. Maybe a bit melodramatic, but so were many photographs from that era."

"The mood was right," I said. "Not the details. Took me till just now to realize what bothered me about it—the rusted barbed-wire fence."

Ms. Ellie shook her head slightly.

"Barbed wire wasn't invented until after the Civil War," I explained.

"Are you sure?" Ms. Ellie asked.

"I have an uncle who collects the stuff," I said. "The first patent on barbed wire was filed just after the Civil War—1868, I think. Even if a few people were experimenting with early varieties six years earlier, you wouldn't find standard commercially produced barbed wire then, especially not in a badly rusted condition."

"I had no idea," she said. "A couple of people spotted the tree before, but in fifty years, you're the first to notice the barbed wire. Impressive!"

I made a mental note to thank Uncle Chauncy.

"So I guessed something fishy was going on," I said aloud. "Of course, I jumped to the same conclusion anyone would."

Ms. Ellie frowned.

"What conclusion?"

"About who did it," I said. "If you didn't know the whole story and suspected that Mrs. Pruitt's famous battle was all a lie, and the documents were faked, who would be the logical suspects?"

Ms. Ellie blinked.

"The Pruitts," she said, nodding. "That never occurred to me."

"Blinded by guilt," I said, shaking my head.

Ms. Ellie smiled.

"The other people who were involved—who were they?" I asked.

"All dead," she said.

"I know, but what were their full names?"

"Paul was Paul Drayer, my brother," she said. "Grant Boyd—a historian, as I said; specialized in medieval studies. Guess he wanted to stay pretty far from the Civil War. And Edwina Ballantine."

"Who married the stodgy professor," I said. "Was that her married name?"

"No, her maiden name. Her married name—"

"Was Sprocket, right?"

She nodded.

Edwina Sprocket, the queen of packrats, from whom we'd bought our house. Former owner of the twenty-three boxes of old papers. Perhaps she hadn't completely turned her back on their youthful prank. Or, more likely, she'd had no idea the original documents from the hoax were still lurking in her attic.

I glanced down at my copies and flipped through them until I found one of the photos.

"That's why Colonel Pruitt's wife looked so familiar," I said. "It's you."

She chuckled.

"And the baby?"

"My little sister's Betsy Wetsy doll," she said. "Look, why the sudden interest in the Battle of Pruitt's Ridge?"

"Mrs. Pruitt was bragging about it to my father this weekend," I said. "I suspect she's planning to use it to fight the outlet mall Evan Briggs wants to build next door."

"Oh dear," Ms. Ellie said. "That would be a tactical mistake—it would discredit the whole effort against the mall. And now you can guess which side I'll take if it comes to a fight over the mall."

"Me, too, for obvious reasons," I said. "I'm also not sure whether it has anything to do with Lindsay's murder, but if there's any—"

"She was murdered?" Ms. Ellie said with a gasp. "Was that the woman they found in Mr. Shiffley's pasture? Oh dear."

"Yes," I said. "I'm wondering if maybe I'm not the first person to have spotted the distinctive tree branch and the barbed wire after all."

"You think Lindsay might have?"

"I don't know," I said. "Maybe she didn't, and it's only a coincidence that she was found at the site of the phony battle, with the leaders of the pro- and antimall forces playing croquet all around her. . . ."

I fell silent. Ms. Ellie was staring down at my desk.

"I hope you're wrong," she said. "About Lindsay figuring out the hoax, I mean. Because if you're right, I'm going to feel responsible."

"If I'm right, maybe you and I are the only people still alive who know something that got Lindsay killed," I said.

"True. I should tell Chief Burke the whole story."

"Wouldn't hurt," I said.

"Mind if I use your phone?"

I shook my head. She squared her shoulders, picked up the phone, and dialed a number. I made a motion to leave, but she waved me back into my seat.

"Debbie Anne? Ellie Drayer. Could you tell

Chief Burke that I have some information that might be related to his murder case? . . . No, it's pretty complicated, and might just be ancient history, but I figure better safe than sorry. . . . No, just have him call me when he gets a chance. Thanks. . . . Fine, thanks. Give my love to your parents."

She stared into space for a few moments.

"Wonder if we did break any laws back then? I imagine the chief will let me know if we did."

"I'm sure there's a statute of limitations," I said.

"Yes," she said, pulling herself together. "On everything but murder. You need any more information, you call me."

"The chief's the one with the investigation."

"Him too," she said as she stood up to go. "You know, if you really want to get rid of the socialites, you should tell them about croquet's unsavory reputation."

"Unsavory? According to whom?"

"It was banned in Boston in the 1890s," she said. "Several prominent clergymen denounced it for encouraging drinking, gambling, and philandering. Men and women playing on the same field. The occasional bare ankle exposed to the leering eyes of the spectators. Young couples disappearing into the shrubbery in search of lost balls. Shocking. I haven't heard of a game that led to a murder before."

"Nice to know we're original here."

She smiled slightly.

"Yes," she said. "Well, nice seeing you."

I watched as she strode out, spine as erect as ever.

Her story would doubtless inspire Chief Burke to take a closer look at any connection between Lindsay and the Caerphilly Historical Society. Which wasn't necessarily good. For one thing, much as I disliked Mrs. Pruitt, I wanted her on the loose, leading the charge against the outlet mall, not locked up on trial for murder. Besides, if Mrs. Pruitt dumped all the actual work of preparing her book on Lacie and her other underlings at the society, odds were that she'd shift the suspicion, as well.

Just then, I heard a commotion outside. Now what?

Chapter Thirty-six

I strode to the barn door and saw that Mrs. Fenniman had returned from church and was standing in the middle of the lawn, waving her croquet mallet around as she talked to the dozen or so people around her. Surely she hadn't taken the mallet to church?

"You should have seen it!" she crowed. Something dramatic, I gathered from the expressions on the faces around her.

"Seen what?" I asked.

"Chief Burke showed up at Trinity Episcopal," she said. "There was Reverend Riggs on the top step, shaking hands with the departing parishioners, and Burke on the bottom step, lying in wait for Henrietta Pruitt."

"He was there to arrest her?" Dad asked.

"No, he had a warrant to search the historical society's office. Came to pick her up to let him and his men in."

"Wonder what happened that made him go through all the trouble of getting a warrant on a Sunday," I mused. Was he already planning the raid on the historical society when we'd called to tell him about the pond?

"Maybe he had it already and was waiting for the right moment to serve it," Michael suggested.

"No, he got it late this morning," Randall Shiffley put in. "Saw Aunt Jane."

"Ah," I said, nodding. Judge Jane Shiffley would be the logical source for a warrant against the historical society. Every other judge in town was either a Pruitt or married to a member of the historical society.

"He may not have been here that long," Randall said, "but the chief knows what he's doing."

"How did Mrs. Pruitt react?" I asked Mrs. Fenniman.

"That's the rich part," she said. "She skipped church! She's on the lam!"

"No she's not," Horace put in. "She's here in the kitchen."

"Oh," Mrs. Fenniman said. "Well, that's as good as being on the lam, isn't it?"

"Don't think she knows about the search warrant yet," Horace said. "If you want to tell her . . ."

He shrugged his shoulders, as if disavowing any responsibility for the consequences.

"Shouldn't we tell the chief she's here?" Michael asked.

"He got one of the other members to let him into the historical society," Mrs. Fenniman added. "A whole troop of them went along to keep an eye on things."

The chief must have loved that.

"That accounts for it," Horace said. "Mrs. Pruitt's hopping made because the other ladies haven't arrived to help with lunch."

"That's right, they volunteered to do today's lunch," I said. "Not that anyone's that interested in lunch yet, after all that breakfast."

"Mrs. P. had a few things to say about that, too," Horace said.

"So we have an irate Mrs. Pruitt in our kitchen," I said. "Should I go try to calm her down?"

"Your mother's taking care of it," Horace said.

Given how Mother felt, I was willing to bet that instead of calming Mrs. Pruitt, she was graciously, tactfully, politely pouring pounds of salt in her wounds. Might as well leave them to it.

"Wonder how long Claire and Lacie will be tied up down at the historical society," Mrs. Fenniman said. "Because I was thinking of getting the game started again."

"Does the chief know that?" I asked.

"Yes, I asked him over at the church."

"Give Claire and Lacie enough notice, then," I said. "No fair saying the game starts in ten minutes and anyone not ready to play is disqualified."

"Says who," she grumbled.

"Says me. I'll complain to the board of regents if you try it."

"It was just a thought," she said, shrugging. "If you don't trust me, you notify them."

"I'll do that," I said. "I think I'll check with the chief, too."

"Hmph. Don't even trust your own family."

Less than anyone, I wanted to say, but I held my tongue and dialed.

"I'm busy," the chief said when he answered his cell phone. Maybe I was behind the times and answering phones with "hello" had become an anachronism.

"I know," I said. "But Mrs. Fenniman said you'd given permission for us to restart the tournament, and I want to make sure we're not going to get arrested for tampering with a crime scene. Is she telling the truth this time?"

"Just stay away from the brier patch," he said. "And the pond."

"We'll make sure there's crime-scene tape around the brier patch and the pond," I said, looking pointedly at Mrs. Fenniman.

"That's easy enough," she said. "Come on, Horace, you can help me."

"I'll gather up the competitors," I said, strolling toward the kitchen door. "By the way, have you by any chance seen Lacie Butler and Claire Wentworth today? I know how to find my team and Mrs. Pruitt, but—"

"Mrs. Pruitt?" he said. "You've seen her today?"

"At the moment, she's sitting in our kitchen drinking lemonade," I said, peering through the kitchen window. Mother smiled and waved at me. I waved back. From the look on Mrs. Pruitt's face, I could almost imagine she'd poured her glass of lemonade before Mother added the sugar.

"Keep her there," the chief said.

"Are you going to arrest her?" I asked. "No sense getting ready to play if one of the teams will be short a player."

"At the moment, I just want to talk to her," he said. "Do you think you can keep her there without mentioning that fact?"

"No problem," I said. "I'll even knock her down and sit on her if you like."

He hung up without replying. Did silence really imply consent?

Chapter Thirty-seven

As I expected, Chief Burke kicked Mother and me out of the kitchen the minute he arrived. I'd have minded more if Mrs. Wentworth and Lacie Butler hadn't arrived in the chief's wake. If I couldn't overhear what he said to Mrs. Pruitt, at least I had a chance of finding out what had happened down at the historical society. An even better chance, since Mother's curiosity was roused. The police officer never lived who could extract more information than Mother when she put her mind to it.

Lacie was obviously excited; even through the poison ivy I could see that her face was flushed and her eyes glittered. She looked like one of my nieces or nephews on the sugar high they always got when their Uncle Rob was in charge of them for more than five minutes. I suspected Lacie's exhilaration had a less innocent origin—had Mother convinced Lacie to do something to trigger the chief's raid on the historical society?

"But what were they looking for?" Mother asked with an air of wide-eyed innocence that suggested she had a very clear idea what the police were after.

Lacie shrugged helplessly, as if abandoning any pretense at understanding the strange and mysterious whims of the law.

"Someone told Chief Burke that Henrietta had been exchanging letters and e-mails with Lindsay Tyler," Mrs. Wentworth said.

"Goodness!" Mother exclaimed. "Why ever would they think that?"

"She was a nutcase," Mrs. Wentworth said. Presumably, she meant Lindsay, not Mrs. Pruitt. I noticed she didn't deny the correspondence. "It was a mistake ever inviting that woman to join the society. A mistake hiring her at the college in the first place. I should have told Henrietta that at the time."

"Mistakes you rectified five years ago," I said. "Only I gather she didn't go quietly."

"No, but she didn't have much of a choice, did she?" Mrs. Wentworth said. "Then she reappeared a few months ago, making the most preposterous demands and accusations. Even threats."

"Reappeared?" Mother said. "You mean at your meetings?"

"No, no," Mrs. Wentworth said quickly. "Or we would have recognized her when we saw the picture. But making phone calls, writing letters, sending e-mails."

"To Henrietta, of course," Lacie put in. "Since she was president. We mostly heard about it from her."

"Yes, of course," Mrs. Wentworth said. "It all fit in with what we'd seen of Lindsay when she was here."

"So we'd have no reason to doubt that Henrietta was telling the truth," Lacie said.

"As far as we knew, she was handling the situation appropriately," Mrs. Wentworth said. "By completely ignoring Lindsay."

"That's what we assumed she was doing," Lacie said. "I know I had no idea . . ."

She let her words trail of and shrugged.

"So what did they find?" Mother asked.

"Who knows?" Mrs. Wentworth said.

"I heard—" Lacie began, then stopped, as if she'd gone too far.

"Heard what, dear?" Mother said. "We won't tell a soul."

"I heard they found some e-mails in the office computer that proved Henrietta had arranged to meet Lindsay the day of the croquet match."

"Where did you hear that?" Mrs. Wentworth demanded.

"The police officers were talking to each other," Lacie said, shrinking back. "I don't really think they noticed I was there."

She shrugged and smiled ruefully, as if to suggest that she was used to people not noticing her existence.

"Oh dear," Mother said. "That doesn't sound good."

"If that's true . . ." Mrs. Wentworth murmured. "I wonder who told them. To search the historical society's offices, I mean."

"We may never know," Mother said, shaking her head sadly. "The police can be so secretive."

"Isn't it more important to focus on the future?" Lacie said. "On what we can do to help Henrietta?"

"Or how to limit the damage her arrest will do to the historical society," Mrs. Wentworth said.

"Yes, of course," Lacie said.

"If you like, I'll suggest to Mrs. Fenniman that we postpone the tournament for a bit," I said. "Until either Mrs. Pruitt is available to play or your team can find a substitute."

"I thought the board of regents had ruled that any player committing a homicide during the course of a game automatically disqualified his or her team from the tournament," Mrs. Wentworth said, frowning.

"Only if the victim is another player, remember?" I said.

"Good idea to have a game plan if Henrietta needs to step back from her normal responsibilities," Mrs. Wentworth said, more to herself than any of us. "I'll make a few phone calls. Line up a few people."

"Very wise," Mother said.

"Lacie," Mrs. Wentworth said. "Do you have the membership directory?"

"In my car," Lacie said. "Why?"

"Go and fetch it. We need to start making some plans."

Lacie blinked and frowned, then got up and left. She didn't look as desperately eager to please as she once had—how frustrating to think you'd achieved a revolution and realize you've only traded one tyrant for another. If, as I suspected, Mother had encouraged the worm to turn, and Lacie had steered the police to Mrs. Pruitt, Mrs. Wentworth might get a nasty surprise if she had any skeletons in her own closet. Or any more cracked Delft chamber pots.

I decided I didn't need to stay while Mrs. Wentworth plotted her palace revolution. If Chief Burke was really releasing the croquet field, surely he'd have no objection to our restarting work on the house.

I strolled out into the yard and spotted something. A car had just pulled up and the town's leading criminal defense lawyer stepped out—the same one we'd hired when my brother had been briefly arrested on suspicion of murder not long ago. Tossing me a perfunctory, preoccupied greeting, he hurried toward the back door with his briefcase tucked under his arm, looking like a football player going for a touchdown. He was admitted into the kitchen. I watched for a few minutes, and he didn't reemerge, so I assumed he was also Mrs. Pruitt's lawyer.

So should I find the Shiffleys and ask how soon they could start work again? Or should I talk to Michael first? Discuss the notion that we might want to go slow on the renovations until we got more information about what was happening with the mall project? Especially considering there was almost no chance Evan Briggs would be arrested for the murder, and every likelihood Mrs. Pruitt would be.

I strolled into the tack room/office and sat down at my desk, still pondering.

"Meg?" I looked up, to see Rob standing in the doorway, holding a laptop computer. "Can I show you something? It could have something to do with—well, you know. The murder and all."

"Okay," I said. "New laptop?"

"No, it's Bill's laptop."

"What are you doing with Bill's laptop?"

"I borrowed it," he said. "Really. He wanted me to look at his résumé. I asked him if I could keep it to show it to someone else from Mutant Wizards."

"His résumé? I'm surprised he let you have the laptop instead of just printing it or e-mailing it."

"It's not a normal résumé," Rob said. "He does computer animation, and he has this animated résumé—pretty cool stuff, really. Hey, I didn't lie— you're on the board, and I can show you the résumé— here."

He set the laptop down on my desk and, after peering at the screen for a few seconds, pressed something. Little cartoon ferrets ran onto the screen.

"That's nice," I said as the ferrets formed a conga line and danced offscreen again. "I gather that isn't what you came here to show me."

"No," he said. "When I was trying to restart the résumé—watch this part with the kangaroos; it's a hoot—I hit the wrong button by mistake and opened his e-mail. I wasn't being nosy, really, but I was looking at the screen, and you know how certain words just pop out at you?"

"For heaven's sake, just spill it," I said. "What did you see in his e-mail?"

"He's been e-mailing Lindsay Tyler," Rob said. "A lot. Like I was trying to get out of his e-mail, and instead I opened this folder full of e-mails to her."

"Show me," I said.

"Okay," he said. Then he hesitated. "Um . . . I'm not really sure I know how to stop this thing."

"Want me to do it?"

"Sure," he said. "Or we could just wait till it ends. It only takes about ten minutes, and there's this part near the end with the wombats—"

"Let me see that," I said, grabbing the laptop. "Before Bill comes looking for his laptop."

My computer skills, though limited, were enough to let me stop the résumé and open Bill's e-mail. After several minutes of poking around, I found the e-mails to Lindsay—237 of them, hidden in a folder named "Accounting 101 study group."

"Yuck," Rob said. "That would have been the last folder I'd've looked in."

"I think that's the idea," I said. "It would be the last folder a lot of people would look in."

Yes, Bill had definitely been e-mailing Lindsay. I paged through, scanning the messages—he'd gathered both sides of their correspondence into the Accounting 101 folder. It began in late September, with Bill politely addressing her as "Professor" or "Dr. Tyler." She'd sought someone to help her with a computer problem. One of Bill's computer-science instructors had recommended him. By October, he was calling her Lindsay, and either he'd solved her computer problems or they'd taken a backseat to discussions of books, movies, music, worldviews, personal histories—I recognized the familiar rhythm of the mating dance. I could pinpoint almost to the day when they'd consummated their relationship in November, and guessed long before Bill did that she was using him for something. It took me awhile to learn what—obviously the e-mails were only a small part of their relationship by that time. Bill was clearly upset about something she was asking him to do—something he carefully avoided mentioning in the e-mails. Something computer-related—he kept pointing out that he couldn't do it from his own machine. That only a few dozen people used the school computer lab. That it wasn't safe.

My jaw dropped when I came to Lindsay's next e-mail.

She was asking him to break into computer systems: Caerphilly College's network, Evan Briggs's corporate system, the county records, even the Caerphilly Historical Society.

She also had definite ideas about where he should attack his targets from. Most of them from the Caerphilly Public Library or from a Kinko's in Caerphilly—not the one the students used, but one a few doors down from Evan Briggs's office. Or from the historical society—she offered to give him a key to the offices.

"Even if they do suspect what's happening, they won't come looking for you. They'll blame someone local. Once we're sure you've gotten everything useful, it wouldn't be a bad idea if you did let them see that someone had hacked into their systems."

Was this part of what Lindsay'd been blackmailing people with—evidence that indicated they were committing computer crimes? Evidence she'd arranged for Bill to plant, so she could stir up contention and muddy the waters by letting the various victims blame one another for the intrusion?

Were the e-mails incriminating Mrs. Pruitt even real?

A pity Jessica, the library aide, hadn't noticed who'd used the library computers while she was on duty. Probably Bill, and maybe if they'd arrested him weeks ago, things might have played out differently.

"Turn my computer on," I said to Rob. "We need to make a copy of these."

"You mean your printer, right?" he said.

"No, the computer," I said. "I mean an electronic copy, not a printout. I'm going to find the mail files and copy them. Push the button on your right. Your other right."

"Wow, you know how to do that?" Rob asked. "Copying the files, I mean?"

"I'll figure it out," I said. "Or we'll call Kevin."

I returned to reading. Bill gave in. He made several weekend trips to Caerphilly. I nodded when I read Lindsay's e-mail suggesting that he register for the eXtreme croquet tournament. He'd have a legitimate reason to be in Caerphilly, instead of having to sneak around. Maybe he could make some local contacts. Find a way to get into the college computer lab.

But Bill was getting cold feet. Or maybe beginning to suspect that Lindsay was more interested in his computer skills than in him. His e-mails sounded increasingly paranoid. Paranoid alternating with just plain angry. He wasn't going to do it. He'd do it, but this was the last time. He wasn't going to do it, and what's more, he'd report her.

Nothing to indicate if he knew that she'd be coming to Caerphilly at the same time he'd be here for the tournament. The e-mails ended the Wednesday before the tournament began. No telling what mood he was in by the time he'd arrived here. To judge from the last few e-mails, he'd been capable of a dozen mood swings in the intervening two days.

From the tone of her last few e-mails, Lindsay was getting tired of putting up with him. Her last e-mail pointed out that he had more to lose than she did. If she turned him in to the college or the local police . . .

"It's Bill!" Rob said.

Chapter Thirty-eight

I whirled, but there was no one in the doorway.

"Sorry," Rob said. "I meant he's the killer."

"He could be," I said.

"It has to be him," Rob said. "I mean, I can't really see someone killing her over a stupid outlet mall."

"That's because you're not mortgaged to the hilt to pay for a house next door to the stupid outlet mall," I muttered.

"But love—passion—sex!" he went on, flinging his arms wide for emphasis and knocking my in basket off the desk. "That's a motive!"

"It's a possible motive," I said. "Hand me that—damn!"

We both started and whirled when we heard a noise in the door.

"Only another sheep," Rob said with a nervous laugh.

"But it could have been anyone," I said. "Bill waving his lethal croquet mallet. Chief Burke asking what we're doing withholding evidence. Dad wanting to see what we've found and managing to reformat Bill's computer by accident. Go stand outside the door. If anyone starts to come in, greet them by name. Loudly."

"Roger," Rob said.

"Take her out with you," I said, indicating the sheep. After snuffling around the floor and snorting as if dissatisfied with the quality of the pasturage, she had begun scratching her back against the door frame.

"She's not hurting anything," Rob said. "This is a barn, after all."

"She's making herself comfortable," I said. "You know what happens once they get too comfortable, and if you won't kick her out, you can clean it up."

"Oh, all right," he said. "Come on, Dolly."

He went outside, shoving the sheep ahead of him.

I found the e-mail folder and copied the whole thing onto a compact disc. Kevin would be proud of me. I put it on the desk. Then I felt a pang of guilt—after all, I'd been nagging Michael about not labeling CDs he made. Nothing worse than having to sort through dozens of anonymous silver discs for something. Especially if the something was important evidence. I grabbed a Sharpie to label it, then stopped. Label it how? Anything really descriptive, like "copies of incriminating e-mails between Bill and Lindsay" would be too obvious.

After a moment's thought, I smiled and printed "Photos of Spike as a puppy" on the CD. Which wouldn't look suspicious to someone who didn't know Spike—like Bill, or even Chief Burke—but would stand out as an oddity to Michael or any of my immediate family, all of whom knew that

Michael's mother had brought Spike home from the animal shelter full grown, with all his bad habits well established. Not that I expected that anyone would need to find the CD in my absence, but you never knew.

I strolled out to where Rob was standing just inside the barn door.

"Finished," I said.

"I can take the laptop back to Bill?"

"No, it's evidence. We're going to give it to Chief Burke."

"Okay," Rob said. "You explain that to Bill."

"No problem," I said. "Right now, we're going to lock the laptop up with the boxes and find Bill. I haven't seen him for a while, have you?"

"No, but I thought I'd avoid him until I could show you the computer."

Outside, I found others already bound on the same mission.

"There you are," Michael said. "Just wanted to let you know that I'm going to take Graham and Tony into town to look for Bill."

"To look for him? Why?"

"Took off this morning in the van and hasn't come back yet," Graham said.

"Damned inconsiderate," Tony muttered.

"Which is not really like him, so we're worried something has happened to him," Graham said.

"And if nothing's happened to him, we can make something happen," Tony added.

"Damn," I said.

"I'm sorry," Rob said. "It's my fault. Maybe he got suspicious because I'd had his computer so long."

"Suspicious of what?" Graham asked.

"How long have you had it?" I asked.

"Since yesterday afternoon," Rob said.

"Great," I muttered.

"But I told him this morning that I'd been too swamped to even look at it yesterday," Rob said. "I said I'd take a look as soon as I could today."

"Why didn't you bring this to me yesterday?" I asked.

"Bring what?" Tony said.

"I didn't figure out how to turn it on until just now," Rob said. "I finally got Horace to help me before he went over to help search the historical society's office."

"And Bill's been missing since morning," I said, turning to Graham and Tony.

"Early morning," Graham said.

"What's he done?" Tony asked.

"You tell me," I said. "We already know he had an affair with Lindsay."

"He did?" Graham said.

"You never noticed?" Tony said, rolling his eyes.

"I just thought he had a crush."

"We know she talked him into doing some illegal hacking," I went on.

"She tried," Tony said. "He wasn't going to do it."

"According to the e-mails they exchanged, he did," I said, holding up the laptop.

"Oh, damn," Tony said. "Pineville will expel him

if they find out. They have a real strict policy on ethical use of computers."

"What's their policy on murder?" I asked.

Everyone gaped at me. Even Rob, who shouldn't have been all that surprised by my question, so I deduced my delivery was effective.

"You don't really think Bill did it," Graham said.

"Damn," Tony said. From the worried look on his face, I suspected the notion had crossed his mind already. Graham didn't look quite as worried.

"I've never known a murder suspect before," Graham said.

"Technically, you've been one since Friday afternoon," I told him.

"Really?" he said, his face lighting up. "That's brilliant! I can't wait to tell everyone at home."

"Getting back to Bill," Michael said. "Where do you think he went?"

"He said he was going to town," Graham said.

"Maybe he fled back to Pineville," Tony suggested.

"More likely, several hundred miles in any other direction, if he thinks Rob found incriminating evidence on his laptop," I said. "Do you know his license plate number?"

Tony and Graham both shrugged. I sighed.

"Come on," I said. "Let's go see the chief."

Chapter Thirty-nine

"I cannot believe he actually suspected me of murder," Mrs. Pruitt was saying for at least the tenth time as she strode up and down the kitchen floor. "Does he realize who I am? What the Pruitt family has done for this town?"

"Get over it, toots," Mrs. Fenniman said as she sighted down the handle of a croquet mallet to make sure she hadn't grabbed a warped one. "Burke doesn't care who you are or what you are. If you'd knocked off Blondie, he'd have arrested you as soon as anyone else."

Maybe sooner. Was it my imagination, or had I seen a brief look of disappointment cross the chief's face when I handed him Bill's laptop and explained what it contained?

"The very idea!" Mrs. Pruitt huffed. "How dare you!"

Mrs. Fenniman shrugged, then took a practice swing with the mallet. A forceful practice swing—was she, perhaps, imagining Mrs. Pruitt's head there on the kitchen floor?

"Really," Mrs. Pruitt muttered, casting another involuntary glance at Lacie and Mrs. Wentworth. Yes, she'd been angry upon learning that they had unlocked the Caerphilly Historical Society's offices for the chief to do his search. But I wondered if she was beginning to regret her angry promise never to speak to either of them again. She hadn't realized that they'd return the favor—and without them chiming in to echo and approve and tut-tut everything she said, her grand pronouncements lacked much of their usual thunder.

"I think Mrs. Fenniman's point was how fortunate you are to have a police chief who will seek justice no matter where the quest leads," Mother said. "I must say, it reflects well on the town and its citizens to have put such an honest public official into office."

"Hear! Hear!" Mrs. Wentworth murmured. Lacie only nodded, and Mrs. Pruitt was clearly withholding comment until she could work out whether what Mother said was a compliment or an insult.

"If we're going to play croquet, we'd better get started," Mrs. Fenniman said. "It'll get dark soon. And someone swiped my night-vision goggles."

Sunset wasn't for another three hours, but an eXtreme croquet game on the cow pasture could take that long. She stalked out the kitchen door, not looking back to see if anyone was following.

"Tell my team I'll meet them on the course," Mrs. Pruitt said to no one in particular. She stuck several things into Lacie's knapsack and strode out.

"We'll see you out on the course," Mrs. Wentworth said to me, as if she hadn't heard Mrs. Pruitt, and made her exit. Was it really an accident that she flung open the door so violently that it almost struck Mrs. Pruitt?

Lacie stopped long enough to rummage through the pack and remove half of the items—presumably, the things Mrs. Pruitt had stashed there. Shouldering her pack—now reduced to a much more reasonable load—she smiled apologetically at us and slipped out of the doorway.

"Oh, dear," Rose Noire murmured. "There's such negative energy in here—I'll have to do a cleansing after the game. I can't imagine what it will be like out on the course."

She shook her head and left.

"For once, I completely understand what she means," Mother said. "I think a cleansing is a splendid idea."

"Yeah, she can burn as much sage and lavender and whatever as she likes," I said.

"As soon as we're well and truly rid of Mrs. Pruitt and her unfortunate associates. Is 'Knock them dead' the appropriate thing to say? Not literally, of course."

"Former associates," I said. "We'll do our best to knock them dead, figuratively speaking."

Mother smiled and waved gaily as I left the kitchen.

The yard was blissfully quiet. The police were all off tracking Bill. Michael had taken Tony and Graham in to town to see if they could rent a car for the drive back to Pineville or if someone had to transport them to an airport. Most of the Shiffleys' trucks were still there, but they'd all gone off somewhere. Sunday dinner with their Uncle Fred, perhaps.

Things were almost back to normal.

"Hurry up, Meg," I heard Mrs. Fenniman calling from somewhere down in the bog.

All I had to do was get through one last eXtreme croquet game. How bad could it be?

Chapter Forty

Okay, it could be pretty bad.

The bickering began at the starting post, when Mrs. Pruitt went over to rummage in Lacie's pack and realized that all her stuff was gone.

"What have you done with my stuff, you little ninny!" she shrieked. "I need my golf gloves! I'll get blisters without them!"

Lacie's initial reaction was a knee-jerk one: She took several steps back, hunched her shoulders slightly, and covered her mouth with her hands, as if to muffle an exclamation. But she recovered quickly.

"I thought she was never going to speak to us again," she said to Mrs. Wentworth.

"And you believe a thing she says?" Mrs. Wentworth replied, shrugging.

They both stood, their hands folded on top of the handles of their mallets, as if to emphasize that both of them were already wearing their golf gloves and in no danger of blistering.

"When's the next meeting of the historical society, anyway?" I asked.

No one answered. Everyone just glared at one another, and at me. No doubt they were thinking the same thing I was. The next meeting wouldn't be pretty. I'd have enjoyed their discomfort if I hadn't had the sinking feeling that their internal battles would distract them from the battle against the outlet mall at a critical moment.

By the time Mrs. Pruitt had fetched her gloves and we got started, the mood was tense, and none of the Dames were playing up to their usual form. Mrs. Fenniman wasn't playing well, either, mainly because she was having too much fun watching the Dames bicker.

Rose Noire kept patting the trees as if to apologize for bringing such negative energy into their space, and waving around a small bunch of herbs. Probably something that was supposed to create harmony and dispel quarrels and anger. Didn't seem to work, but at least the poisonous atmosphere in which we played was sweetly scented.

Even our referee was off his game. At the third wicket, Rob opened up Spike's carrier to let him out for a pit stop without noticing that the leash wasn't attached to his collar. Spike was out of sight in seconds.

"Damn," Rob said. "Now what'll we do if we run into any cows?"

"Call Mother and Dad back at the house," I said. "Have them keep an eye out for Spike."

"He was heading away from the house," Mrs. Fenniman said.

"That was just to fool us," I said. "He'll double back in a minute or so."

I was the only one playing up to my usual form. Above it, in fact. Every time I approached my ball, I would push all my anxieties and resentments out of mind and focus on the ball, trying to make each swing as clean and solid as I could. Like chopping wood or hammering iron, whacking croquet balls was a great way to take out your frustrations. With each long, powerful drive, I pulled farther ahead. Tiger Woods had nothing on me today.

By the ninth wicket, I was so far in the lead that I couldn't even hear their squabbling. In between the occasional radio calls for me to take a shot, I could enjoy the peace and quiet of my solitary ramble through the woods.

At least I could have enjoyed it if I'd known how to turn off my brain.

I kept wanting to call back to the house myself, to find out if they'd heard anything about Bill. Worrying if I'd overreacted to the e-mails.

Don't be silly, I told myself. The chief reacted the same way. And he had prior knowledge of the hacking problem—more knowledge than I did.

But what if Bill wasn't guilty? Not guilty of murder, anyway, only convinced that everyone would assume his guilt once they saw the incriminating e-mails and discovered his involvement in the computer break-ins?

We'd find out sooner or later. Right now, the sooner I could get through this croquet game, the sooner I could go home, put my feet up, talk to Michael, and revel in the luxury of an empty house. Emptier, anyway; we'd still have various family members underfoot, but not the Dames, the Briggses, the Clones, or the Mountain Morris Mallet Men.

"Turn, Meg," my radio advised.

I lined up my shot and whacked the ball perfectly, lofting it into the air. It not only went in the right direction; it easily cleared a particular nasty patch of thorny bog.

"Sweet," I muttered. Then I grabbed the radio, shouted "Done!" into it, and set off after my ball.

When I emerged from the wood, I found Dad talking to someone standing on the other side of a barbed-wire fence. When I got closer, I recognized our neighbor, Fred Shiffley.

"There's your ball!" Dad said, pointing to where it lay, nestled in the middle of smooth stretch of grass. "The wicket's over by the stream."

"Thanks," I said. "Any news about the manhunt?"

"Not yet," Dad said. Fred Shiffley shook his head.

"They really sure that poor boy did it?" he asked.

"I don't think they're too sure of anything yet," I said.

"You ask me, they should still keep an eye on that Pruitt woman," Mr. Shiffley said.

"Any particular reason?" I asked, leaning my mallet against the fence. "Or just on general principles?"

Mr. Shiffley smiled slyly.

"Recognize this place?" he said. I looked around. Yes, I recognized it. On Friday, when I'd played far worse, I'd spent an inordinate amount of time disentangling my ball from the barbed-wire fence.

"The fence!" I said. "It's the one in the photo about the so-called Battle of Pruitt's Ridge."

Mr. Shiffley nodded.

"Anyone who'd pull a stunt like that would do anything," he said. "Inventing something that never happened and trying to pass it off as history. If someone has no respect for the truth, do you really expect them to respect the value of human life?"

"But Mrs. Pruitt didn't invent the Battle of Pruitt's Ridge," I said. "None of the Pruitts did."

"If they didn't who did? Because it sure as hell never happened."

"Ellie Drayer did it," I said.

"Ms. Ellie, the librarian?" he said, shaking his head. "I can't imagine why she'd do that."

"This was over fifty years ago, when she was in college," I said. "She and a couple of her friends did it to play a prank on the Pruitts."

"Well, I'll be," Mr. Shiffley said, and broke out laughing. "Pruitts sure fell for it, didn't they?"

"The *Clarion* published it, and the whole story came out, and for some strange reason, the *Clarion* never published the truth about the hoax."

Mr. Shiffley snorted.

"That's because old Tiberius Pruitt owned the *Clarion* back in the fifties," he said. "No way he'd

print anything that made the Pruitts look like the
fools they were. Wish I'd known the whole story
sooner."

"I bet Mrs. Pruitt does, too, now that the truth is
out," I said.

"If I'd known the joke was on the Pruitts, maybe
I'd have played along," he said, still grinning. "Sup-
ported the whole campaign to have their phony bat-
tlefield declared a historical site when she first
started working on it eight or nine years ago."

"Even though it would torpedo selling your land
for the mall project, having it declared a historical
site?"

"History did happen here, you know," he said,
his smile fading. "Not the showy history the Pruitts
are interested in. My family's farmed this land
since 1753. House isn't that old—Yankees burned
what was left of the original in 1864—but there's
stones in the old graveyard from before the Revolution. Stones for Shiffleys who died in six or seven
different wars. And the women who bore them or
married them, and kept the farm going after they
left. That's history, too, but I guess it's not good
enough to save. Not important to anyone outside
the family."

"It should be," Dad said with the mix of envy and
melancholy that sometimes crept into his voice
when other people talked about their family history.

"If you feel like that, why are you selling your
farm?" I asked.

"Not like I want to sell," Mr. Shiffley said.

"Financial problems?" Dad asked.

"We're getting by," Mr. Shiffley said. "But I'm getting along. Can't keep farming forever. Getting harder and harder, waking up in the morning to do the milking."

"You can't find find someone besides Evan Briggs who wants to buy it?" I asked.

"Not to farm it," he said. "Hell, I've tried for years to get one of my nephews to come in with me. Let me start training him to take over the farming, and after a year or two, the missus and I could build us a smaller house—I'm thinking a cottage down by the river. Less housework for her, and I'd be near enough to help out. Leave them the farm when we go."

"What a wonderful opportunity!" Dad said. "Aren't any of them interested?"

"They want the land all right," Mr. Shiffley said. "They're not really interested in farming it. Soon as Bess and I went, they'd sell it, just like that. Farming's hard work. Young people aren't interested."

Dad shook his head in sympathy. I felt slightly annoyed.

"They never struck me as lazy," I said, sticking up for my generation. "They've done great work for us." Apart from the duck pond, which wasn't their fault.

"Getting top pay, too," Mr. Shiffley said. I couldn't exactly argue with that. "And don't tell me they're always there the minute you want them. Like to work hard for a spell, then take it easy for a longer spell, those nephews of mine. Farming's a seven-day-a-week job, fifty-two weeks a year. They know that. Not stupid, any of 'em. I didn't say they were lazy anyway. Just not cut out for something as tough as farming."

"But why Evan Briggs and the damned outlet mall?" I asked. "Almost anything would be better than that."

Mr. Shiffley snorted.

"Yeah, that's what my nephews said. They lined up a classy developer. Guy promised he wasn't going to build cheap little houses on postage-stamp lots. He'd divide it into ranchettes. Nothing smaller than five acres."

He snorted again in disgust.

Maybe not as nice as having a farm next door—it would mean several dozen new neighbors. Still better than the outlet mall. Why did Mr. Shiffley sound so disgusted?

"Ranchettes," he repeated. "Hell, I don't care how large the lots were, it'd still be just a bunch of houses for rich people from the city to play farmer in. I like the outlet-mall idea better—nothing tasteful and classy about that. If it's not going to be a working farm, the hell with it."

An idea began to grow in my mind.

"Yes, the outlet mall's spectacularly horrible," I said. "That's the whole idea, isn't it?"

"What do you mean?" Dad said. Mr. Shiffley looked at me with one eyebrow cocked in curiosity.

"I imagine it's causing quite a fuss, now that word's getting around about your plan to sell out to Mr. Briggs," I said.

"Meg!" Dad said. "I think 'sell out' is a little harsh."

"But I bet Mr. Shiffley doesn't," I said. "He's hoping everyone will be so outraged that something will happen. Some plan to turn it into a park—that's why you've kept your nephews from telling the truth about the Battle of Pruitt's Ridge, isn't it? Or maybe someone will appear who can afford to buy the land to keep it as a farm—maybe not for as much money as Mr. Briggs would pay, but enough for you to live on. If no one comes forward to help you save the farm, well, then we're all stuck with the outlet mall, and serves us right."

Mr. Shiffley looked at me for a few moments; then his mouth quirked into a brief, wry smile.

"Smart girl, that," he said to Dad. Then he turned and stumped away down the slope toward his house.

"Fascinating," Dad said.

I glanced over. He wasn't looking at Mr. Shiffley. He was standing with his hands on his hips, slowly sweeping the landscape with his gaze and nodding slightly.

"Dad," I said. "What are you—"

"Meg! Turn!" Rob's voice informed me over the radio.

"You go on with your game," Dad said. "I need to ask Mr. Shiffley something."

"Dad! Wait!"

But Dad was off and running. And here came Lacie Butler, stumbling through the underbrush, squeaking with dismay whenever she tripped over a root or branch, eliminating the option of pretending I couldn't find my ball or hadn't heard the radio.

I gritted my teeth at having to play croquet when everything exciting was happening somewhere else and turned to greet Lacie.

Chapter Forty-one

"Oh dear," Lacie said, with the usual anxious quiver in her voice. "High grass. You didn't see my ball land, did you?"

I shook my head.

"Are you sure it came this way?" I said. "Last time I heard, you were over at the fourth wicket."

"I was," she said. "Only *somebody* roqueted me over this way."

Great. Not only were she and Mrs. Wentworth refusing to speak to Mrs. Pruitt; they were even refusing to say her name.

"Dad and Mr. Shiffley and I were talking here for quite a few minutes," I said. "We didn't see it."

"Oh no!" Lacie exclaimed, clapping her hands to her mouth as if the loss of her ball were a real disaster instead of just an annoyance.

My mouth fell open. I suddenly realized how Lacie could have gotten poison ivy on her face. Not from falling face down in a patch of it—after all, this time of year there weren't any patches, just vines. She'd handled one of the vines with her golf

gloves, then spent the next hour or so transferring
the urushiol oil to her face every time she exclaimed
in mock horror and put her hands over her mouth.

"Turn, Meg," the radio said.

I started, and pretended I'd just been zoning out,
not staring at Lacie.

"Let me take my shot," I said. "Then I'll come
help you look for your ball."

"Oh, no, I couldn't ask you to do that," she said.
"I'm sure I can find it. Don't worry about me."

Exactly what I was hoping—even expecting—
her to say. I breathed a sigh of relief and strode
toward where I'd left my ball.

"I'm sorry," she said from behind me. "I can't let
you do that."

I looked over my shoulder and froze. Lacie was
pointing a gun at me.

"Okay," I said, playing it light. "If you're that
impatient, I'll help you look for your ball before I
take my turn."

"Don't move," she said. "I don't know how you
figured it out, but obviously I can't let you go and
tell the police."

"Tell them what?" I asked.

She shook her head as if disappointed by my attempts at subterfuge. Not very convincing attempts—
I was distracted by the gun. I'd had guns pointed at
me before, and every other time, despite all Dad's
mystery-inspired lectures on the subject, the only
thing I could remember was the gun's enormous size.
Cousin Horace had told me that most civilians re-

acted that way. Even the smallest gun looks Really Big when you're looking at the business end of it.

But the gun Lacie was holding looked remarkably tiny. You could hardly see it in her hand, and she didn't have particularly large hands for a woman. I had to work hard to shake off the thought that it was only Lacie and her silly little gun. Thinking that way was just as dangerous as being frozen with fear. As Cousin Horace had also remarked, a .22 will kill you just as dead if the bullet hits the wrong place. Something about Lacie suggested that I shouldn't take a chance that she was a bad shot. Maybe it was the sudden disappearance of her usual simpering mannerisms. Or perhaps the surprising steadiness of the hand holding the gun. With my luck, they probably had marksmanship contests down at the club in between golf and tennis matches.

"You don't really think you can get away with shooting me, do you?" I said.

"Oh, I rather think I can," she said with a vacant smile. "I'll just go bash one of the others over the head with your mallet and leave the gun nearby. It will look as if she shot you in self-defense."

"Won't work unless you lure one of them over here," I said. "Hard to have us killing each other in a deadly hand-to-hand confrontation if we're not even within sight of each other. Besides, won't they trace the gun to you?"

She frowned. Then a pleased expression crossed her face.

"You're right. I'll bash one of them over the head

and run back here. I can say I saw you do it and then I ran away, and you chased me here and I shot you. That will work nicely. And who would wonder at my bringing a gun along, with a vicious murderer on the loose?"

Great. I might have just helped her figure out how to get away with it.

She frowned again.

"I just need to decide whether it should be Claire or Henrietta," she said in a petulant tone.

"Mrs. Pruitt's treated you the worst," I suggested. Keep her talking.

"Yes," she said. "And after everything I've done for her. The way she gave me such a hard time about that stupid book—how was I to know the paper had gotten it all wrong? But I don't think she'll bother me much from now on. And Claire has been quite bossy today. I don't think that bodes well for the future, do you?"

"Probably not," I said. "Look, if you're going to kill me anyway, at least tell me why you did it."

"So you can keep me talking until someone shows up to rescue you? I think not."

"Probably Mrs. Pruitt's idea," I said as if to myself.

"It was not!" Lacie hissed. "All she did was complain about how Lindsay was going to ruin everything. I figured out how to get rid of Lindsay, and make it look as if Henrietta had done it, so I'd be rid of her, too. Give someone else a chance to run the historical society for a change."

"Someone else like you?" I said. "Too bad; it looks as if Claire Wentworth's got her eye on that job."

"Yes," she said. "So I guess it's really Claire I need to get rid of now."

She smiled as if I'd helped her solve a thorny problem.

"Meg, did you hear me?" my radio said. "Turn!"

"They'll come looking for me in a minute," I said.

"So I'd better hurry." She lifted the gun. "Hold up your mallet as if you're about to strike me; I want the proper angle."

Yeah, right. I shifted my gaze. My eyes widened.

"Oh my God," I murmured.

"What now?" she snapped.

"If you're very still, maybe he won't charge," I said.

" 'He'?" Lacie echoed.

"We are in a cow pasture, remember?" I said. "He's bad-tempered, though I suppose it's only because he's being protective of the herd."

"I'm not falling for this," she said. "There's no bull behind me. Now pick up your mallet and——"

She froze as a snort and the sound of a hoof striking stone revealed that there was something behind her. A look of panic and indecision crossed her face—now, that was more like the Lacie I knew. I was just planning how to make my counterattack when the damned sheep baaed and gave the game away.

"It's only a sheep," she said. She moved slightly, so she could see both the sheep and me.

"A ram," I said. It was possible; how could anyone but another sheep tell under all that wool? "I don't like the way he's looking at us."

Unfortunately, the sheep had lost interest in us. Any minute now he—or she—would wander off, instead of staying around where I could use it as a diversion.

The damned sheep put its head down and began cropping grass.

"See," Lacie said, focusing back on me. "Now lift the—"

"BAAAAA!"

The sheep bleated and leaped into the air like a woolly Morris dancer, then came down and galloped off. Lacie had to dodge, and I made a run for it, but unfortunately, I was right in the middle of the smooth stretch of grass that I'd been so happy to see when my croquet ball landed there. Now I'd happily have traded the grassy sward for someplace boggy and thorny that offered more cover.

"Stop or I'll shoot!" she said.

I ignored her. I figured my only chance was to keep running and hope she wasn't really a good shot.

"I mean it!" she said.

I heard a small bang—much like a car backfiring—and something nicked my heel. It was more surprise than pain that made me trip and fall.

Great, now I was a stationary target. I scrambled to get to my feet. Another bang made me flinch, but I didn't feel anything. I glanced back.

Lacie was hopping on one leg and shaking the other while flailing with the gun at the small black-and-white ball of fur attached to her ankle.

"Get it off me!" she shrieked. "Get it off!"

Fortunately, she couldn't quite reach Spike, but I figured as soon as the first shock was past, she'd remember that she was holding a gun, not a club. I turned back to go to Spike's rescue, though the pain in my ankle cut my speed.

She had stopped shrieking by the time I grabbed my croquet mallet, and she'd put both hands on the gun and was aiming at Spike with that demented smile on her face, when I got near enough to bring the croquet mallet down as hard as I could.

No, not on her skull, though it was tempting. I smashed her wrists. The shot went wild, she screamed, and Spike let go of her ankle long enough to bark a few times before chomping down again on a meatier part of the leg.

I pulled out my handkerchief and picked up the tiny little revolver by the barrel.

My radio crackled.

"Meg, what's going on over there?"

"I've found Spike, and I've found Lindsay's killer. Call Chief Burke. Tell Dad to bring his medical kit over."

"Um . . . okay," Rob said.

"Has she taken her shot?" Mrs. Pruitt said in the background.

"And tell Mrs. Pruitt the game is over," I said, raising my voice. "They lose. House rules. Spectators are fair game, but if you try to murder one of the other players, your team's out. Period."

I could hear Mrs. Fenniman's whoops of laughter even without the radio.

Chapter Forty-two

With my eyes closed, I could still hear the victory celebration going on outside the barn, but I didn't have to watch. Dad had settled me in an Adirondack chair just inside the barn doorway so I could watch if I wanted, but I preferred to doze. I sipped my Merlot and carefully put my good left leg up beside the bandaged right one on the cushion.

"You doing okay?"

I opened one eye and saw Michael hovering over me, holding the Merlot bottle. I assessed the level in my glass and held it up for a refill.

"How's the party?" I asked.

"Fine," he said. "If you want me to tell everyone you need peace and quiet, I can do that."

"Let them get it out of their systems," I said, closing my eyes again. "This will be the last party we have until the damned construction is finished."

"Speaking of the construction," Michael said.

I waited to see what he was going to say, then finally opened my eyes.

" 'Speaking of the construction,' " I repeated.

"It kills me even to suggest this, but maybe we should hold back—until we know what's happening next door."

I smiled. Evidently Michael, who had just returned from taking Tony and Graham to Richmond to catch a flight home, hadn't heard all of the news.

"I mean, if Briggs really does get permission to build an outlet mall there . . ."

His voice trailed off.

"Yes, Mr. Briggs," I said. "Is he still here?"

"He was, briefly, but he went home."

"Figures," I said. "He went home to mope because someone else bought the farm."

"Oh no!" Michael exclaimed. "You mean she killed someone else before she went after you? Or—you don't mean Mrs. Briggs . . ."

"Not bought the farm as in died," I said. "I meant that someone else is purchasing Mr. Shiffley's land."

"Bad news for Briggs, I suppose," Michael said. "Not necessarily good news for us. I suspect anyone willing to beat Briggs's price is planning to do something equally awful with the land."

"No one beat Briggs's price," I said. "But someone did make Mr. Shiffley a better offer."

"Who?"

"Dad. Who has no intention of building an outlet mall on it. Or a subdivision. Part of the deal with Mr. Shiffley is that the place will stay a working farm."

"Meg, that's wonderful!" Michael exclaimed.

"Well, it's better than the outlet mall," I conceded. Michael evidently hadn't considered my family's ability to drive us bonkers in ways far more subtle than Mr. Briggs's outlet mall. Dad had already begun planning for his orchard of heritage fruit trees. Rose Noire had put in her bid to use part of the land for growing organic herbs and spices. Sammy and Horace were straining at the leash to begin digging for her. Mother, impatient at the slow progress of our renovations and at our unwillingness to adopt all her most expensive suggestions, was already hard at work on a plan for refurbishing the farmhouse.

"So we can go ahead with the construction," Michael said.

"As soon as the Shiffleys get their hammers back. In the meantime, we can have them fill in the leaky duck pond. We don't need it any longer. Mr. Shiffley has a perfectly good cow pond that can double as a duck pond."

"How big a duck pond?" Michael asked.

"How big does do we need for one little duck?"

"One little duck? Take a look."

I opened my eyes and saw Duck proudly crossing the yard, leading five baby ducklings.

"That's impossible," I said.

"We're in farm country," Michael said. "She could have found a drake."

"Yes, but she's been too busy laying eggs all over the place to hatch any."

"Meg, isn't it wonderful?" Rose Noire exclaimed, racing over to my side.

"Bloody puzzling, if you ask me," I said. "Where'd they come from?"

"Seth has a friend who raises ducks," she said.

Seth? Oh, Mr. Early. "He brought them over this evening. You're supposed to put them under the foster mother when she's asleep, to make sure she accepts them. Duck woke up and accepted them immediately. She brought them out to show off!"

I worried when one of the ducklings strayed and Duck hurried to chivy it back in line, using the same technique that had worked so well on the sheep. But she was much gentler with the ducklings. She was obviously preening as she paraded them around the yard.

For that matter, Seth Early was preening, too, at the success of his present, and oblivious to the lethal glances he was getting from Cousin Horace and Deputy Sammy.

Not my problem. I closed my eyes again.

"How are you, dear?" Mother asked, placing a cool hand on my forehead.

"Fine," I said. I opened my eyes and saw her and Mrs. Burke standing beside me.

"Tell the chief I'm sorry about the wild-goose chase," I said.

"No problem," Minerva Burke said. "After all, he was a criminal—Henry's been trying to solve the hacker case for months now."

"Good," I said.

"He's pleased as punch," she went on. "Now the only unsolved case on his books is that bizarre sheepnapping Saturday night."

"Terrible," I said, closing my eyes again.

"For some reason, Seth Early's uncharacteristically calm about it," she said. "No telling why."

"No telling," I echoed.

"Did I tell you the good news," Mother said, "about the Caerphilly Historical Society?"

I opened my eyes again.

"It seemed obvious that the society needed new leadership," Mother said.

"You're not planning to run, are you?" I asked.

"Me? What a thought. We only plan to weekend here. No, Minerva's decided to run."

"Time to shake up this town," Minerva Burke said.

"Excellent," I replied "Town needs shaking up."

"The society's done a dreadfully poor job of fighting inappropriate development under the current leadership," Mother said. I nodded.

"I do hope I can count on you to help organize the committee on architecture and design," Mrs. Burke said. "We need people with artistic credentials on that."

"Artistic?" I said. "I'm a blacksmith."

"An ornamental blacksmith, dear," Mother said. "Which means you can also provide an all-important practical knowledge of craftsmanship and technique."

I was stunned into silence. This was the first time I could remember Mother actually referring to me as a blacksmith. She normally referred to me as a craftsperson on the grounds that it didn't sound quite as unfeminine. Yes, she'd added "ornamental," but still, I was so surprised, I forgot to protest. Taking my silence for consent, Mother and Mrs. Burke both nodded at me, then strolled away arm in arm.

Glancing across the yard, I could see Fred Shiffley chatting amicably with several men about his own age—probably his brothers and cousins, the older generation of Shiffleys, given the physical resemblance. Several of the Shiffleys had pulled out pencils and were now sketching diagrams on the sheets of plywood we'd set up to serve as tables, and arguing about the sketches.

"What are the Shiffleys doing?" I asked when Michael came back and handed me a plate of food.

"Planning the cottage they're going to build for their Uncle Fred and Aunt Bess," Michael said.

"Seems to be causing arguments."

"Ah, but it's a good kind of arguing," he said. "They're all happy about how things turned out. Which reminds me—remember the last time we talked about setting a date for the wedding? You said we needed a way to arrange a small private ceremony without mortally insulting the several hundred relatives who expect an invitation?"

"I remember," I said, wincing. "It's not that I want to raise impossible obstacles—"

"I've figured out how to do it!" he exclaimed. "All we need to do is—"

"Michael!" Dad exclaimed, appearing in front of us. "Come on—we need one more to make up the side!"

I glanced over to the lawn, where nearly two dozen people had lined up in formation, waving croquet mallets or hockey sticks. They were a little deficient in the bell department, thank goodness—only two of them had regulation sets of Morris dancing bells, though several others were making do with bells that looked as if they'd been hastily scavenged from the family Christmas decorations and tied to the wearers' shins with various bits of yarn and string. Half a dozen Shiffleys were tuning up a variety of musical instruments.

"You were saying?" I asked.

"I'll tell you all about it later," Michael said, indicating with his eyes that he didn't want to talk about it in front of Dad. Not that Dad would have noticed—he was too interested in dragging Michael toward the Morris dancing.

"Michael! Wait!" I called.

He pulled free of Dad's grip and took a step closer.

"No Morris dancing at the wedding," I said.

"Yes, ma'am," he replied with a grin and a crisp salute. "I'll try to get it out of my system beforehand."

With that, he ran off to join the dance.

Read on for a sneak peek
at Donna Andrews's next mystery

The Penguin Who
Knew Too Much

Now Available from
St. Martin's/Minotaur Paperbacks

Chapter One

"Meg! Guess what I found in your basement?"

I looked up from the box I was unpacking to see Dad standing in the basement doorway, his round face shining with excitement.

"A body?" An unlikely guess, but Dad was a big mystery buff—perhaps if I amused him, he'd stop playing guessing games on moving day.

"Oh, rats—you already knew? Well, how soon will the police get here? I need to move the penguins—we don't want them any more upset than they already are."

He disappeared down the basement stairs without waiting for an answer. I abandoned my unpacking to call after him.

"Dad? I was joking. Did you really find a body? And why are there penguins in our basement? Dad!"

No answer. Should I go down to see what was happening, or call the police? Damn! I closed my eyes and counted to ten. Normally counting to ten calmed me, but today it just gave me time to realize how much more could go wrong elsewhere in the house. On cue, I heard the crash of something breaking, followed by a sheepish "Oops!" from my brother, Rob, in the front hall. In the living room, Mother ordered a brace of cousins to move the sofa to yet another location. She'd been at it for an hour, and so far only three pieces of furniture had made it from the truck to the house.

In the dining room, Mrs. Fenniman, Mother's distant cousin and closest ally, was singing an Italian aria, changing pitch every dozen notes, which meant she'd had a few martinis already and we'd have to redo the walls after she'd painted them.

I'd only reached seven when Rob interrupted me.

"Meg? You know that big cut-glass punch bowl? Is that a particular favorite of yours?"

"Don't you mean *was* it a particular favorite?" I asked as I pulled my cell phone out of my pocket. "And no, but Mother was quite fond of it, so see if you can sweep up the pieces before she notices. Broom's over there."

"Right-o."

I dialed 911. I wasn't sure the situation quite warranted 911, but I hadn't memorized the nonemergency number for the Caerphilly Police Department and I had no idea which box contained the phone book.

"Hello—Debbie Anne?" I said when the dispatcher answered. "This is Meg Langslow."

"Meg! How's the move-in going? And what's the problem?"

"Slowly. And the problem is that Dad says he's found a body in the basement."

"Oh, Lord," Rob said. He stopped in the doorway, broom and dustpan in hand, the better to eavesdrop.

"Is he serious?" Debbie Anne asked after a moment. "I mean, if it's just some kind of practical joke—"

"He sounded serious," I said. "And I thought I should call you first instead of wasting time going to look myself, and possibly disturbing a crime scene."

"I'll tell Chief Burke you said so. If it turns out to be some kind of mix-up . . ."

Her voice trailed off. I knew what she was thinking. Quite apart from the major-league practical jokers in my family, there was Dad, with his well-known mystery obsession.

"If it's a mix-up, I'll call back right away," I said, and hung up.

"Did he really find a body?" Rob asked.

"So he says."

"Don't you think you should have checked before calling the cops?"

"If he was pulling my leg, I'll let him explain it to Chief Burke."

"I still think you should check for yourself."

"I'm going to—want to come?"

Rob, who fainted at the mere idea of blood, shook his head and hurried back to the hall.

I took the stairs to the basement.

The smell hit me first.

Not the rank smell of a decaying body or the tang of newly spilled blood, both of which I'd had a chance to experience while tagging along after

Dad—less while he pursued his medical practice, of
course, than during his repeated attempts to involve
himself in murder investigations, like the protago-
nists of the mystery books he read by the dozen.

No, this smell was a cross between a barn in dire
need of cleaning and a fish market that had lost
power for a few days. I deduced that I was smelling
penguins. The stench wafted from the unfinished,
far end of the basement, the part under the library
wing, where the concrete floor gave way to packed
dirt.

I also heard muted honking and trilling noises. I
followed my nose and ears.

I should have brought a flashlight. This side of
the basement was not only unfinished, it was unelec-
trified. And to get to the far end, where Dad was, I
had to traverse a part near the stairs that the pack rat
former owner had turned into a perfect warren of
ramshackle storage rooms.

"Chief Burke? Is that you?" Dad appeared
around a corner, carrying a flashlight.

"He's on his way," I said. "Where's the body?"

"This way!" Dad was grinning with obvious delight at showing off the house's exciting new feature.

Not a feature that had been there when my fiancé,
Michael, and I bought the place, I suspected. The
rambling three-story Victorian house had been so
packed with junk by the previous owner that we
hadn't initially realized quite how badly in need of
repair it was. But I'd spent several months crawling
over every inch of the place, getting rid of decades

of clutter, and then several more months supervising the repairs—at least the ones we'd decided we had to do before moving in. For that matter, we'd been living on-site for months—camping out first in the ramshackle house and more recently in the barn while the house was repaired. Surely by now I'd have noticed a body lying around, even in this remote and as-yet unrenovated corner of the basement.

Dad and I emerged from the maze of storage rooms into the larger, dirt-floored open area. A couple of battery-powered Coleman lanterns hung from the ceiling, casting enough light for me to see the room. I didn't spot any penguins, though I could hear and smell them nearby. And I could see an excavation near the center of the room.

"Oh, wonderful," I said. "You didn't just find a body. You dug one up."

Chapter 2

Gazing at the hole, I felt slightly reassured. Surely, if the body had been buried, it would turn out to be an old one after all. Little more than a skeleton.

"Yes," Dad said. "And not even buried very deep. It was remarkably easy to uncover—what were they thinking?"

He shook his head solemnly, as if to express his dismay at the shoddy professional habits of the modern criminal class. Or perhaps at Michael's and my shoddy housekeeping skills.

"It's not as if we're in the habit of tilling the soil down here," I said. "Did you suspect it was here, or did you have some other good reason for digging a hole in the middle of our basement floor?"

"For the penguins," Dad said. "I knew they'd be much happier with someplace to swim. So I was going to put in a pond—one of those preformed plastic ones."

"Of course. A pond," I said. It made sense coming from Dad, who had always had a fascination with water features. He probably loved having the penguins as an excuse. "But why not outside?"

"They're penguins," he exclaimed. "You can't expect them to stay outside in the heat of a Virginia summer! In here, we can give them some air-conditioning."

It would be a neat trick, with this end of the basement not even electrified—I could already see the giant industrial extension cords snaking through the house. And I shuddered to think what it would do to our electric bill.

"I started digging yesterday," he went on. "But then I realized that I didn't know how big a hole I needed. So I went to Flugleman's garden store last night and got the precise dimensions. And almost as soon as I started work this morning—voilà!"

He pointed to his excavation. I grabbed one of the overhead lanterns, picked my way carefully to the edge of the hole, and peered in. I didn't exactly see a body—more like a hand sticking up by itself out of the dirt. But even though I had refused to follow in Dad's footsteps, becoming a blacksmith instead of a doctor, I had enough grasp of basic human anatomy to deduce that if the hand wasn't still attached to a body, it had been at one point. Probably, from the size of it, a full-grown male body.

Though hands could fool you. I glanced down at my own, which were largish for a woman's hands. Of course, at five feet, ten inches, so was the rest of me. And my work as a blacksmith wasn't exactly conducive to maintaining elegant feminine hands.

Mother had long since given up chiding me for ruining them at the forge. Even Michael didn't pretend to find my hands beautiful, but he had pronounced them capable-looking, and made it sound like a higher compliment. One of his many positive traits.

Our subterranean visitor's hand, like mine, looked well used rather than well cared for. Capable. On the large side. And hairier than most women's hands.

So judging from the hand, our uninvited visitor was male. And either he worked with his hands, as I did, or he had done something useful with them in his off-hours.

And he probably hadn't been buried beneath the basement floor all that long, I realized, with a sinking feeling. Now that I was closer, I could smell decay, even over the penguin poop. If he'd been there since the late Mrs. Sprocket owned the house, I wouldn't have smelled anything at all. Or seen enough of him to make all these deductions.

"How recently did he die?" I asked. "Or can you tell from just the hand?"

"Longer than a day," Dad said. "Or decomposition wouldn't be detectable. And there's no rigor, so presumably it has worn off. But not much longer."

"So we're talking days, not months or years, right?"

"Of course," Dad said. "You could figure that out yourself."

"I hoped I was wrong," I said. "It would be so much easier if we could blame him on the previous owner. Anyway—ow!"

Someone—or something—had goosed me. I stumbled forward, barely avoiding the hand. My foot landed on a soft, warm body that squealed and wriggled frantically out from under me, almost toppling me over onto the hand. I glanced around to see a throng of penguins milling about us.

"Oh, dear, they're loose again," Dad said. "There really isn't any place down here that will hold them. Help me take them outside, before they spoil the crime scene."

"A little too late to worry about that," I said. The penguins had discovered the hand and were poking and nibbling at it with their beaks, though luckily they hadn't decided that it was edible.

"Grab a fish and lure them outside," Dad said, taking a bucket down from an overhead hook and handing it to me.

"Yuck," I said, but I followed orders. I grabbed something cold and slimy from the bucket and headed for the other end of the room, where concrete steps led to a set of old-fashioned slanted metal doors that provided an outlet to the yard. Behind me, I could hear Dad gently shooing the penguins. I barely had time to swing open one side of the door and scramble out before they caught up, nearly knocking me down in their eagerness to get to the fish.

I threw the fish into the yard, tossed a few more after it, and then looked around for a place to stow the penguins before they wandered off to visit the neighbors.

The duck pen. It wasn't as if our resident duck and

her adopted ducklings spent much time in it. I opened
the gate, dumped most of the remaining chum at the
far end, then stood waving a fish as a lure until I had
all the penguins inside. Dad shut the gate behind
them, and I climbed over the fence to freedom, or at
least the absence of penguins underfoot.

"Good thinking!" Dad said as he put one foot up
on a rail and leaned his elbows on the top of the
fence. The veteran penguin wrangler, resting after a
successful roundup. "That should take care of them
for the time being."

"For the time being," I repeated. "At least until
you can take them back where they belong. And just
where is that, anyway? Not in our basement, I as-
sure you."

"The Caerphilly Zoo," Dad said. He had pulled
out his handkerchief and was mopping his face and
the shiny expanse of his bald head. "Patrick asked
me to foster them for a while."

"Patrick?"

"Patrick Lanahan. The zoo's owner. It's just until
he gets through this bad patch he's having."

"What kind of a bad patch?" I asked. In our family, "bad patch" was a convenient euphemism. It
could cover anything from brief cash-flow problems
or minor marital discord up to a felony conviction
with a sentence of twenty to life.

"Only temporary, of course," Dad said.

"Of course. What's wrong down at the zoo?"

"The bank was going to put a lien on the property. And if he hadn't moved the animals out, the
bank might have seized them, too."

"Oh, so these might even be hot penguins," I said. "Great."

"Don't be silly, Meg," Dad said. "The bank didn't want to seize the penguins. What on earth would they do with them if they did? They gave Patrick plenty of time to foster out all the animals before they filed the lien."

"To foster out all the animals? Dad, how many animals did you take, anyway?"

"Only the penguins," Dad said, as if hurt by my distrust.

"Ah. Only the penguins," I repeated. Suddenly the throng of black-and-white forms busily exploring the duck pen for escape routes looked small and relatively harmless. I tried to remember what other animals they'd had at the zoo. Nothing particularly dangerous, I hoped. Still, penguins were better than hyenas, weren't they? And hadn't the zoo had at least one elderly, ill-tempered bobcat? "So you're stuck with the penguins until Patrick can pay his bills?"

"Just until he finishes negotiating an agreement with a new sponsor," Dad said. "Which should be any day now."

He was looking at the empty fish bucket with a slight frown.

"Remarkable, how much fish they eat," he said. He glanced at the penguins, then back at the bucket, and sighed.

"Dad, just how long have you had these penguins?"

"Only two weeks."

"They haven't been in the basement for two weeks, have they?" I asked. I thought I'd have noticed penguins, but perhaps the preparations for the move had made me less observant than usual.

"Oh, no—I've been keeping them over at the farmhouse." Although he and Mother still lived in Yorktown, about an hour to the south, a few months earlier he'd bought the farm adjacent to our new house, partly to save it from development and partly so they could come up to Caerphilly whenever they felt like meddling.

"Why couldn't they just stay there?" I asked.

"With your mother coming up today? I didn't think she'd be pleased."

"And you thought I would?"

"I knew you'd cope better than your mother."

"You mean you knew I'd complain less."

"Oh, look! There's Chief Burke!"

As the chief's car pulled up, Dad hurried out to meet him, visibly relieved that something had interrupted my line of questioning.

"Glad to see you!" Dad exclaimed, reaching to shake the chief's hand as he stepped out of the patrol car. "Though I'm sorry it had to be under these circumstances."

"Just what are the circumstances?" the chief asked. His normally cheerful brown face wore a faint frown. "Debbie Anne had some fool story about you finding a body in the basement."

"Yes—extraordinary, isn't it?" Dad said. "Let me show you."

He made a dash toward the side yard, where the

battered metal cellar doors were located. The chief and I followed more slowly, and saw Dad's head disappear into the opening just as we turned the corner of the house. The chief looked at me.

"You've seen this body?" he asked.

"Yes. Part of it anyway—the hand. The rest's still buried."

"Lord," the chief said. "And here I was hoping for a quiet Memorial Day weekend."

He walked over to the basement doors and frowned at them for a few moments. Since the doors weren't doing anything to merit disapproval, I suspected that he wasn't really all that keen on going inside. I glanced down through the doors myself and could see why. Now that my eyes were used to the bright sunlight outside, I could see little more than a few steep steps disappearing into the gloom.

"Chief?" Dad called. "Are you coming?"

"Coming," the chief called. "I don't see what he's in such an all-fired hurry about," he grumbled to me. "Body's not going anywhere, is it?"

"You know how excited he gets about murders."

The chief only rolled his eyes. Then he put one foot carefully on the first step, and I watched his head drop lower with each step until it vanished into the basement.

Should I follow, or stay outside to keep an eye on the penguins?